T0005399

Savor

AND

Intoxicated

By Monica Murphy

The Billionaire Bachelors Club Series
Crave • Torn
Savor • Intoxicated

Lancaster Prep Series
I'll Always Be with You • Promises We Meant to Keep
Birthday Kisses • A Million Kisses in Your Lifetime
Things I Wanted to Say, But Never Did

One Week Girlfriend Series
A Drew + Fable Christmas • Five Days Until You
Four Years Later • Drew + Fable Forever
Three Broken Promises • Second Chance Boyfriend
One Week Girlfriend

The Players Series
Playing to Win • Playing by the Rules
Playing Hard to Get

The Callahans Series
A Callahan Wedding • Making Her Mine
Fighting For You • Meant to Be
Addicted to Him • Falling For Her
Close to Me

The Rules Series
Safe Bet • Slow Play
In The Dark • Fair Game

Dating Series
Blind Date • Wedding Date
Rate a Date • Hate to Date You
Holidate • Fake Date
Save the Date

Savor
AND
Intoxicated

A BILLIONAIRE BACHELORS CLUB ROMANCE

MONICA
MURPHY

AVON

An Imprint of HarperCollinsPublishers

This is a work of fiction. Names, characters, places, and incidents are products of the author's imagination or are used fictitiously and are not to be construed as real. Any resemblance to actual events, locales, organizations, or persons, living or dead, is entirely coincidental.

SAVOR. Copyright © 2014 by Monica Murphy.

INTOXICATED. Copyright © 2014 by Monica Murphy.

All rights reserved. Printed in the United States of America. No part of this book may be used or reproduced in any manner whatsoever without written permission except in the case of brief quotations embodied in critical articles and reviews. For information, address HarperCollins Publishers, 195 Broadway, New York, NY 10007.

HarperCollins books may be purchased for educational, business, or sales promotional use. For information, please email the Special Markets Department at SPsales@harpercollins.com.

Originally published separately as *Savor* and *Intoxicated* in the United States by Avon Impulse in 2014.

Designed by Diahann Sturge-Campbell

Library of Congress Cataloging-in-Publication Data has been applied for.

ISBN 978-0-06-338302-9

24 25 26 27 28 LBC 5 4 3 2 1

Table of Contents

Acknowledgments

As always, I'm thanking my husband and children for putting up with me while I work extra hard at my desk, giving myself eyestrain while I stare at the computer all day and night. You are all so awesome and supportive and rarely complain (ha ha). What would I do without you?

To the readers—I would be nothing without your continued enthusiasm and love. Thank you, you all mean the world to me. This book (and this entire series) is a little different and I hope you love reading it as much as I've enjoyed writing it. Hopefully we can't go wrong with sexy billionaire bachelors . . .

A big thank you to my editor, Chelsey Emmelhainz, for slapping my words around and making this book so much better. To the entire team at Avon for their enthusiastic support of this series—y'all rock. To KP Simmon and Kati Rodriguez for keeping me straight. And to Katy Evans for loving Archer from the very, very beginning.

Savor

Chapter 1

Matt

"Can you become addicted to someone's smell?" My voice is nonchalant, my thoughts turbulent. I keep my gaze locked on the woman I'm talking about. The one I think I'm slowly becoming addicted to though my brain is screaming at me that this particular addiction is a huge mistake. Bad for me. Bad for everyone.

Ivy Emerson turns to look at me, her expression incredulous. My friend's fiancée and the mother of his future child also happens to be one of the best interior designers in all of the Napa Valley *and* she's working for me. "Who exactly are you talking about?"

Hell. I actually said that aloud? I didn't mean to.

We're sitting in my office, the door wide open, allowing me the perfect view of the outer lobby, where my assistant's desk is. Bryn James. Miss James, she of the intoxicating scent that makes my head swim and my cock hard.

Also she of the bland wardrobe and quiet ways, meaning she's not my usual type. So why the attraction? Why does her scent drive me fucking crazy?

It makes no damn sense.

"No one in particular," I lie with a shrug. Ivy has stopped by to go over the latest invoice for her services. Combine her astronomical costs with Archer Bancroft's wealth and these two will end up taking over the entire world. Or they'll just buy it all.

"You're such a liar," she mutters, shaking her head. "And you're also in denial."

"About what?" Grabbing a pen, I scribble my initials on the invoice as Ivy settles into the chair across from my desk. "Give this to Bryn and she'll cut the check for you. Do you want it now or would you like to come by and pick it up later?"

Ivy smiles. "You're also a classic avoider, aren't you? Ah, men. You're all the same."

I frown at her, wondering what she's referring to now. I've known Ivy since she was a teenager, when I became good friends with her brother, Gage, and her now fiancé, Archer. The problem with knowing Ivy for that long is she constantly crosses professional boundaries when we work together. She has no problem telling me exactly how she feels.

Most of the time, like now, I don't want to hear it.

"Ivy." My voice lowers, and I glower at her, but she smiles at me as if she thinks I'm one big joke. The woman is completely oblivious. "When do you want your check?"

She waves a hand, the bracelets clasped around her wrist jangling with the movement. "Just drop it in the mail. Bryn will know what to do and where to send it. She's so efficient, don't you think?"

"Extremely." I push the invoice farther across the desk, closer to where Ivy's sitting, hoping she gets the hint. I'd like her gone, so I can get back to work. Get back to possibly researching if one really could become addicted to another's scent. I've heard about pheromones before.

"She also smells amazing. I've asked her before what perfume she uses, but she won't tell me. I think she wants it to be her secret." Ivy's grinning so widely I bet her cheeks hurt.

Damn it. Why the hell did I ask her that question anyway? It just popped out of my mouth without thought, which I've been prone to doing lately when I stare at Miss James for too long.

As in, I stop thinking. My brain just shuts down. All I can do is watch and imagine what she might do if I pushed her onto her desk, grabbed hold of her long, dark hair, tugged her head back, and kissed her with all the pent-up intensity that's been brewing within me since she started working for me.

Which is basically the day I first took over the winery. She came along with it. A built-in assistant, just for me. The previous owner had called her a gift.

Quite the tempting gift. One put on this earth—and right outside of my office—to make me freaking crazy with need.

All because of the way she smells.

Oh, and that sexy little voice of hers. The one she doesn't use much since she's so damn quiet. And all that hair—hair she keeps tightly bound in a bun or restrained in a sleek ponytail.

There's something going on under those bland, downright unflattering clothes too. I can tell. I'm not an idiot. She's hiding breasts and an ass that are probably pretty damn amazing.

Of course, this could all be wishful thinking since I'm still bothered by the fact that I'm attracted to my assistant—my very plain, yet very tantalizing employee.

It makes no damn sense.

"Forget I ever asked that question," I growl at Ivy, which only makes her laugh.

God, she's infuriating. I don't know how Archer can stand her sometimes.

"Don't be so cranky. It's okay to admit you have a thing for Bryn." Ivy leans forward in her chair, a secretive smile curling her lips. "I have a feeling she has a thing for you too, you know."

I do know. And I can't act on it. Bryn James works for me. She's my assistant. She's by my side constantly; we spend more time with each other than probably anyone else in our lives, especially lately what with the winery's grand reopening approaching. She's a representative of my business. If I were to fuck around with the help and the relationship fell apart, I'd be in huge trouble. She could screw me over financially every which way by suing me for sexual harassment and I'd be left with a limp dick in my hand and a ruined business.

Yeah. Not going to take the chance. Saw it happen with my father. Not going to let it happen to me.

"It doesn't matter. Nothing can happen." I send Ivy a stern look. "And this conversation can never leave this office." Glancing over her shoulder, I try to see if Bryn is at her desk but the chair is empty.

Thank Christ.

Ivy's expression goes solemn and she holds up three fingers. "This conversation stays here. Scout's honor."

"You were never a scout," I mutter, afraid she's making a promise on an untruth. She'll probably just blab to everyone. Or specifically Archer and Gage. I don't need to hear their shit.

And I am worrying way too much over this.

She laughs again. "I won't say a word, I promise. But I need to tell you something, Matt." She leans in close, her voice dropping. "She's got a major crush on you. You might not see it, but it's there—sounding in her voice, shining in her eyes, every time she looks at you, talks about you. The way her body turns into yours every time the two of you are together . . . it's pretty obvious. A body language expert would have a field day with you two."

Body language expert? What the hell is Ivy talking about? "I have no idea what you're referring to, but office crushes are just that. Crushes. Harmless attractions no one ever acts on. Period. End of story."

This is what I keep telling myself. I can't pursue anything with Bryn, no matter how much I'm tempted to. Not only would it be wildly inappropriate, dating my assistant, but we come from two different worlds. She seems nice and normal, quiet and unobtrusive, and I am anything but. My life has been a circus sideshow for years.

"I get it. You're trying to do the right thing, and I admire that. So, of course you don't see anything beyond an efficient assistant in Miss James."

Well. Ivy's not too far off the mark. When I first met Bryn, she hardly said two words, kept her head bent when I spoke to her, and offered lots of yes-sir and no-sir answers. She had this way of almost blending in with the walls, like she didn't want anyone to notice her.

So I didn't.

As we got comfortable working together though, something happened. I'm thinking Ivy had a hand in Bryn's slow transformation. She actually makes eye contact when she speaks to me, and she's become somewhat animated. Started to wear bolder colors as well, drawing my attention to her chest though I keep my eyes averted as best I can.

These subtle changes made me notice all of the little things—like the color of her eyes (blue), how her hair looks (like silk and I want to touch it), and the tempting fullness of her lips (they're fucking spectacular).

Her gaze lingers when she looks at me and sometimes so does mine. Her smile softens, her voice drops lower when she speaks, sparking my imagination. Would she sound like that right before I kissed her? Took off her clothes? Took her to my bed?

Yeah. All of those are dangerous thoughts. I almost prefer the old Miss James. The one who was like the wallpaper—boring and nondescript. Mean to say, but hell, the last thing I need is a distraction.

And she's become the biggest distraction I'm currently facing. The very last one I need.

"She's a great assistant. That's it. Stop trying to make something out of it that it's not," I say, sounding like an irritable old man.

"Oh, come on. You can admit you're attracted to her. You won the bet, Matt—fair and square." Her eyes sparkle. "Give in now and Gage and Archer can't give you any grief over it."

"I think you just like giving me shit," I tell her.

The million-dollar bet—like I've collected anything from either of those asshole friends of mine who owe me five hundred thousand each. When we were at a friend's wedding reception almost a year ago, they'd readily agreed to my suggestion, like fools. I'd proposed that the last single man standing would win one million bucks. It had started out as a joke. I figured Archer and Gage would be the last guys to fall in love, especially Archer. I never believed they'd take me or the bet seriously.

But surprisingly enough, they did. And I started to realize that I had them.

Archer had gone first. Gage fell right after him. They hadn't been able to hold out for even six months. Hell, Archer ran out the very night we made the bet and hooked up with Ivy.

Crazy. It's like the bet spurred them on to find a woman and fall in love.

Ivy's laughter pushes me from my thoughts, and I glance up to find her standing, snatching the invoice from my desk and clutching it in her hand. "I do like giving you shit. And I should go. It was lovely as ever to spend a few minutes in your company, Mr. DeLuca. Can't wait to see you next week when we start putting everything together for the reopening."

"See ya," I toss out, but she's already gone, escaping my office and dropping the invoice off on Bryn's desk before she disappears completely from view.

I lean back in my chair, scrub my hand across my jaw, the scruff on my face abrading my palm. I need a shave. I need a fucking vacation. I've been doing nothing but work, work, work, since I picked up this winery on a whim.

I thought it would be fun. Something different. I'd been looking for something to do after my spectacular demise from the National Baseball League.

I'd spent my formative years on a baseball field. I lived and breathed that shit and turned it into a career. I'd planned on lasting much longer than my father ever had. Planned on having a better career than he did too.

That had all come crashing down when I was running backward on the field, ready to catch a fly ball and fucking tripped. On what, I can't even remember. My own feet? No one could figure it out.

All I know is I was on top of the world, practicing for a big game, and then I was in the hospital ready to be put under for extensive knee surgery.

My career was over and I'd only played eight seasons. My

entire life had changed completely, and I was at a loss as to what I should do next.

Archer kept trying to encourage both Gage and me to come to the Napa Valley. And once I was pushed into early retirement, I decided to go on the hunt for an interesting investment and possible distraction.

Within days, I found it—an established winery that had once been the pride of the area and had fallen on hard times when the patriarch died. The winery was in foreclosure. Before it went to a bankruptcy auction, I scooped it up for a song.

And found myself with a handful of employees—including one Miss Bryn James—looking at me as their personal savior.

Turned out the problem hadn't been the employees or the wine that was produced. It was the squandering of money on the part of the eldest son who'd taken over and spent lavishly on everything and nothing. He'd bled the company and his family's coffers completely dry—left it to flounder with lackluster marketing, dated labeling, and no projected plan for the next six months, let alone the next five years.

The place had been destined to fail.

So I snapped up the property, slapped my name on it, and the DeLuca Winery was born. I've worked these past months nonstop, preparing for the grand reopening. The majority of the locals, especially the local vintners, think I'm a joke. That I'm the big, bad, and early retired baseball player Matthew DeLuca coming into town and playing like I know how to own a winery. Like I came here looking for a hobby and the winery is it.

They're sort of right, not that I'd ever admit it.

I want to prove them wrong. I want to show them I know exactly what the hell I'm doing. I want respect. Unlike my father, who'd held respect in his hands time and again and then crushed it until it disintegrated into dust.

I'm nothing like him. He's a joke. The public tried to make me out to be a joke too. And they probably will again. I need to prove once and for all that just because I'm Vinnie De-Luca's son, that doesn't mean I'm just like him.

That's why I need to stay far away from Miss James. She's sweet, but she's a female who works for me. And that could cause all sorts of trouble.

Trouble I absolutely do not need.

Bryn

I settle in behind my desk, grabbing the invoice Ivy left and add it to my stack of things I need to do before I leave for the day. Lately I don't make my escape until past six, but today I have a feeling I'm going to stay even longer.

With the grand reopening happening in little over a week, there's still so much to do. Plus I guess I need to make some time to go shopping this weekend with Ivy and find a dress. Not that Matt doesn't pay me well, but I really can't afford such a splurge, especially on a dress I'll probably only wear once before I shove it into the back of my closet.

Still, I want to look my very best for Matt—as a representative of the DeLuca Winery of course.

Of course. It doesn't matter that you think he's so gorgeous your head spins every time he looks in your direction. Or when he flashes that smile. Or when you spend time in his office, just you and him, working together, his voice a low murmur, his clean masculine scent lingering in the air, driving you wild. The way he looks at you when he thinks you're not paying attention. Like maybe he wants to slowly strip your clothes off and run his hands all over your bare skin. Followed up by his mouth.

Sighing, I hang my head, staring at my keyboard before me. Having the hots for my boss is just about the stupidest thing I've ever done. And I've done plenty of stupid things in the past.

I roll my eyes and start typing. Even my thoughts go round in circles. I make no sense in my head, worrying about the going-nowhere crush on my boss. So how can I ever make sense when I'm talking to Matt? I get around him and my brain literally short-circuits. He approaches my desk, and I feel a little dizzy. He smiles at me, and my heart skips about five beats.

What's worse? I've gone down this road before. And not only a crush; I let my former boss chase me around his desk a couple of times, his quick hands grabbing my ass. My breasts. I'd slapped him away but giggled. Then I'd gone and let him kiss me.

A lot.

Then I found out he had a wife and children and, oh my God, I'd wanted to die. I quit the very next day. I'd been all of nineteen, scared out of my mind and afraid his wife would come after me. And with just cause, since I kissed her husband. How could I do such a terrible thing? What was wrong with me?

You were born with that pretty body and that gorgeous face, my grandma told me long, long ago. *It will bring you nothing but trouble girl. Y'all are too pretty for words.*

I grimace, my fingers poised over the keyboard in mid-tap. Great. Now my grandma is haunting my thoughts. But those words she said—and what happened with my old boss—are the reason I began downplaying my looks. My face caused me so much trouble.

When I was a little girl, the known pervert who lived in the trailer three spots down tried to drag me into his car. I'd done what my mama always told me to do if someone ever tried to snatch me up—I spit in his face and ran away.

And when I was in high school and three jocks from the football team cornered me in the empty gymnasium, shoved me to my knees and were ready to take turns using my services—by sticking their dicks in my mouth—until their coach found us and told them to get lost. No one ever talked about it again.

That had been the absolute scariest moment of my life, beyond the town pervert.

So when my former sweet-talking boss worked his magic charms and somehow I found myself kissing him with all the pent-up desire of a naive, nineteen-year-old girl who's read too many romance novels, it's no surprise that my silly dreams were crushed in an instant.

My silly dreams were always crushed. And the one thing that always got me in trouble was my too-pretty face.

I moved away, left Texas and headed for California, the land of dreams and fortune. I tried my best to stick it out in Hollywood, thinking if I had the looks, I may as well try and use them.

Instead, I realized quickly I was one of a bazillion pretty faces. I nabbed one local commercial for a TV station that only aired during late-night programming. I posed at a couple of car shows in a bikini and had to slap at all the men's grabby hands when they tried to rub my thigh or pinch my butt.

Dejected, I started searching online for a job. Any job,

anywhere, I didn't care, I just wanted out of Hollywood. Yet again, my dreams were smashed into bits. No one wanted to give me a job unless I had sex with them. Or gave them a blow job. For some reason they all wanted blow jobs.

Perverts.

Finally I came across a help-wanted ad on Craigslist for a personal assistant in the Napa Valley. That would get me out of Hollywood but keep me in California so I wouldn't have to return home and hear how everyone thought I was an epic failure.

So I transformed myself. I got the job and started wearing no makeup, pulled my hair into a bun or ponytail, and found a new wardrobe that consisted of neutral-colored, downright baggy clothing. I was a shadow of my former self. I was quiet. And I was a damn good worker.

Unfortunately, the previous owner of the winery was a terrible boss.

When he lost all his money and the property went into foreclosure, I thought for sure I'd have to return to my dusty hometown, the place where dreams went to die. I'd started packing my bags, looking for a way to sell what little furniture I had in my crap apartment that I could barely afford when my very own personal hero came into my life and changed it forever.

Matthew DeLuca.

The sexy-as-hell former pro baseball player was forced into retirement with a career-ending knee injury. With his movie-star good looks and the easygoing smile, he walked into the building and declared in that deep, rumbly voice of his—the one that stirs my body to life every time I hear it—that he was going to change our lives for the better.

And he did.

Not only did he give us all the back pay that our former employer cheated us out of when the last few paychecks started bouncing, he gave all employees of the Chandler Winery, now under the name DeLuca, a raise and then asked if we wouldn't mind working a bit of overtime the next few months in preparation for the winery's reopening.

He didn't have to ask any of us twice. We were more than willing to do whatever it took to make our new boss happy. And to put more money in our pockets.

Not only did Matt save my life, he was also a good boss. Fair, intelligent, generous, he pushed me hard to want to perform at the best of my ability. And he didn't try and chase me around his desk so he could steal a kiss.

Though I wish sometimes he would.

"Miss James, could you prepare an updated list of who will be attending next week's party?"

Matt's crisp, business-like tone shakes me from my thoughts, and I glance up to find him standing in front of my desk, a concerned expression etched into his features. His brow is wrinkled, his head tilted to the side, as if he's trying to figure out exactly what's wrong with me.

Certainly can't tell him that *he's* what's wrong with me, now can I?

"Yes, sir." I give him a close-lipped smile, my new standard since my old one was bright and toothy and caused way too many problems. Gave men the wrong impression.

"You have plans to attend, correct?" One dark brow rises as he waits for my answer.

My mouth goes dry, I lick my lips, and notice the way his gaze falls to my mouth for the briefest moment before he looks me in the eye once more. "Correct," I say, mimicking him. I need to be there to make sure everything goes well. Even though I'm beyond intimidated to even show up.

What if . . . what if he brings a date? I'll be devastated. I'll have to pretend everything's fine and carry on with my job, but inside, I'll die a little.

Which is dumb. Dumb, dumb, dumb.

"Good." He nods once. "I need you there."

"I'll be there," I say weakly, thankful I'm sitting down since my knees feel a little wobbly. Heaven help me, I like the fact that he said he needs me there.

That he needs *me*.

"Thank you." Matt nods again and heads toward the doorway that leads outside. "I'll be out in the orchard. Text me if you need me."

"Will do. And have fun," I call to him, my gaze dropping to his jean-clad backside. He'd dressed casually from the very start, considering he spent much of his time out in the vine-yards, learning what it took to produce a quality grape that would, in turn, produce a quality wine. He wears jeans and button-down shirts that he often rolls up to the elbow, re-vealing those strong, tanned forearms that make my mouth water.

On occasion, he shows up in a suit. Usually when he has a meeting at the office with someone important. An investor, a wholesaler, and the like. Those days are the worst. My con-centration is shot. The man can fill out a suit like no other. Those wide shoulders and broad chest, the dark hair that's a little longish in the back—a throwback to his baseball play-ing days, I swear. His thick, brown hair waves at the ends in the most appealing way. As in, always making my fingers itch to comb through it.

I barely restrain myself. The man is like a drug, and I'm hopelessly addicted. Not only hopelessly, I'm happily addicted. It's ridiculous, how much I think about him.

But he doesn't seem to think about me whatsoever.

My cell phone rings, and I see that it's Ivy, so I answer. I don't like taking personal calls at work. Not that Matt's ever said anything, but it doesn't feel right.

And not that I get a bunch of personal calls. I don't have a lot of friends since I'm still relatively new to the area. I don't have a boyfriend because men are nothing but trouble, and my grandma certainly never calls me. She acts like I don't even exist most of the time.

"You must come shopping with me this Saturday," she declares when I answer.

Dread sinks my stomach to my toes. I wanted to. I let her talk me into it. But the more I've thought it over, the more I've realized I can't afford the places she shops at. She's loaded. I am definitely not. "Ivy, I appreciate you wanting to take me out, but I really can't spend too much money on the dress," I explain to her, turning my chair so I can stare out the window that faces the nearby vineyards.

I can see Matt out there, talking to the field manager, his hair gleaming in the sunlight, his white button-down stretched across his shoulders in the most appealing manner. "I'm going to hit up Ross or someplace," I go on. "That's more the price range I'm looking at for this."

"You are so not going to Ross." Ivy sighs, sounding completely bent out of shape. "I have a plan and you're a part of it so you must come shopping with me. And I'm bringing a friend. You'll adore her. She's my brother's girlfriend and she's a total sweetheart."

Great. I know Ivy's brother, Gage Emerson, is a high-powered real estate hotshot who helped Matt find the winery in the first place. He's rich and gorgeous. Just like Matt. Just like Ivy's fiancé, Archer Bancroft.

And then there's me, little ol' Bryn James from Cactus, Texas, who grew up in a double-wide and was dirt-poor my entire life. I shed my skin like the snakes that lived beneath our mobile home and started a new life. Here, in California, the Golden State.

Some of the gold's become tarnished since I got here, but it's nothing a little polish can't fix.

"Sounds—"

"Like your worst nightmare?" Ivy laughs while I sit there in shock. How did she know? "I like you, Bryn. A lot. And I think you like me too."

"I do," I say automatically, sounding like a robot.

Ivy laughs harder. "You just need to . . . loosen up. You're too uptight. Do you have any friends? A boyfriend? Do you ever wear a color besides brown or tan?"

"Hey." My feelings are hurt even though all Ivy's saying is the truth. "I bought those bright tops at the Gap last month on your recommendation."

"I know. And I'm proud of you for making the effort. But you need more color, Bryn. You're so pretty—and don't deny that you are because trust me, you *so* are. Let's do your hair or take you for a makeover or something." Ivy pauses. "Please? It'll be my treat."

"No way. Uh-uh. I don't want your charity." I turn away from the window and focus on my computer screen, my vision going blurry. Usually when someone wants to do something nice for you, they always expect something in return.

At least, that's what always happens to me.

"It's not charity, I promise. I just . . . I'll explain everything to you on Saturday. We could all meet for lunch, I'll tell you everything, and then we'll shop around downtown. How does that sound?"

Like a nightmare. Like a handout. I should say no. I don't want to feel beholden to anyone. Bad enough I feel that way toward my boss. I owe him so much and he hasn't a clue.

I don't want Ivy to feel like she has to take care of me either. So embarrassing.

"Just say yes, Bryn. Come on." Ivy's tone is cajoling, and I give in because I'm a weak suck, and I can't help myself.

"Fine. I'll do it. But I have final say on everything, okay? All the shopping options and whatnot," I tell her, my voice firm.

"Yay! You won't regret this, I swear." I can literally hear the excitement in her voice. Maybe this shopping excursion means more to her than I originally thought. "Oh, and Bryn?"

"Yeah?"

"Don't tell Matt about this shopping trip, okay?"

"Ooookay."

Well.

That was weird.

Chapter 2

Bryn

We meet for lunch at Ivy's friend's place of business in downtown St. Helena. The Autumn Harvest Bakery and Café is super cute and super popular, if the crowds of people in line to purchase sandwiches, baked goods, and coffee drinks are any indication. The moment I walked in I wondered if we'd be able to find somewhere to sit.

Until I noticed a pregnant Ivy waving frantically from a table on the far side of the café and relief flooded me.

I wind my way through the crowded restaurant, my gaze going to the menu, which is written in chalk on a giant blackboard hanging above the counter. The soup and sandwich options sound amazing and my stomach growls in anticipation.

Yikes. Hope that doesn't happen when I meet Ivy's friend. Talk about making a tacky first impression.

"Bryn! So good to see you." Ivy hops up from the table and envelops me in a hug like I'm her long-lost friend. I return the gesture, oddly touched by her affection since I never really get that sort of thing anymore.

I withdraw from Ivy first and smile at the woman who's now standing next to her. She's young, with long blonde hair pulled back into a loose ponytail and cool, assessing blue eyes. "This is my friend Marina Knight," Ivy says, gesturing at

Marina with a wave of her hand. "She's the owner of Autumn Harvest and my future sister-in-law."

"Stop, please." Marina rolls her eyes. "Your brother hasn't made it official yet."

"Trust me, he will." Ivy laughs. "Marina, this is Bryn James. She's Matt's assistant."

"Oooh." That long, dragged out sound is telling. "I've heard lots about you." I both dread and long to know what they've said.

"Nice to meet you," I tell Marina as I shake her hand. All formal and business-like, I sound good. Calm and collected when usually this type of stressful situation tends to bring my Texan out.

It took me over a year to learn how to talk without all those twangs and y'alls, but it sure doesn't take much for me to slip right back into it if I don't watch out.

"Great to meet you too," Marina says with a touch too much enthusiasm. "Ivy's told me so much about you."

Really? I'm stunned. I figured they might've gossiped about me in passing, but that's it. Why in the world would Ivy talk about me to her friend? I'm so in the dark this afternoon I'm scared I won't survive it.

We all sit down and Marina goes over the menu, explaining what she thinks are the best dishes and expounding on their specials of the day. Once we've decided, she calls one of her employees over and he takes our orders—a special perk of being with the owner.

Everyone else has to stand in line and place their order at the counter.

"So Ivy said you want a makeover."

"I never said any such thing," I tell Marina, sending a surprised glance in Ivy's direction. She maintains an expression of innocence, looking downright angelic. I see her devil horns peeking through her hair though.

"Come on, Bryn. You wouldn't refuse a pregnant woman, would you?" Ivy blinks at me, the epitome of sweetness and light and my hard feelings at being pushed into something I didn't want to do melt a little.

"You're going to use that excuse as long as you can, aren't you?" Marina asks, rolling her eyes.

I know right then I'll like Marina.

"The entire pregnancy, absolutely," Ivy confirms, smiling. "Bryn, I can tell you're uncomfortable with this, but please. I'm a hormonal pregnant lady who wants nothing more than to have fun today. And having fun means finding you a gorgeous dress and going to the spa."

Just the word *spa* has dread curling in my stomach. Spa equals expensive. I should know. I've never been to one because I can't afford it.

"You're scaring her, Ivy," Marina says, her voice low. "Stop laying it on so thick. Maybe you should tell her the truth."

The truth? That sounds ominous. But there's no truth to be told, at least not yet. Ivy merely smiles at me, then changes the subject. We talk about everything and nothing while we wait for our food, Marina and Ivy chattering on while I interject when asked. Other than that, I remain silent, drinking in the cute yet hip atmosphere of the café.

Our lunches finally arrive and I dive right in, holding nothing back. I'm freaking starved and usually I eat at home, rarely going out, only because I know hardly anyone. And, since I don't cook, I eat pitiful meals that consist of Lean Cuisine microwaved meals or premade salads I pick up at the local grocery store. After I finish, they always leave me feeling empty and unsatisfied.

Kind of like my life.

Halfway through my sandwich, I realize the other women aren't eating. Glancing up from my plate, I catch both Ivy and Marina staring at me like I'm an alien who just landed on planet Earth.

I slowly chew what's in my mouth then swallow, setting the sandwich carefully on my plate. "Um, do I have something on my face?"

Marina shakes her head. "Do you never eat? Because you're acting like a starved woman."

"I don't get out much," I admit, feeling infinitely stupid.

"Give her a break and take it as a compliment. Clearly she loves your sandwiches," Ivy says, her smile kind.

"I'm not giving her a hard time. I just . . . we don't normally see girls our age devour a sandwich like that," Marina explains.

This makes me feel even worse. I'm an absolute pig. But I eat such crappy meals, and I really don't think a soup and sandwich indulgence will do me any harm.

"Being pregnant is absolute freedom. I love eating without worry." Ivy takes a huge bite out of her sandwich for emphasis.

"You're not pregnant are you, Bryn? That's not your excuse, right?" Marina asks.

I'm horrified at her question. Pregnant? Heaven forbid. "Absolutely not," I say with conviction.

Ivy bursts out laughing, pressing a hand to her chest. "Well, thank goodness. That would've torn our plan to shreds."

Okay. I'm done with the mystery. I feel like I'm their little project, and I don't like it. "What exactly is going on here?"

"What do you mean?" Ivy asks.

"I feel like you've invited me here for lunch under false

pretenses." I hate that I'm skeptical of everyone, but I can't help myself. My entire life I've always felt like someone wants something from me. It's made me throw up walls and become ultradefensive.

I have no idea what they're up to and it's making me uncomfortable.

"Just tell her Ivy," Marina mumbles, making me even more nervous.

These women in the Napa Valley are weird. And I thought Hollywood was full of strange people.

"Oh fine." Ivy blows out an irritated sigh. "I wanted this to be a surprise, but you're getting too twitchy. We want to try and pair you up with Matt."

I gape at her. Wait. What? "Are you talking about Matt—as in my boss, Matt DeLuca?"

Now it's Ivy's turn to roll her eyes. "Do you know another Matt?"

Well, I went to school with Matt Short, but he's still back in Cactus, running his daddy's welding business last I heard. "But he's my boss," I stress, thinking of another boss I had. The one with the kids and the wife and the wandering hands, the one who literally chased me so fast around his desk we probably wore a path in the carpet.

"So?" Ivy waves her hand, dismissing my concerns. "I think he has the hots for you."

I refuse to let that bit of information spark hope in my chest. Forget it. "I doubt that. I'm his assistant." Who wears drab clothing and tries to be efficient but forgettable.

"So? Attraction is attraction." Ivy shrugs, taking a bite from her sandwich.

I watch her and Marina eat, the both of them completely

unaffected while inside my nerves are in chaos. It's one thing to be attracted to my boss and keep my feelings secret.

It's quite another to have others notice that there might be something between us and actually want me to act on it.

"I'm not his type," I finally say, unable to come right out and say what I really feel.

I dress like this and act like this on purpose. I don't want Matt DeLuca's attention. I don't want him to notice me!

Lately though, I do. I have to fight it every day. It would be so easy to throw on a short skirt and a revealing top, saunter into his office, and lick my lips before flashing my sauciest smile. Wear my hair down and flip it over my shoulder, thrust my chest out and let him get a look at my breasts because even I can admit they're pretty nice.

But I don't do any of that. It's not worth the trouble.

"I think you're hiding beneath that exterior. I've never seen you look better than right now," Ivy says matter-of-factly.

I'm wearing a red T-shirt and a pair of jeans, and my hair is in a high ponytail. Not a lick of makeup is on my face and the jeans fit my curvier self from a year ago so they're kind of saggy. Not the most flattering thing I own.

"Gee thanks," I mutter.

"I'm being serious. The way you dress, the way you present yourself to everyone, it doesn't feel real. It's like you're doing your best to hide." Ivy contemplates me, her gaze roving over my face, and I almost want to squirm, she's making me so uncomfortable. "You have a beautiful face."

Oh, no. "Thank you," I say uncertainly.

Ivy narrows her eyes, nudges Marina with her elbow. "Like, really beautiful. You could pass for Angelina Jolie. Don't you think, Marina?"

"Please." I've been told that once or twice. Usually by some lecherous, so-called director I'm reading a script for who's hoping to get in my panties before he'll give me the part. I don't miss Hollywood at all. "I look nothing like her."

Now it's Marina's turn to scrutinize me. "Yeah, actually you kind of do look like her."

My appetite evaporates, just like that. I stare at my half-eaten sandwich, sad that I can't enjoy it any longer.

"Where are you from anyway, Bryn? I don't think you've ever told me," Ivy says.

"I came here from southern California." I shrug, being deliberately vague.

"And where did you come from before that?" Marina asks. "You have a slight accent."

Crap. I thought I'd banished that twang for good. "Fine. I grew up in Texas," I say with a sigh. "A little town I'm sure you've never heard of."

"Now I'm dying to know," Marina says.

I'd come to California to forget my past and start fresh. I want a new chance, to be a new me. Not sit over lunch and reminisce. "Cactus, Texas, population three thousand-two hundred. Right at the tippy-top of the state," I say.

Ivy grins. "You said 'tippy-top.'"

My cheeks are hot. "I guess I'm still a bit of a hick." I am such a hick. And in this town full of rich people, where everything is beautiful, and lush, and green, I'm nothing but a simple girl.

"You are not a hick. You're adorable." Ivy smiles and picks up her glass of ice water, sipping from the straw. "Let's finish lunch and go shopping before my mid-afternoon exhaustion sets in."

"We're going to Ross, right?" I ask weakly, knowing there wasn't a Ross Dress for Less anywhere near St. Helena.

"Absolutely not," Ivy says firmly, Marina nodding in agreement.

"There are a few boutiques nearby where I think we'll find something. Something amazing to knock Matt's socks off," Marina says.

"Why are you two so determined to hook me up with Matt?" I shouldn't even consider messing around with my boss. And I don't get why these two women are so willing to set their friend up with his assistant—as in me. It makes no sense.

"He's lonely. I swear, in all the time I've known him, I've never seen him with a woman more than once," Ivy explains. "He's a bit of a serial dater. He needs to find a steady woman. One he can count on."

Ugh. Well, that's not good. That means he's a commitment-phobe.

"He was a pro baseball player," I say, my voice dripping with sarcasm because *come on*. "You're telling me he had a hard time finding women?"

"No, certainly not. But he does have trouble finding a good one," Ivy says.

"But he's definitely the least cynical of the three," Marina adds. "Which is to your advantage, Bryn. He's not such a non-believer."

My head is bouncing from one to the other, like I'm watching a tennis match. I have no idea what to believe, who to believe. It all sounds like dreamy, Cinderella-type stuff.

And I'm not one who believes in the fairy tale.

"Such a nonbeliever of what?"

"Why love, of course."

Matt

"Y ou, my friend, are a grumpy asshole." Gage points his beer bottle in my direction before he takes a swig, Archer chuckling and nodding in agreement.

Assholes. The both of them. Calling *me* a grumpy asshole. I have reason to be grumpy. I'm working my fingers to the bone trying to get this winery in top shape so I don't become the laughingstock of the Napa Valley. All while they're perfectly happy and content, living with their women, established in their careers. Hell, Archer's getting married soon and having a baby.

I've had to start completely over. And it sucks.

"Both of you cheated," I grumble, peeling the label off my beer bottle, shredding it to bits, and leaving a mess on the table for someone else to clean up.

And I really don't give a damn.

We're at the golf resort's lounge, having a beer after an intensely sucky game on my part. I just want to go home.

Or drown my sorrows in plenty of beer.

"Hell no, we didn't cheat, you sore-ass loser. I won fair and square. It's not our fault you never have time to play golf anymore," Archer says, his look pointed as he watches me from across the table.

Wasn't that the truth? I have no time for anything anymore. It's all about the winery. Makes me worry—and I've had this worry more than once since the moment I made the purchase—if I've done the right thing. The winery is a huge responsibility. I have a great staff helping me run it, but damn.

I need a break.

Thought golfing eighteen holes with my best friends would be a great way to ease some stress. Instead, it seemed to stress me out even more. My game was bad. My focus shot. I took endless phone calls, texted more than I swung, and generally pissed everyone off—including the fourth guy we didn't even know who was paired with us to play.

Now here we sit in the nearly empty lounge—it's a Saturday afternoon, so I can only assume all the men have gone home to their wives—talking about my shitty mood.

I really hate when I'm the focus of their attention. I know my friends mean well but right now, I don't want to deal.

"You know what your problem is?" Gage asks, interrupting my thoughts.

Looks like I have no choice but to deal. "Please. Enlighten me," I drawl, preparing myself for some sort of insult. It's how we usually operate together. We're friends, we take care of each other, celebrate the ups, mourn the downs, but in the end, we always, *always* give each other shit.

We could count on each other for that.

"You need to get laid." Gage jabs his finger in my direction. "And quick."

Hell. He was close to the money, if not right on it. I can't remember the last time I got laid. I'd been detrimentally injured over a year ago during practice, for the love of God—*practice*—and that put me out of commission for months. My career, as well as my mind, was blown.

I had no time for women during that dark period of my life. Hell, I'd been a fucked-up mess, mourning the loss of my career, my life as I knew it, and I even lost a little bit of myself. My relationship with my dad became even more strained—no surprise. He'd been so proud of me for following in his footsteps and playing in the major leagues. It was his only source of pride when it came to me. Once he lost that, he lost interest.

Completely.

When I became strong enough, I went through physical therapy on my way to recovery. I was so focused on that I didn't care about women. And once I healed, I went in search of an investment, a new career, a new focus, and that ended up taking all of my time, so now . . .

Here I am. Grumpy and . . . yeah, in dire need of some sexual attention.

Problem? Only one woman has snagged my attention, and I still can't figure out why. Or figure her out. Bryn is a mystery.

And I want to solve it. Solve her.

Christ. Even thinking those two benign words makes me break out in a sweat.

"You're right," I finally say, deciding to own up to it. "I haven't gotten laid in months." Too many months to mention, the number was so embarrassingly high.

"Knew it," Gage says grimly. "You need to get out more, my friend. Hit up a bar or something."

Grimacing, I shake my head. That sounds like my personal nightmare. "The bar scene is not for me. I don't have time for that sort of thing."

"You'd have a flock of women surrounding you the minute you entered," Archer says, his brows raised as he tips his head toward me. "I hear the gossip around this town. All the single women under the age of fifty are thrilled that former pro baseball superstar Matt DeLuca is living here. They want a chance with you."

"You're the most eligible bachelor in the entire area," Gage adds.

Holy shit. These two have spent way too much time with their women. "You guys sound like a bunch of gossiping hens. Are you for real? Did you really just say I'm the most eligible bachelor?" I pause. "And that all the single women under the age of *fifty* are interested? I mean, what the hell?"

"Hey, there are a lot of women out there who don't care if they're older than you. They're looking for a man, doesn't matter his age," Archer says, a hint of a smile curling his lips.

That little smile makes me want to punch him. "And how do you know this?" Anger and embarrassment war within me. It's bad enough the entire community is waiting with baited breath for me to fail in the winery business. Worse, there's supposedly a line of single women desperate to get their claws in me?

I swear I'll never have any respect in this town. None. Zero.

"I hear talk. I've lived in the Napa Valley for a while now. I have a lot of connections. Ivy's gained a lot of connections in a short amount of time with her work. We're in the know and things are definitely being said about you," Archer explains.

"Marina has lived here her entire life. She's heard plenty lately. There's a lot of gossip that goes down in that little bakery of hers, especially in the morning when everyone's grabbing a coffee," Gage says. "She says the buzz is heavy about the winery, about you. Everyone's curious."

Holy hell. This just . . . sucks. I don't want to be the mockery of the Napa wine country. I'm trying to start a new life here. Become a different person. Not be known as the hotshot player son of former hotshot player—and notorious hothead—Vinnie DeLuca. Dad played for the Oakland A's years ago when I was a little kid and earned his reputation as a troublemaker from the very start.

Many in the profession expected me to follow in his footsteps. I showed talent early. I was a cocky asshole in high school because I knew I was damn good. But I wasn't a mean asshole who always tried to get in fights. That's more my father's style.

I never wanted to be like him, not like that.

Ever.

"So everyone's gossiping about me and my potential love life," I say through gritted teeth.

"Well, yeah, and so are we because we're concerned, man. You're working too hard. You need to relax and live a little. You've always been a little intense when it comes to your career," Archer says.

I study Archer, see the worry filling his eyes. Yeah, we all give each other shit, but he's being serious. He's concerned for my welfare and I appreciate that.

"The minute this reopening party is done, I'm going to tone it down," I vow, feeling like I'm making some sort of solemn promise. "You're right. I can't continue to work at this pace; it'll drive me into an early grave."

"Hell yeah, it will. You gotta find balance," says the second biggest workaholic I know, Gage.

Balance. I really have no idea what it is or how to get it.

"And you gotta get laid," Archer adds with a chuckle. "We gotta find you a woman. I'm sure Ivy has some single friends."

"So does Marina. She knows everyone," Gage says.

Now they want to set me up. Great. "I can find my own woman, thank you very much."

"Really? Because you're doing a pretty piss-poor job of it at the moment." Gage laughs and Archer joins in.

"Like I have time," I mutter. Realization hits, and I decide to go in for the kill. "And hey, maybe I'm waiting because I'm in need of my payment."

"Payment?" they both echo, like it was rehearsed.

I want to knock them both upside their heads.

"Yeah, that little bet we made months ago? I'm here to collect," I say, my voice smug. "So pay up."

"We don't owe you shit," Archer mutters.

"Who's the last man standing, hmm? I want my million dollars." I could funnel it right back into the business. Hell, I'd probably give these two bastards a share of the profits from what I'd reinvest. I'm fair like that. I take care of my friends.

"There is no way I'm paying you. That was a bullshit bet," Gage protests.

"You're only saying it's bullshit because you lost." I drain my beer and set the empty bottle on the table with a loud *thunk*. "I expect payment within seven days."

"Oh, listen to you, all formal and shit. How about we make this a little more interesting." Archer leans back in his chair, a gleam in his eye.

Anticipation rolls through my brain, hums through my blood. "I'm open. What are you talking about?"

"Give us sixty days. If you're still single within that time period, we'll pay you fair and square," Archer says.

"But—" Gage starts, but Archer silences him with a look.

"Sixty days? How about thirty?" I laugh. "I won't be with any woman in thirty days, especially in a relationship with one."

"Thirty? That's too short. None of us expect you to be in a relationship in thirty freaking days," Archer says. "Make it forty-five."

"Forty-five?" Gage asks. He sounds horrified. "I still think that's too short. How about ninety? That's more reasonable."

"We never said this bet was reasonable," I reply calmly. Freaking cheapskate Gage. "Forty-five days or you pay up now. It's your choice." I know I won't be in any sort of relationship in that amount of time. Give me a break.

"I want to add a stipulation." Archer grins. "No sex either. So no relationship, no sex, no one-night stands, nothing for you, Matt, for the next forty-five days. You withstand it, you'll get your million bucks . . . plus another two-hundred fifty thousand to make it interesting."

"No freaking way," Gage says.

"Yes way, jackass. We're doing it," Archer says, not even letting him argue.

"Fine. Deal," I say firmly. I've gone this long without sex, what's another forty-five days? I can handle it.

"God, you disappoint me. You're so confident. I'd think you'd at least want to get some on occasion, you know?" Gage shakes his head, but I ignore him.

"I'm agreeing to this," I say. "I'm sure you two losers need the time anyway to gather up the funds to pay me, so I get it. I can be a patient guy. No problem. But in forty-five days, I want my money. No excuses, no bullshit. Six hundred and twenty-five thousand each."

"Then we have a deal," Archer says, a sly grin on his face. The asshole is up to something, I can tell.

And I don't like it.

"Whatever. Deal," Gage says much more reluctantly. The guy hates nothing more than wasting money, and I'm sure he views this payout as the ultimate waste.

"So I hear Ivy's taken your assistant out for lunch and

shopping today," Archer says, his voice casual. Too casual. "What gives?"

"Really?" Curiosity fills me. I knew Ivy had taken a liking to Bryn and Bryn felt the same. But I didn't realize they'd become that close.

"Yep." Archer nods. "I heard something mentioned about a makeover."

"Marina went with them too," Gage confirms.

Shit. Now I'm really starting to sweat. Bad enough I'm attracted to Bryn despite her boring clothes and uninspired appearance. It was her damn scent. God, she smelled fucking fabulous. Sweet and fruity yet floral and with this hint of spice that I can't quite put my finger on.

"Yeah, Ivy sent me a picture as a matter of fact. Couldn't quite figure out why she'd do that since, you know, I'm not interested in any other woman but her." Archer shrugs then grabs for his phone. "Then she texted that I needed to show you."

He hands over his phone, and I look at the screen, my mouth going dry. It was a picture of Bryn in a chair at a salon, wearing a close-lipped smile, her almost-black hair cascading around her face, down past her shoulders in luxurious waves.

"Whatcha think?" Archer asks before he bursts into smug laughter.

Damn. I'm in huge trouble.

Chapter 3

Matt

I came into work early Monday morning so I could walk the fields and inspect the vineyards alone before anyone else got there, my new absolute favorite thing to do. I'm not a sit-in-the-office kind of guy. A nine-to-five job holds absolutely no appeal. When I bought the winery, I didn't know shit about wine besides the fact that I liked some, but I definitely wasn't a connoisseur. More like an I'll-drink-some-wine-if-you-have-nothing-else type of guy.

I preferred beer.

But I've since learned there's a science to wine making. It's a formula, with a bit of luck thrown in for good measure. The grapes have to be just so. The weather has to be a certain way to insure that.

A variety of factors play into it. Some we have complete and total control over and others . . .

We're at the whim of their command, which drives those scientist brains absolutely crazy.

There's more to my spending time out in the fields this particular morning. And it all has to do with a particular woman. I'm avoiding the office because Bryn will arrive soon, and I don't want to see her. That picture Archer showed me haunted my thoughts the rest of the day. Hell, the rest of the weekend. All that hair—I could only imagine slipping my fingers through it. Wrapping those long, silky strands around my fist and giving it a tug. Pulling her in so I could kiss her. Burying my face into the soft mass and inhaling her delicious scent.

She had on a red T-shirt in the picture, that mysterious little close-lipped smile, and makeup on her face. I could tell because for the first time ever, I really noticed her eyes. They were crystal blue like a perfect summer sky.

Needless to say, after thinking about Bryn a little too much, I took a shower and jerked off. This new addition to the bet with Archer and Gage is going to kill me. I couldn't even run out and find some anonymous chick and fuck her. I could lie, I guess. Keep it from them.

But I wouldn't feel right about that, and besides, they'd figure me out. They always do. I don't like liars. My father is a consummate one. Seeing how his lies always ended up getting him in trouble, I purposely keep myself on the straight and narrow. I'm brutally honest. Always.

Archer knows it too, that motherfucker. It was like he set that entire deal up. He knew I was interested in Bryn and he knew she would tempt me. Always one step ahead, that guy.

The field employees start to slowly trickle in, and my phone starts blowing up with emails, text messages, and phone calls. The workday has officially kicked off, so I decide to pack it in and reluctantly head for the office. I know Bryn's there; I see her car in the parking lot. As I walk through the vineyard, I go over the various scenarios that could be awaiting me within the building:

Bryn, wearing her hair down and clad in some sort of sexy skirt and button-up shirt combo with her cleavage on display.

Or Bryn, back to normal with her hair pulled into a tight bun and the baggy beige ensemble I've come to depend on.

Worse, maybe there will be a combo Bryn sitting behind her desk: hair down, beige pants and top on, those pretty eyes enhanced with cosmetics, all of it designed to drive me absolutely wild with lust. That Bryn just might do me in—every facet of her on display, making me want her.

Clearly I have too much time on my hands if I'm coming up with all of these ridiculous thoughts. I need to focus on the most important task at hand. Today's Monday and the grand reopening is Friday. There's still so much to do for this giant event it's not even funny.

And Bryn is pretty much handling everything—consulting me along the way, of course.

Hell.

I enter the building, the cool air greeting me. It's blessedly silent, and I walk down the hall toward my office, nerves eating at my gut as I roll up first one sleeve, then the other of my navy blue button-down. I'm wearing jeans and my work boots, thankful for the casual atmosphere. Every time I have to put on a monkey suit, I feel ridiculous, uncomfortable.

So not my thing.

I enter the outer office where Bryn's desk is and stop short, my eyes widening at the sight before me. It's Bryn, bent over the file cabinet that sits just behind her desk, her very fine ass waving in the air as she searches through the files.

The fact that I can actually see the shape of her ass tells me she's wearing something completely different than usual. Second clue, there's not a hint of beige or tan or khaki in sight.

The dress is black, with a delicate floral print in hints of green and turquoise. The flared skirt stops just above her knee, which means if she was bent over the cabinet much farther, I'd be looking at her panties.

Just the word *panties* makes my entire body twitch in anticipation. Those long, bare legs make my gut twist and her scent washes over me, sweet and so uniquely Bryn I'm afraid I might do something fucking crazy.

Like sneak up on her, wrap my hands around her waist, and tug her close. Let her feel exactly what she does to me.

Deciding I shouldn't surprise her, I clear my throat, letting her know I've arrived. A little gasp escapes her and she stands up straight, pushing the drawer in with a loud slam as she turns—in black high-heeled shoes that fuel all sorts of instant fantasies—to face me.

"Matt! Um, Mr. DeLuca, good morning." She runs her hands down the front of her dress, her expression self-conscious, her movements agitated.

The dress fits her like a dream. I can see the shape of her full breasts, the nip in her waist, the flare of her hips. Her arms are completely exposed, slender and graceful and she lifts one, smoothing her elegant hand over her hair in a most definite nervous gesture.

Her hair just so happens to be pulled back, but not like usual. It's in a loose braid, and a few wisps curl around her face, emphasizing the exotic slant of cheekbones I've never noticed before.

Good God, my assistant is smoking-ass hot.

"Morning," I say, clearing my throat, but the word comes out more like a strangled croak. "You look . . . ah . . . nice."

She darts behind her desk and lands in her chair, pulling it up close, almost like she's using her desk as some sort of protective shield. Too late, I've already seen her, and I wholeheartedly approve. "Thank you."

I don't know what else to say. All sorts of questions are running through my brain. Like, *What happened? Why did you go shopping with Ivy and Marina? What made you decide to give up beige? Is this a temporary thing or permanent, because I don't know if my heart can take it, seeing you like this every single day.*

Instead, I go for the safe and boring. It's easier. Less risky.

"Did you have a nice weekend?" I slowly approach her desk, noticing the way her fingers shake slightly when she picks up a pile of paper, straightens it, and then puts it to the side.

Interesting.

"I did, thank you. How about you?" She picks up a pen and taps it against the edge of her pursed lips. Lips covered by a slick of pale peach gloss, I might add.

It was fucking great. I went and golfed with my best friends, we made a new bet that I can't touch any woman—including you—for the next forty-five days, and then I saw a picture of you and your new look. I jerked off twice, not that seeing your photo with all that sexy-as-fuck hair is related—no, not at all. Then I come to work and see you like this, and all I can think about is how much I want to get my hands on you. All over you.

"It was fine," I answer, stopping just in front of her desk. She looks up at me, and my gaze drops to the elegant line of her neck, her exposed collarbone. She's wearing a delicate gold necklace with a little charm dangling from it. I can't quite tell what it is.

All I know is I want to fucking kiss her right there, where her skin is probably soft and sweet and scented. Follow the thin, tempting line of the necklace, kiss her all around her neck, her nape, her collarbone. Lick and nibble and make her moan.

"Is there anything in particular you'd like me to do for you this morning?"

Her sweet, sultry, and slightly trembling voice knocks me from my thoughts and turns them even dirtier, if that's possible.

Why yes, Miss James. I'd love it if you could perch your pretty little ass right on the edge of your desk, slowly lift your skirt, and spread your legs so I can see what you're hiding under there. Maybe lick your peach-glossed lips and say something subtly filthy like, "I've got something I'd like you to do, Mr. DeLuca. How about . . . me?"

I blink, hard. Twice. Trying to push the image of Bryn inviting me to fuck her from my head, but it's just no use. She's all I can see. Her hands braced behind her on the desk, her spread legs dangling, the skirt of her dress bunched around her waist. I can imagine her wearing skimpy black lace panties, panties I can see right through.

She fucking works for you! Get your mind out of the gutter.

Damn, the state board of equalization could have a field day with me. I'm a pervert of the highest degree.

"Let me make a few calls and check my emails. I'm sure there's plenty I'll need you to do today, like usual. This week is going to be a busy one," I say, my voice brusque as I turn away from her desk and head toward my office door. "You'll probably need to work late all week, just warning you."

That statement conjures more images, ones I hurriedly push out my brain so they don't clog it all up and distract me again.

"I don't mind," she calls after me. "I have a list of things I'm going to follow up on. I'm calling the caterer right now because there are still a few unresolved items, including the final headcount for the party Friday night. I'll come see you in a bit so we can go over everything."

"Sounds good," I say as I open my office door and slam it shut behind me.

My breathing erratic like I just ran around the bases at top speed, I collapse in my chair. Exhaling loudly, I lean my head against the back of it, staring at the ceiling. Bryn's pretty face, those sexy glossed lips, still forefront in my mind.

Holy hell. She looks freaking amazing. Combine all that with her heady scent, her sensible work ethic, that curvy figure, her dependability, those damn black shoes that are giving me heart palpitations, and I'm a dead man.

Forty-three days, and I can't touch a single woman, or I risk a million-dollar-plus loss. And it's not that I need the money, it's the principle of the matter. I won the initial bet fair and square. Now those two so-called friends of mine have changed it up and put me in a bind.

It's my own damn fault though. I'm the one who agreed to it in the first place.

Worse? All I can think about is touching a woman. Well, a particular one. Sitting a few feet away from me. The same woman who just so happens to work for me.

And the only person I can blame is myself.

Bryn

Matt slams his office door with a finality that makes me jump in my chair. My heart racing, I rest my hand over my chest, feel it flutter against my palm like the furiously fast wings of a hummingbird. I hadn't expected him to walk inside at that particular moment—with my butt in the air. I was searching through the file cabinet looking for an invoice I know I paid after just receiving a past due notice in the weekend's mail.

So embarrassing, him catching me like that. *God*.

I found the paid bill. Had started ruffling around looking for something else, I can't even remember what, when I heard him clear his throat. God, he'd surprised me. I'd nearly leapt out of my skin when I turned to find him standing there, looking as gorgeous as can be. Per his usual, if I'm being truthful.

Not the way I wanted to make an impression. No, I'd planned on sitting behind my desk when I first saw him this morning. Calm, cool, and efficient, offering a bright "good morning" with an equally bright smile. Watch him stare at me in total shock.

Well, I got the shocked stare, that is for sure. But I also noticed how his gaze had been zeroed in on my backside when I was bent over before it rose quickly to meet my eyes. He didn't say anything about my change in appearance beyond the standard "you look nice."

Nice.

How boring is that? Then he went on to ask if I had a nice weekend too, like nothing had changed, nothing was different. Not that I want him to be a slobbering idiot like my creeper old boss. But I thought I'd at least thoroughly impress Matt with the dress, the hair, the makeup, and the shoes.

God, the shoes. They're pinching my toes and I don't think I've been here even an hour.

I'd expected at least a "you look pretty" comment or something. Anything really.

But it was the same old thing. Back to work. Gotta keep on it, we're so busy, and I need you to work late, Miss James, blah, blah, blah. Just like his usual self.

Instead of disappointment, I should be glad. I should be

relieved and thankful he didn't leer at me and tell me how sexy I looked and could he get a hand up my skirt or anything like that. My old boss spoke to me like that all the time. He literally asked if he could feel up my "titties" one afternoon. I really hate that word. I'd worked as his receptionist for two whole weeks when he asked that particular question.

I'd been so surprised I'd politely told him, "I don't think so."

I don't think so. I'd been so naive and shocked, I'd even giggled when I said it, which probably gave him the wrong idea.

That I'd willingly let him kiss me and touch my so-called titties within two months of that first request probably gave him the wrong idea too.

Sighing, I rub my forehead, run my hand over my hair. I'd planned on wearing it down and decided at the last minute I couldn't do it. The dress, the makeup, and the shoes were bad enough. The hair, my one crowning glory as my grandma always called it, would've made it more than obvious.

My daily appearance as the drab, neutral Miss James is a complete facade. How I'm dressed at this very moment, I'm more like my old, sexy, too-pretty-for-her-own-good Bryn self.

Shopping with Ivy and Marina had been so much fun though. Those girls ran me ragged all Saturday afternoon and into the evening. That little pregnant and supposedly exhausted Ivy was the fastest of us all, too. She pulled out so many things for me to try on, I'd been stuck in one dressing room after another, all over downtown St. Helena.

I'd broken out the credit card and bought a few new pieces of clothing for work, this dress being one of them. Then they took me to a salon, and I got my hair cut. I can't remember the last time I had it trimmed, and it felt so good to have it professionally shaped and styled, some of that heavy weight cut off since my hair is so thick.

When they offered the free makeover, I decided why not. What could it hurt? Not that I don't know how to apply makeup. I have an entire box of the stuff at home, stuffed under the sink. I haven't busted it out once since I arrived in St. Helena. I was a new person and this version of Bryn James didn't wear makeup.

The makeup artist was good and Ivy and Marina were beside themselves when it was all said and done. The new hair, the new face—they couldn't stop going on about how fabulous I looked.

Or how fabulous they thought Matt would find me.

Those words made me nervous. I wasn't doing this just to get a reaction out of Matt. I also did it for me. To bond with these two women who felt like they could be true friends. Had I ever really had friends? When I was little, yes, I had a bunch of them. I ran around with a group of kids who lived in the trailer park with me. But as I got older, filled out and got curves, the boys started paying attention to me in a different way.

And the girls didn't really like me anymore.

Shoving those unpleasant thoughts from my mind, I remember the last store we went into before going out to dinner. They'd been ready to close up shop, the employees irritated that we'd come in. Ivy had spotted a dress in the window she declared perfect for me to wear to the grand reopening and I'd reluctantly agreed.

The moment I put the magenta dress on, I knew Ivy had been right. It felt silky on my skin, with thin straps that wrapped over my shoulders and an almost completely exposed back. A deep V in the front showed off my cleavage, and the slightly fitted skirt hugged my hips and thighs, stopping just above my knee. The dress was sophisticated and gorgeous and sexy. Marina and Ivy practically peed themselves they'd been so excited to see me in it when I emerged from the dressing room. I turned this way and that, smiling and laughing with them as I imagined what Matt might do when he saw me in it.

Then I slipped back into the dressing room, caught sight of the price tag, and gasped in surprise.

It cost almost my entire month's paycheck.

Immediately depressed, I took the dress off, slung it back on the hanger, and fled the dressing room, leaving the dress inside, mumbling to both girls that I'd changed my mind and didn't want it. Marina followed me outside in shocked disbelief, trying to convince me I needed to march right back in there and buy that dress.

I'd been too distraught to even wonder what Ivy might be doing.

Ivy joined us within moments, her expression serious and clutching a shopping bag. She thrust it toward me, her jaw set, her mouth thin.

"Don't you dare refuse this. It's my gift to you. For all the birthdays and Christmases you have coming up," Ivy said.

I'd wanted to cry as I accepted the bag, but held it together. Her kindness surprised me, especially from a woman I barely knew. My own mama wouldn't look twice at me anymore since she was too busy out living her own life. I haven't seen her since I graduated high school and she'd only come for the ceremony before she left again with her boyfriend. And my grandma would rather give me crap than a present.

It was the nicest thing anyone had ever done for me before, besides Matt repaying our bounced paychecks.

Now the dress is ready to be worn, sitting in my nearly

empty closet. I can't wait. I absolutely cannot wait to put it on and see what Matt does when he gets a gander of me.

Probably nothing. He'd probably say, "You look nice, Miss James," and leave it at that.

My fist curls of its own volition, and I thump it on top of my desk, making everything sitting on the surface rattle. *No.* I refuse to accept another non-reaction from Matt. I know he's my boss. I know I shouldn't be doing anything like this. It's risky, stupid, and I could potentially lose my job or at least ruin it forever.

I still want him. The consequences be damned. I want Matthew DeLuca.

And I'm starting to think I'll do anything to make it happen.

Chapter 4

Bryn

"You work too hard."

Matt glances up, his dark gaze meeting mine. Lines of exhaustion are around his eyes, his normally lush mouth turned into a slight frown. His dark brown hair is in complete, sexy disarray and his shirtsleeves are shoved up almost past his elbows, as if he'd done it impatiently.

Which he probably had, knowing him.

For the past two days, he's been working constantly preparing for the grand reopening. Considering it's already Wednesday and we only have two days left to prepare, I've been here right along with him, helping wherever I can.

He's beautiful despite the air of tired frustration that hangs over him, and I realize in that moment that I'd love nothing more than to grab him. Slip in between his chair and the desk, settle on the edge and pull him into me by his tie. Kiss him until he forgot all about the winery and the grand reopening and the party and everything else.

Until all he could focus on was me, a more than willing woman with her tongue in his mouth and her hand in his hair, her other hand gripping his tie so he can't get away. And he wouldn't want to get away. He'd kiss me harder, grip my waist, push my skirt up and . . .

Yes. I want to kiss his troubles away. And he'd probably think I lost my mind if I even attempted it.

"I have to work hard," he says with this rueful smile that doesn't look real. No, it looks as tired as the rest of him. "Trying to make sure this all comes together properly, you know? We only have a few days left and it's crunch time."

That's his new favorite phrase—crunch time. He's been saying it since Monday, when he had a staff meeting and told everyone we needed to basically get our asses in gear and get this place in tip-top shape.

I've worked past six the last two evenings and tonight it's almost seven. I'm starving, but trying to ignore my growling stomach. I'm also wishing for my drab uniform of old because hey, dressing like you don't care also means you dress comfortably.

Today I'm wearing a new black pencil skirt that makes it hard to take wide steps and a pretty, delicate white shirt that makes my boobs look huge, not that boss man has noticed. Oh, and I'm wearing the new damn shoes I've worn all week that I've somehow gotten used to—sort of.

My toes scream with joy every night when I slip the shoes off, and I might have Band-Aids on the back of my ankles, but I'm making them work. Matt's appreciative looks every time his gaze drops to my feet for even the briefest moment make all the pain worth it.

Despite parading the new wardrobe in front of him for the last three days, it's like he's hardly noticed. I know Matt's distracted, his brain completely preoccupied with this grand reopening party. It's so important to him, for the winery to be successful, for him to do something other than play baseball. I think he's afraid no one takes him seriously, and I totally get that.

But I'm dying for him to notice me. Really, really notice me. I've done just about everything I can to get him to see me, but it's like he looks right past me.

Rather frustrating.

And I want him to like me for more than my looks too. I know he appreciates the work I do for him and admires "the way I handle things so efficiently"—this is a direct quote, one he said to me only yesterday. But what about me? Bryn James, the woman? I may be just some hick from Texas at the mere age of twenty-two who's hardly lived, and I'm definitely not sophisticated like the women he probably prefers to date or screw or whatever, but damn it, I want a chance.

If I were bold and brave, I'd *demand* a chance.

I take care of the man, and he doesn't even realize it. I make sure he eats. I make sure he goes home. I handle his schedule, knowing where he needs to be or what he needs to be doing at all times. I make sure all the little details that he might've missed are handled. I'm here for him always. Always.

And he doesn't really care.

"Are you hungry?" I ask, my stomach grumbling yet again and reminding me that yes, indeed *I* certainly am.

He shrugs those impossibly broad shoulders. They look even broader when encased in starched white cotton. He's still wearing a tie, though it's loosened around his neck, and the first button of his shirt is undone, tempting me to unbutton it even more and see what he's hiding beneath the fabric.

Like I don't know. I might've spent a few hours Googling Matt DeLuca. It was easy—the man has a ton of photos out there. Some of those pictures are mouthwateringly good because holy hell, the man's body is perfection. He's posed for a few magazines over the years wearing little, and I said a small prayer of thanks when I stumbled across those after I first started working for him.

I might've gone in search of those photos again last night. Staring and drooling and wondering what the heck I can do to garner this man's attention. How much more obvious do I need to be?

He'd dressed to impress today because he met with reporters from a local news station for a video interview about the winery earlier this afternoon.

Matt most definitely impressed me. I love it when he wears suits or at least a dress shirt and tie, which is not often enough in my humble opinion.

"I'm kind of hungry, I guess," he finally answers, his gaze locked on the computer screen as he taps away at the keyboard with his typical index-finger pecking. I have no idea what he's working on, but it's definitely holding his interest better than I am. "But I don't have time to eat."

"Want me to bring you something then?"

He looks at me once more, peering over the top of his monitor, his gaze narrowed, his expression skeptical. I'm sitting across from his desk, feeling a little rumpled, a lot tired, and wishing I looked as perfectly sexy as he does. "You don't need to do that," he says carefully. "Maybe you should go on home, Miss James. It's late. You've put in a long day."

What, go home to an empty apartment and more Lean Cuisine? I don't think so. "I don't mind picking you up something to eat, Matt . . . er, Mr. DeLuca." I try to keep it formal between us, and he does the same, but we both slip on occasion. There's something a little fun about addressing him so properly. Makes my wicked thoughts of him all the more lurid. "I could call in an order from somewhere you like and have it here for you within thirty minutes."

"I don't know. I'm not even sure what I'd want." He rubs his hand along his jaw. I can hear the rasp of stubble against his palm, and my knees literally go weak. I would love to know what that slightly rough face would feel like against mine, or even better—how it would feel between my thighs.

Thank goodness I'm sitting down, or I swear I'd collapse because my legs are so wobbly.

"I'll take care of everything," I say, my mind scrambling as I stand. "I'll order some food and deliver it to you before I leave for the night." I start to leave the office, wondering if he prefers Italian or Chinese when he says my name in that deep, delicious voice of his.

I stop and slowly turn to find him looking at me, his expression one of pure gratitude. "Thanks a lot for taking care of me these last few days. I know I've kept you far busier than you should be."

Smiling, I try to ignore the mass of butterflies fluttering in my stomach at his words. "You're welcome. And it's my job, right? I'm just doing what I'm supposed to."

"Not necessarily a part of your formal job description, but I suppose." He smiles. "You should join me." At my confused look he explains further. "For dinner."

"Oh, I-I couldn't." I shake my head at the same exact moment my stomach decides to grumble loudly, and I rest my hand over my front, horribly embarrassed. I can feel my cheeks heat, and I'm tempted to duck and run.

But I stand my ground instead, trying to pretend it didn't happen.

Soft laughter escapes him as he quirks an eyebrow at me. "Not hungry, huh?"

"Fine. I'm starving." I roll my eyes. Are we flirting? It feels like it but . . . not. Ugh, he's so confusing. "But I'm sure you don't want to eat with me. We spend enough time together, don't you think?"

"Do you want to eat with me?" he asks, his dying laughter replaced with this foreign gleam in his eyes. "I don't mind if you don't. Come on, Bryn. Let's have dinner together at my desk. It'll be exciting." He laughs. "We can go over the caterer menu one more time. Exciting right?"

"All right," I agree, trying my best to stomp down the giddy sensation that wants to take over but it's so hard. It's bubbling to the surface ready to burst out all over Matt. "Let me find a restaurant. What do you prefer, Italian or Chinese?"

"Italian, of course," he says, and I'm thankful.

I prefer Italian too—especially the DeLuca variety.

"Damn, this is good," Matt says as he eats another forkful of lobster ravioli. "And you said the restaurant is nearby?"

Enraptured with watching him eat, I nod silently, but realize he's not even paying attention to me, so I answer, "Yes, they're not too far from here. Little place that doesn't look like much but is packed inside."

So packed, I drew quite a few stares as I went to the register and purchased the food, waiting for the bag to be brought out. I could tell they weren't tourists. They were probably wondering who the heck I was and not like I could announce it to everyone. I stood there, smiling shyly at everyone who was blatant enough to check me out.

This city, the entire area, has a very small-town feel. I understood. Whenever a stranger showed up in Cactus, everyone went crazy wondering who they were. It set the gossips buzzing for days.

That's what I've turned into. I'm the girl who sparks gossip and makes people wonder who the heck I am. Even when I was trying my best not to get any attention whatsoever, it still happened.

"What did you get?" Matt points his black plastic fork at me. His eyes are alight with interest.

We're sitting at his desk just as he said, eating quietly and occasionally making conversation. These low sounds of complete male satisfaction leave him every once in a while, setting my blood on fire, but I try to ignore them. My dinner is delicious too, something I rarely indulge in because Italian food goes straight to my hips, but who cares?

Tonight—not me.

"Mushroom ravioli," I answer just before I take another bite of crusty, warm bread.

"Are you a vegetarian?" he asks.

"Please, I'm from Texas." Oh crap. That was sort of a sarcastic and shitty thing to say. I need to watch my mouth.

"Really? I had no idea." He looks at me, his gaze intense. "Tell me more."

I shrug, wishing I'd never opened this can of worms. "There's not much to tell."

"Now I doubt that, Miss James," he drawls softly. "We're sharing a meal together so at the very least you could make polite conversation."

He's not going to let this go, I can tell. "Well, you asked for my boring life story so here it is. I grew up in Cactus, Texas, a small town with one stoplight. Wait, there's another, so make it two." I tap my fingers against my lips, trying to decide what I can and can't tell him. Not the bad stuff, which there's a lot of. No-good daddy, and a too-young mama who never stuck around much or seemed to care. Gruff but lovable grandma who gave me lots of words of wisdom but wasn't the best at showering me with affection.

This is probably why I seek out love in all the wrong places. My head is just flat-out screwed up.

"I was raised by my grandma," I finally say. "My mom was real young and not around much."

"That's . . . too bad." He looks a little uncomfortable, like he doesn't quite know how to react.

Probably shouldn't have told him that, damn it.

I make a face. "Don't feel bad. My grandma is awesome. A real sweet old lady who makes the best church cake you've ever had." Sort of. Kind of mean, actually. She's the type that sits on her front porch with a shotgun and threatens strangers who come on her property that she'll shoot their asses off if they take one step farther. No joke.

My life in Cactus is a cartoon cliché of epic proportions, I swear.

Matt frowns. "Church cake?"

"Oh, you know. A big ol' made-from-scratch chocolate sheet cake that everyone at the church social can have a piece of. With some of the best, rich chocolate frosting you've ever tasted." I sigh, missing Grandma's chocolate church cake something fierce. Grabbing at a mint the restaurant provided, I tear off the wrapper and pop it into my mouth, but it's a poor substitute for chocolate cake.

"Ah, now I see it." When I look at him oddly, he smiles. "Your accent. I heard it when you were talking."

I clamp my lips shut. I start talking about home and out comes the Texan like I can't help myself. "I left Cactus when I was nineteen, and I've never been back." And I don't really miss it either. I talk to my grandma when I can, but it's not like our relationship was super close. I had no friends. And I had a wife out to hang me by my hair for messing around with her husband though she thought we'd been up to much worse. She'd found out about me pretty quickly after I found out about her, and it had been such a nightmare dealing with her.

Thank God I never slept with him. I heard he got some other poor girl who worked for him knocked up, his wife promptly left him, and he ended up marrying the mistress.

That would've been me if I'd continued with him. My life stuck married to some loser insurance salesman who can't keep his tongue in his mouth or his dick in his pants, fooling around with every dumb young girl who works for him.

A shudder moves through me at the thought.

"So how about you?" I ask, desperate to change the conversation. I push my empty plate away from me, the bread sitting in my stomach like a lead weight. Sure had been good though. "Tell me your life story."

He smiles, stabs his fork in the last lobster ravioli standing. "Raised by my father after my mother died when I was four. Always loved baseball because he was a former pro, and I wanted to follow in his footsteps. So I did, got injured, was forced into early retirement, came to Napa on my friend's recommendation, and bought the winery. That's it."

Well, didn't he simplify that completely? I need to take lessons from him for the next time I get nosy questions. "You summed that up pretty well."

"I figured you Googled me anyway, so you probably already know everything." His cheeks turn ruddy, and I wonder if he's actually blushing. "I sounded like a complete ass right then."

"It's okay," I say. "I did Google you," I admit, my own cheeks heating. There'd been all the photos from his underwear ad campaign. Those had been rather . . . enlightening. "A while ago, after you took over the winery. I wanted to find out more about my new boss."

"You hadn't heard of me before, when I played baseball?"

"No, not really. I don't pay much attention to sports, and if I do, the only one I care about is football." At his raised brows, I shrug. "I am from Texas after all."

Matt

Well, I guess I can forgive you for your football love, considering you're from Texas and all," I say, smiling at her.

She returns the smile, a brilliant, toothy flash, and then it disappears as fast it came. Disappointment fills me, but I ignore it.

The more I talk to Bryn, the more I like her. I'm fascinated with her being from Texas only because that's the last place I figured she'd be from, for some reason. I assumed she was a local, just like everyone else who worked for the DeLuca Winery.

The more she spoke of Texas, the thicker her accent got. It was cute, hearing her talk about grandmas and chocolate cake. She didn't drop too many other details though. Made me think there's a lot more going on behind the scenes.

I wonder if she's hiding something. I know I wish I could—my past, my entire life history is out there for all the world to read and see, thanks to Vinnie DeLuca and his escapades.

She's actually a little feisty which I didn't expect. But

I've only known the other Bryn. The beige-wearing, never-looking-at-me version. This new Bryn, with the sophisticated yet sexy clothes, the gorgeous hair, and the mildly sassy attitude is a pleasant surprise.

I like that she actually ate a meal too. I've dated women before who pick at their plates or only order a piece of lettuce and a glass of water. Not only did Bryn down almost her entire meal, she also scarfed down on bread, just like I did.

Had no idea a woman with a healthy appetite was so arousing.

"Sounds like your career was cut super short, huh." She winces. "Sorry, I probably shouldn't have brought it up. I'm sure you don't like talking about it."

"It's all right. Just a fact of life, you know?" I shrug, pretending it doesn't bother me that I lost my baseball career, but it does. It hurts tremendously. "I miss it, but life goes on and brings you new challenges."

She raises a delicate brow. "And I'm sure the winery is a challenge."

"Absolutely it is—an interesting one though. Lots of hard work, but I believe it's going to reward us in the end." I said *us*, like she's an integral part of this winery, which she is to me.

I wonder if she knows exactly how much I value her. And I'm not talking about her salary or how much I'm making off this venture or anything like that. I'm referring to how much I need her help. How stuck I'd be without her.

Of course, it's not all about finances and how much money you make, right? I have enough money to last me ten lifetimes. My dad may be a loudmouthed jerk who loves to make his troubles public, but he's a rich loudmouthed jerk. I think that's what allowed him to be so crazy through the years. When you're rich, you're eccentric. When you're poor, you're flat-out strange.

Either way, growing up with my father was quite the experience. He expected me to be just like him. So I tried my best to emulate him as much as I could, but I did it with my pro baseball career.

Until the unfortunate injury that took me out of the game permanently. Dad just about lost it. I swear he was ready to disown me and it hadn't even been my fault. Though it was already on shaky ground, our relationship hasn't been the same since.

Now I try my best to avoid being lumped in with my father.

"I'm sure it'll work out. I think you might have the golden touch," she says, her voice soft, her smile . . .

It's such a pretty smile. She's pretty. Beautiful. I stare at her, momentarily captivated and I shake my head, banishing my wayward thoughts.

I wonder what she meant when she said that I have the golden touch. I fucked up one career by complete accident. I'm working extra hard to make sure this one goes off without a hitch.

Now I can only hope everything sticks to the plan. We're two days out. The grand reopening kicks off Friday afternoon and runs into the late evening, with all sorts of press events, a tour of the vineyards, a wine tasting, and finally, the party starts at six. There will be food, plenty of DeLuca wine, and live entertainment.

I'm exhausted just thinking about it.

"Well, I should get back to work," I say as I point my fork at her. When I get time, I need to go back and check out the restaurant Bryn picked up our dinner from. It was the best damn meal I've had in ages.

Wonder what Bryn would say if I asked her to go with me. Like on a date.

"You're going to stay and work some more?" she asks incredulously.

I swallow and nod. "Yeah. There are a few things I need to wrap up here before I can go home."

"Do you need me to stay and help?" She blinks at me, those crystal-blue eyes sucking me right in and tempting me beyond reason.

Staying late at the office with Bryn, I can imagine all sorts of things happening. Like her spread out on my desk, her lips swollen from my kisses, her hair a sexy haphazard mess.

I need to stop thinking about Bryn in such a sexual manner. I need to get over my attraction to her. Focusing on work is far more important than figuring out how I'm going to get my hands beneath my assistant's skirt.

Yeah. I sound like a sexist jackass even in my head.

"No, you can go home. It's already well past eight. You've done more than enough." I drop my fork on my empty plate and toss my napkin on top of it.

"Oh, don't worry about that. I'll pick it all up." She grabs the to-go bag from the floor and starts gathering all of the garbage before she fills the bag with it. She picks up my empty plate, bending over slightly and offering me a delicious view straight down her shirt.

Her bra is white, lacy, and her breasts strain against the delicate fabric. My brow breaks out in a sweat at the tantalizing glimpse, and I keep my eyes trained at that spot for as long as I can before she straightens up and her breasts are out of view.

Damn, the woman is too hot for words.

"I'll toss this in the trash on my way out," she says from

over her shoulder as she exits my office and heads for her desk.

I sit in my chair, immobilized as I watch her. The sway of her hips mesmerizes me. Her walk is pure seduction. That black skirt fuels my imagination, what with the way it hugs her every curve. Her ass just begs for my hands to touch it.

Get a fucking grip, man. She's your assistant. You can't go there.

Ignoring the negative thoughts running through my head, I stand and pull my wallet out of my back pocket, flipping it open. "I owe you money for dinner, Bryn."

"I can cut myself a check tomorrow if you'd like. We can write it off as a business expense, you know," she says as she rummages through her desk. "It's no big deal."

She's always thinking, my assistant. "I'd rather give you cash right now, if you don't mind." I head for her desk, as I start to pull out a couple of twenties. "You kept the receipt, right?"

I'm so intent on digging through my wallet I don't realize I'm right in front of Bryn until it's too late. I run straight into her, our bodies colliding, and I reach out, my wallet dropping from my hand to the floor as I wrap my arms around her waist to keep her from falling.

"Oh!" She grips my shirt to keep herself from slipping in those heels she's wearing, and her soft, delicious curves nestle up close. I rest my hands tentatively on her back, just above the curve of her ass as she tilts her head up, her wide-eyed gaze meeting mine. "I'm sorry," she murmurs, her tongue sneaking out and moistening her lips.

Shit, why did she have to go and do that?

"Uh, I'm the one who should apologize since I wasn't looking where I was going," I say, my brain stuttering to a halt at having her in my arms. I tighten my hold on her just the slightest bit. She feels damn good. Too good. My skin is electric, my hands itching to search her body, and I realize I should shove her away. End this conversation now before it has a chance to get completely out of hand.

"All right then. Maybe you should." Her fingers curl tighter into my shirt, fingertips brushing against my skin, and I feel her touch to the very depths of my bones, even through the fabric. My breath sticks in my throat as I stare at her, completely fascinated with the sultry expression that crosses her face. "Apologize, Mr. DeLuca."

"Sorry, Miss James," I whisper, making her smile. Damn, that smile is gorgeous. Everything about her is gorgeous. Why did I never notice her like this before? Well, I did get hung up on her scent, but told myself it was nothing. That she was nothing special.

Was I such a shallow bastard that form-fitting clothes and makeup was what it took to really make me notice her?

But there's more to this woman. She's smart and always there when I need her, which is often. I try my best to be fair and not always take, take, take, but I've been pretty damn selfish since I took over the winery. I've been living and breathing this place for weeks and months.

Bryn has stood by my side the entire time. Always there with what I need, guiding me when I'm lost. She keeps me on task.

And I'm a lust-addled idiot because all I can think about is how much I want to kiss her. Taste her. Strip off her clothing and see her naked for the first time.

My head is descending like I have no control over it, and she's tilting her head back as if in waiting, the smile fading, her lips parting. Warning bells clang in my brain. What am I doing? I think I'm going to kiss her.

Yep, I'm definitely going to kiss her and find out what those delicious lips finally taste like. And when I finish kissing her, I'm going to press my face into her hair and breathe deep her addictive scent. Inhale it until it fills my lungs and makes my head spin. I can smell her now, her fragrance wrapping all around me, drugging me, and I close my eyes just as my mouth settles on hers.

The kiss is soft. Light. Simple. I'm testing her, testing myself. She doesn't run, doesn't so much as jerk in my hold. No, it's worse. She should pull away from me and slap my face. Or at the very least, stomp on my foot, tell me I'm a bastard and that she quits. I'd let her go because it's the right thing to do.

Pulling her into my arms and kissing her is the absolute wrong thing to do.

Instead, she sighs against my lips. The softest, sexiest little sound I think I've ever heard in my life and then her hands are smoothing up my chest, curving around my shoulders as she steps closer, clinging to me as if for dear life.

That's it. The sign I've been looking for despite the flash warning repeating in my head:

Step away, step away, step the fuck away, asshole.

I ignore it. I can't resist her. I don't *want* to resist her. All those soft, delicious curves press against me, her breasts to my chest, her legs tangling with mine. She's taller with those fuck-me heels on and I'm tempted to slide my hands down, curve them around her ass and see what she might do.

With the way she's responding to my mouth on hers, I have a feeling she'd like it.

The kiss is still simple, the both of us seem to be waiting for the other to make the first move. I revel in the simplicity for a minute, wanting to etch this moment into my mind, so I don't ever forget it. The way she feels in my arms. The little sounds she makes in the back of her throat, a combination of sighs and whimpers that are beyond arousing. She tastes like mint, sweet and fresh, and I slant my head, parting my lips, ready to take it deeper.

But unbelievably, she beats me to the punch, opening to me as her tongue darts out for a tentative lick against mine—a wicked little flick that sends my body into overdrive, my cock straining against my trousers. Fuck, I want her. I could drown in her.

I'm done for.

Chapter 5

Bryn

Oh God, he's kissing me. Really kissing me, our tongues doing a delicate dance that gets deeper, wetter, hotter with every second that passes. I clutch at him, slide my hands from his shoulders to circle around his neck, one hand in the thick, soft hair at his nape, holding him to me.

His muscular arms tighten around my waist, like steel bands holding me close and my skin tingles at the possessive way he touches me, kisses me. This is exactly what I've been wanting for months, since I first started working with Matt. When he walked into my life and pretty much saved it, so I didn't have to pack my bags and return to Cactus, totally ashamed and a complete failure, just like everyone thought I would be.

I've fought this dizzying attraction for Matt for what feels like forever, especially this last week, and I think he has too. Over dinner, the connection only seemed to grow, like a tangible presence.

Why else would he so readily kiss me? I know it was an accident, us running into each other, but it feels so natural, being in his arms. He couldn't deny he was attracted to me any longer and now, alone in the dark, hushed, quality of the office, with no one else close by, we can finally give in to our attraction and take it a step further.

"Bryn." His voice is agonized, sending shivers down my spine when he whispers against my lips. "We shouldn't do this," he says, breaking our kiss completely.

I stroke the back of his head, still lost in the lingering sensation of his mouth moving over mine. God, the man can kiss. I'm thankful he's got a hold of me, or I'd probably melt onto the floor. What did he say again? "Wait . . . what?"

"We shouldn't do this," he repeats, pressing his lips to the spot where my pulse throbs wildly at my neck before he withdraws the slightest bit, putting distance between us.

Staring up at him, I realize he's dead serious. His expression is somber, his eyes almost . . . pained. He's putting a stop to this.

And making me feel like a humiliated fool.

"Fine." I take a deep breath and drop my hands from where I gripped his neck. "You're right. We should definitely not do this."

I sound like every silly romance I love to read when I'm not working like a dog. And I'm so pitiful it's embarrassing.

"I'm—sorry, Bryn. I got carried away." He lets go of me, and I step backward, feeling bereft without being in his embrace.

"I'm sorry too." I smooth my hand over my hair, then jerk my top back into place, running my hands over my skirt. My hands are shaking, and I release another shuddery exhale, desperate to get myself back together and quick.

No way do I want him to see how much he affects me, especially after he so soundly rejected me.

He bends down and snatches his wallet from the floor,

flipping it back open and peeling out two twenty-dollar bills from within. "Is this enough?"

"For what?" My mind races. What is he giving me money for? He better not be paying me off because of the stupid kiss. And if he thinks my lips are only worth forty dollars, then I'm completely insulted.

"For the dinner you paid for," he says, his voice gentle as he holds the twenties out toward me. "Is it enough?"

"It's fine," I snap, snatching the money from his fingers and clutching it tight in my fist. I feel so incredibly stupid I don't know what else to say.

So I say nothing at all. Just turn my back on him, grab my purse from where I left it on the corner of my desk, and flee the building, never once looking over my shoulder. I don't even notice the tears streaming down my cheeks until I'm in my car, sitting in the driver's seat and desperately trying to stab my key in the ignition yet somehow missing every single time.

I burst out crying in earnest, my vision blurring, and finally get the key in. I turn it, the engine starting with its usual dependable, gentle roar. I press my forehead against the steering wheel and let the tears fall silently. No sobbing, no cursing, no shaking my fist at myself or the man who kissed me so sweetly, so passionately, I don't know if I'll ever experience another kiss like it again.

Bright headlights shine on me every time a vehicle passes, and I wince, lifting my head. I swipe at the tears dampening my cheeks, blowing out a frustrated breath. I need to get out of here. Sitting around crying and feeling sorry for myself is not the way to handle this. I've always been a pull-myself-up-by-the-bootstraps kind of girl. It's the Texan in me; the tough take-no-prisoners attitude my grandma's instilled in me ever since I was a little girl.

A pervert chases after me and tries to abduct me? No problem, spit in his eye. My old boss tries to get in my pants? No worries, just quit. A variety of Hollywood jerks proposition me for a blowjob?

Yeah. Just walk. Find another job. Find another boss, another man with too much power who knows how to quietly devastate me with just a look. A touch. A kiss.

Throwing my car into reverse, I back out of the parking lot and drive out of there so fast, my tires spin, spitting up gravel. Determination steels my spine, fuels my anger. I refuse to let someone make me feel weak all because I'm a woman. I keep doing that. It's been a pattern my entire life. I change my look to stop men from seeing a pretty face, then let myself be convinced it would be smart to go back to my usual ways and of course, I get in trouble. But forget it.

No man has ever held me down.

Ever.

"Oh my God, what happened to you?"

I glance up from the letter I'm typing to find Ivy standing in front of my desk, her expression one of pure disappointment mixed with horror. Straightening my shoulders, I smile at her, going for subdued.

"Whatever do you mean?" I ask calmly. It's only been a few days since I last saw her. I know she's going to give me an earful.

She waves a hand at me, her gaze drinking me in as her nose wrinkles. "The tan-colored everything—it's back. And your hair is in a bun, and you're not wearing any makeup.

Why? What happened? I thought you bought yourself a new wardrobe. In fact, I know you did—I was with you."

It's pointless to try and make a man fall for me who so very clearly doesn't want to. Despite the devastating kiss, the intimate conversation, and his hot eyes drinking me in every chance he could get, I needed to go back to my original look. I wear the color beige like a suit of armor. Protecting my heart from failure.

"I did. I wore my new clothes, tried my best to impress Matt, and it backfired. It was an utter failure." Reaching beneath my desk, I pull out the bag that contains the gorgeous dress Ivy so generously bought me to wear for tomorrow. "I'm returning this to you. I appreciate the gesture, but I won't be needing it after all."

Ivy takes the bag as if in a daze, opening it to peek inside before she turns a determined glare on me. "Oh no, you don't. Don't you dare return this to me because you think I spent too much money on it. This is my gift to you."

"No offense, but I don't want it." I sniff delicately, hoping she'll forgive me but God, I'm still just so angry at Matthew-the-jerkwad-DeLuca. "There's no point in wearing it, so I'm giving it back to you. Hopefully you can still return it to the store."

"What? Why is there no point in wearing it? What happened?" Ivy gapes at me.

I flick my head in the direction of Matt's closed office door. He's kept it closed all day, hardly talking to me beyond the occasional request, said in a painfully polite voice. I'm just as bad, replying with a crisp "yes, sir" every time he asks me to do something for him, earning an irritated look in return.

"What did he do?" Ivy's voice drops to a whisper.

Shaking my head, I roll my eyes and it sort of hurts. Probably has something to do with my hair scraped into a bun so tight I swear it's pulling on my entire face. Who needs a facelift when you give yourself a hairdo like this? "I can't talk about it here. Not now."

"I refuse to accept this." Ivy deposits the bag on top of my desk, her expression practically daring me to deny her. "You're wearing it tomorrow night whether you like it or not."

"It's not that I don't like it, you know." I take the bag and throw it back under the desk, knowing I just totally wrinkled the dress. I'm going to have to iron the crap out of that thing tonight if I'm really going to wear it tomorrow. "The whole reason for you buying it was to impress a certain someone who, trust me, won't be impressed whatsoever."

"You're talking in circles and I can't stand it." Ivy starts for the door, waving her hand. "Come with me."

I follow her outside, the sun bright and warm on my chilled skin as she leads me behind the building. She turns to face me, and I cross my arms, feeling defensive. The last thing I want to do is argue with my new friend, but I also really don't want to admit to her what happened between Matt and me last night.

It's embarrassing.

"Give me all the details. Tell me what that stupid Matt did to you to make you revert to your old ways." A shudder passes over Ivy. "I hate the beige, I hope you know."

I do too, but I don't admit it. Better to act like this is more my style and hide behind it than reveal that I actually can look . . . pretty without the beige. I wear it like armor, fighting against all my vulnerabilities. "It's embarrassing."

"It'll only be between me and you. Oh, and Marina. She'll want to know what's going on," Ivy says.

"You can't tell Archer. And Marina can't tell Gage. This is our little secret," I say, pointing my finger at her.

"I'll keep my lips shut. Scout's honor." She holds up three fingers, then starts giggling, which makes me even more nervous.

"I can't take you seriously if you're laughing," I tell her, exasperated as hell. If Matt finds out I'm outside talking to Ivy, he might get mad. He's a ball of nerves today what with everything finally happening tomorrow. Tense and stressed and the bad, weird vibes going on between us aren't helping matters any.

"I'm not laughing about this. I told Matt the same thing, scout's honor, when he was telling me something last week." She frowns, tilts her head. "I can't believe it's only been a week since Matt and I had that conversation. A lot has happened since then."

"What conversation? What did he tell you?" I'm totally testing her. If she tells me what he said there is no way I'm confessing to her what happened last night.

"Ah, ah, ah. I'm not falling for that." She smiles. Dang, she's good. "So spill."

I explain everything. How Matt seemed interested since I ditched the beige. That I stayed last night and brought him dinner, which we ate together. How I was about to leave when we ran into each other and the next thing I knew, we were kissing.

And it was amazing.

"Then it was over. He said we shouldn't be doing this, gave me forty bucks, and sent me on my way," I finished miserably.

"Wait a minute, he gave you forty bucks? What for?" Ivy practically screeches.

"Shhh." I shake my head, wanting to laugh but not really

finding the situation that funny. Maybe I will someday, but not at the moment. "It was for dinner since I paid for it."

"Oh, thank God," she mumbles and this time I do laugh. I can't help it. "I thought he was trying to pay for your services or whatever." The entire story is just absurd.

"I thought the same thing!"

Then we're both laughing, leaning against the building as if we need it to hold us upright.

"So I'm guessing now he's ignoring you?" Ivy asks once she's composed herself.

I nod, my laughter dying. "I didn't help matters when I left last night. I didn't say a word to him, just turned and fled like my feet were on fire."

"And then you show up this morning in your beige ensemble and it's back to normal." Ivy sighs. "What a mess."

"I don't know what else to do. His rejection, it . . . hurt," I confess, pressing my lips together to prevent myself from saying anything else. She's my friend, but we're not that close. I don't want her to think I'm a total idiot by divulging my past. I've had a lot of crazy stuff happen to me. Beyond the perverts and the crazy bosses and the Hollywood creeps looking for blowjobs, I had boyfriends who weren't that great either. Men look at a pretty face and decent body and think I'm easy.

I change the way I dress and Matt kisses me. Then he pushes me away. And I wanted him to notice me. Deep down inside, I want to be more to Matt than just his assistant.

I'm stupid to be upset because I brought this on myself, but I can't help myself. When it comes to men, I flat out don't think rationally.

I don't want Ivy to think I'm crazy. Even though I sort of am.

"You need to be defiant in the face of rejection, my friend. And he didn't reject you because he doesn't want you. He's probably trying to do the right thing," Ivy points out.

Hmm. She might be right. Matt seems like a pretty stand-up guy from what I've witnessed. I know he'd never set out to purposely toy with me or anything. "It won't work," I tell her, my voice firm. "He's my boss, I'm his employee. I don't know why I let you two convince me something like this *could* work."

"No, no. Don't you dare give up. I won't let you." Ivy grabs hold of my upper arms and gives me a little shake before releasing her hold. "You're going to wear one of your new outfits tomorrow. No neutrals allowed, okay? Matt needs you on your best behavior and that means you looking your best too. There's a lot at stake tomorrow."

She's so right. Tomorrow is by far the most important day of his newfound career. "Fine, okay. I'll wear my other new dress. Not even a fleck of tan in sight."

"Good." Ivy smiles. "And then tomorrow night, you're going to the party, and you'll be wearing that dress. You'll greet everyone, be an impressive representative of DeLuca Winery even if it kills you. You will make Matt so proud he'll know without a doubt what a valuable employee he has in you. If he happens to also see you as a beautiful woman, then so be it."

Where is she going with this? "And?"

"And if he makes a move, fabulous. But I'm going to warn you." Ivy's expression turns scarily solemn. "If he doesn't make a move, don't be surprised. He tries his hardest to do the right thing, especially because of his father."

"What do you mean, because of his father? What's wrong with him?"

Ivy makes a face. "Vinnie DeLuca has a total slime-ball

reputation and embarrasses Matt constantly. They pretty much don't talk anymore."

"Slime-ball reputation? Like how?" Curiosity fills me.

"Womanizer. Liked to start fights, especially when he was playing pro baseball. There were rumors he took steroids and that he gambled and cheated a lot." Ivy shakes her head. "Matt's always tried his hardest to distance himself from his father and his horrible reputation. He's always been a pretty straight arrow."

And here I come along, going from boring and bland to obvious and desperate at warp speed. No wonder he kissed me and then rejected me. He's most definitely trying to do the right thing.

While I've been trying to do the wrong thing.

"I feel like a jerk," I say with a sigh.

"You shouldn't. We encouraged you." Ivy sighs as well. "I feel like a jerk too."

"I'll wear the dress. But I won't try and flaunt myself in front of Matt or anything. It's wrong. He doesn't need that sort of trouble or guilt." I kick at a rock, feeling crappy for doing the right thing.

"You amaze me, you know that? Matt's lucky to have you by his side."

"I really hope he feels that way," I say, my heart twisting in my chest.

Matt

Matt's lucky to have you by his side.
I really hope he feels that way.

I didn't mean to eavesdrop on Bryn and Ivy's conversation, but I came upon it by accident. And when I realized they were talking about me—and specifically my dad—I had to stick around and hear what they said.

I hated hearing what Ivy said about Dad, but there's no denying that she spoke the truth. He is a slimeball and has a terrible reputation, one I try to distance myself from as much as possible.

That's why I had to push Bryn away last night. I couldn't take that amazing kiss we shared any further no matter how badly I wanted to. And damn, I really wanted to.

Listening to Bryn say she felt like a jerk over what happened last night made me realize that she wanted it as bad as I did. I'd firmly believed I'd pushed myself on her. After she left without saying a word, my concentration had been shot, and I'd closed up shop. Drove home frustrated and horny, going over what happened between Bryn and me over and over again, trying to figure out how exactly how I let it happen. That kiss. Pulling Bryn into my arms. Touching her.

Yeah. A huge mistake, not one I can forget easily either.

It had been tremendously hard having to face her this morning, though somehow she made it easier on me by appearing in a beige outfit again, hardly looking at me, like I scared her. This Bryn I knew and understood, or so I thought. I'd been dealing with wallpaper Bryn for months and I was used to her like this.

It's gorgeous, elegant, sexy-as-fuck Bryn that does me in and makes my head spin. Not only does she look amazing, but she becomes bolder with the stylish clothes and the beautiful hair. She moves with confidence, looks me in the eye, talks to me.

Seeing her this morning in her usual beige getup tripped

me up but only momentarily. Hearing her voice, watching her, and all I saw was the real woman behind the facade. She can hide all she wants in drab colors and severe hairstyles; I know who she is beneath the surface.

And I want more despite wanting to do the right thing.

She confuses me. I thought by pushing her away, it would solve all my problems. Instead, I feel like I have a whole bunch more.

Moving away from where Ivy and Bryn are still talking, I head toward my car and take off, going to my last quick appointment for the day, a meeting at my local bank with a possible investor.

My cell rings not two minutes after I pull out of the winery's parking lot and I check the screen to see it's my father. Speak of the devil. It's like the old man could sense someone was talking about him, thinking about him. Against my better judgment, I answer it—best to face him now than prolong it and have him harassing me tomorrow.

"Son." Vinnie's voice booms through the speakers of my car since I have my phone on Bluetooth. "It's been a long time."

He always acts like there's no reason we haven't spoken for months. "What's going on?" I ask, cutting right to the point.

"Ah, you're always full of the kindness for your old man, aren't you?" Vinnie chuckles, and I grit my teeth, wanting to hang up on him so bad it's killing me. "So I hear your fancy winery is having its reopening tomorrow."

"It sure is." He's never shown one iota of interest in the winery other than when I told him I bought it, and he said "that's nice" in his usual distracted, completely self-absorbed voice.

We never discussed it again.

"I was hoping I could get an invite."

Unease slips down my spine, and I clear my throat. "I thought you were more of a hard liquor fan," I say, trying to sound like I'm joking.

"Well, I'm not a big drinker of wine, I agree, but I want to be there when my only son shows off his new winery. It's going to be a proud moment, I'm sure."

A proud moment I absolutely one hundred percent don't want him to be a part of. "Are you sure you want to come? It'll be boring. Hardly anyone there that you know besides my friends."

"Anyone from baseball?" he asks.

Yeah. A few people, and I definitely don't want him around them. He tends to get in heated arguments whenever they discuss baseball and specifically his past in both the game and the league.

But shit, how can I refuse him? He's my father.

"A small handful but not a lot," I tell him, keeping my gaze focused on the road ahead of me. I hadn't even bothered sending him an invitation for tomorrow. I wonder if he's pissed. I wonder if this is some strange way for him to get revenge on me for ignoring him.

I wouldn't put it past my father. He's just that type of guy.

"I saw a write up in the paper," he explains. He still lives in the Bay Area, having been born and raised there. We were both lucky to be included in professional teams close to where we grew up. My dad always attributed it to the DeLuca curse—an apt word considering how crappy both of our pro careers became. "And realized this was going down tomorrow. I won't be able to attend the day events—I saw you're doing a tour and a wine tasting and all that good stuff—but I'd love to show up at the party tomorrow night if you'll have me."

"That can be arranged," I say, regret filling me in an instant. I hope this isn't a mistake.

"Great, good! I can't wait to see you. It's been far too long, son. I miss you."

Yeah, right. "It'll be good to see you too, but you do understand I'm going to be busy the entire night and won't have much time for miscellaneous chitchat." I won't have much time for his calculated reminiscing over our sometimes troubled past either. He loves to do that too and push me into a guilt spiral.

Our relationship is twenty levels of fucked up, I swear.

"I understand completely," he assures me. "I'll just be there basking in your glory, always the proud father. I won't disrupt your little party tomorrow night, I promise. Don't worry about me."

That he's describing tomorrow's event as "my little party" already sets me on edge, the asshole. I swear he says those sorts of things on purpose. I don't believe a word he says.

And I hate that I feel this way.

After he hangs up, I ponder over how I can handle the problem that is my father. I wonder if Bryn would help me. But if I set Bryn in my dad's sights, he'll probably try and make a pass and she'll end up beyond insulted.

Yeah. That's a risk I really don't want to take. Do I have a choice though? It's like my dad needs a babysitter and only a specialized few will do.

Still, I definitely don't want to subject Bryn to my rude bastard of a father.

Chapter 6

Matt

"The place looks fabulous, man." Archer slaps me on the back so hard, I take a step forward, wincing when pain shoots through my knee. It still hurts. It'll always hurt. "You pulled it off. I bet everybody will have DeLuca Winery falling from their lips come tomorrow."

"Thanks, but the party only just started," I say, ever the grim reaper as I worry about anything and everything. The grounds are crowded with people, the lot filled with cars, including the dirt field we opened up specifically for the event.

My father still hasn't arrived which worries the shit out of me, but I can't sweat it. Maybe he'll never come at all. I figure I won't be that lucky. He knows how to put a damper on any party, big or small.

The image of my father crashing into the party, loud and drunk and making me look like a fool, has set me on edge. I need to do something to take that edge off and quick.

"You're all gloom and doom today, asshole. Perk up. Life is good," Gage says, saluting me with his glass before he takes a swallow of a DeLuca Cabernet.

"Don't be so mean," Marina chastises as she slips her arm through Gage's. "It's an amazing party, Matt. I know everyone's impressed."

"Thanks, Marina." Her words mean a lot to me since she comes from one of the oldest families in the area. If anyone knows what's going on in the Napa Valley, it's Marina Knight. That I can impress her and she hears nothing but good things from those she knows, lets me breathe easier.

A little bit easier, at least.

My name is on the label, on the sign out front, on the building. It's a surreal feeling, finally seeing the fruition of months and months of hard labor, sweat, and tears.

The day's events came off without a hitch. The tour was a success, heavily attended by many, including plenty of local media. The wine tasting had been a nerve-wracking experience but soon turned into complete relief. Almost everyone enjoyed what they sampled, though there had been a few naysayers, but that was to be expected.

Bryn led the tasting, composed and elegant and thoughtful and amusing. She'd enraptured everyone, talking so enthusiastically about the wine and the DeLuca name and what it's going to mean to the Napa Valley in the coming years. Hell, even I believed my own hype.

She'd been utter perfection, and I never got a chance to thank or praise her. I still haven't seen her arrive tonight and that surprised me. I figured she'd be here already.

I need her to be here already.

Gage and Marina head for one of food tables, and I glance around, checking out the crowd. I notice that the small live band is tuning up and getting ready to play. The weather tonight is perfect, not too cold, though I have outdoor heaters going on low to fill the air with warmth. There's a gentle breeze rustling the majestic oaks that are all over the property. White lights are strung in the trees surrounding the courtyard, illuminating the party without being too bright.

There are bars set up on each corner of the courtyard, and they all have long lines, everyone wanting a glass of one of the new DeLuca wines. Servers move through the crowds with their trays, offering appetizers or flutes of sparkling wine.

It has all come together so perfectly, and I owe a lot of that to Bryn. But where is she?

"Matt! Your party is fabulous." Ivy comes at me, her pregnant belly so obvious it's preceding her. Archer stands at her side as she comes for me, enveloping me in a perfume-scented hug. "I can't believe how beautiful everything looks. Where's Bryn? I wanted to praise her too. I know she's done so much for you."

"She has. And you've done an amazing job too you know." I kiss her cheek before I let her go, thankful for all her decorating input. Everything looks freaking amazing because of her. Her design skills and expertise were just what I needed to ensure the grounds and the interiors looked modern yet stayed true to the authenticity of the winery in times past.

"I'm so glad you like it." She smiles, then notices Marina and Gage waiting in line. "I'll be right back. I want to talk to Marina."

Archer and I watch her go before Archer turns to me, a knowing smile on his smug-as-hell face. "Been diddling the help yet?"

Unease slips down my spine. "What the hell are you talking about?"

"Ah, don't pretend with me. I know your assistant has the hots for you, and I hear the feeling's mutual." Archer takes a sip from his glass. "Ivy talks. Her and your Miss James have become awfully close."

"What did Ivy tell you?" No way did Bryn tell Ivy about

what happened a few nights ago, when I kissed her then pushed her away.

"Not a whole hell of a lot. Just that the two of you have been circling around each other in the office for far too long and that Bryn finally got herself a new wardrobe and some courage. I hear the dress she's wearing tonight is a plan to knock you completely on your ass with lust for her," Archer warns.

I swallow hard. Great. So she's going to be wearing a dress that makes her look like utter perfection? I can withstand that. No problem.

Shit, I hope I can.

She hadn't worn an uninspired beige outfit earlier today, and I was thankful for it, though she impressed me so damn much I probably wouldn't have even noticed. She'd shown up dressed to perfection in a fitted deep purple dress, her hair pulled back into a sleek ponytail that wasn't so severe as her usual hairstyle. She'd looked beautiful. Assured and elegant, she was a fine representative of the DeLuca Winery.

"She's my assistant, nothing else," I tell Archer, needing to convince myself as well. "I know you've seen the pictures of when she got the makeover and you've given me endless shit, but I can't do anything about it. She works for me. I won't risk anything between us for fear it could go horribly wrong in an instant. She could turn against me and ruin my ass. Get me on sexual harassment charges or whatever."

"Oh, I get it. Tell that to Ivy though, since she's still hell-bent on getting the two of you together," Archer says, his gaze roaming lazily over the crowd much as mine had only a few moments ago. "Hey, isn't that her? Your Bryn?"

I jerk my gaze to where Archer's staring, and I do a double take, my eyes widening when I see her.

Damn, she's . . . unbelievably gorgeous. I thought she was hot when she showed up in that black printed dress on Monday, but right now, she's just fucking beautiful. There are no other words for it.

"That's her," I say, watching as she walks the far parameter of the courtyard, her head turning this way and that as she seemingly takes everything in. A small smile curves her plum-colored lips and she pushes her long, inky-colored hair over her shoulder, stopping to talk to someone, laughing at whatever he said before she pats the man on the shoulder and keeps moving.

Jealousy moves through me, and I tell myself to knock it off. She can look at and talk to other people, especially if we're not together. Hell, even if we were together, I have no right to tell her what to do or who she talks to.

But I'd like that right. I sound like a complete Neanderthal but damn it, I want Bryn to be mine.

Still.

"She's a fucking looker man," Archer utters. "I'd get it if you gave up the million bucks for a piece of that."

Fury burns through my blood, and I glare at Archer. "Don't talk about her like that, you bastard. You could at least show the woman some respect," I tell him, my voice like steel.

"Ah, don't get your panties all twisted," Archer says, smiling as he shakes his head. "I love how caveman we all get when we're with the women we love."

"I never said I was in love with Bryn." I've worked with her for six months and have only just noticed her as a woman, though her scent has been driving me crazy pretty much since day one. But there's absolutely no way I'm in love with her. It's way too freaking soon for that.

I can't deny that I'm attracted to her though. Ever since

that kiss, I can't stop remembering what she tastes like—how she felt in my arms.

"Yeah, well you're looking at her like you want to lick her from head to toe." Archer laughs when I glare at him. He cut too close to the truth. "See? You like her, DeLuca. It's okay. You can admit it. And as soon as the two of you fall into bed together, make sure you let us know so we can rescind the bet and let it die a happy, empty death."

"Hell, no. I'm going to win that bet, no matter what," I say with utter conviction.

"Keep dreaming," Archer says, clapping me on the back much like Gage had done earlier. Only this time, I keep my footing. "It's about damn time we see you show some interest in a girl. You've been celibate for far too long."

I don't even notice when Archer moves away from me. I keep my gaze locked on Bryn as she moves through the crowd, crossing the courtyard, seemingly coming right for me. The dress she's wearing fits her like a dream. A daringly bold magenta color, it stands out in the crowd of mostly black. The silky fabric clings lovingly to her breasts and hips. Her shoulders are exposed, the straps are thin and the skirt ends just above her knee in a gentle flare.

The color is beautiful on her, bringing out the flush in her cheeks. Her hair is done: long, wavy black-as-midnight locks. She spots me and a secretive little smile curves her lush lips as she approaches on silvery-colored stiletto sandals that shimmer in the light.

She looks like a fucking fairy princess brought to me just for this night. I'm tempted to take her hand, say screw the party, and find somewhere private where we can be alone and naked together.

What the hell is wrong with you?

Bryn James. That's what the hell is wrong with me. The problem? I like this problem. Hell, I'm reveling in it. I shouldn't want her, but I do. I shouldn't think about her in this manner but I can't stop. Hell, I even dream about her.

Sweaty, wicked dreams that leave me aching for her every time I wake.

"Sorry I'm late," she says, stopping in front of me. Her scent carries on the breeze, deliciously sweet, and I inhale as discreetly as possible. My dick twitches, and I will it down. Now is absolutely not the time, but it has other plans, every one of them involving me and Bryn and the two of us naked. "I had to get home and change real quick, and traffic was a nightmare getting back out here."

"You haven't missed much," I tell her, letting my gaze blatantly roam over her before it settles on her chest. All that exposed skin is a fucking distraction. "You look amazing."

The smile grows and my body tightens in reaction. "So do you."

I'm wearing a suit, and I'm as uncomfortable as ever, but I'll take her compliment. "Thanks. Did I tell you I thought you did a fantastic job earlier at the wine tasting?"

"Oh really? No, we never talked, and I was sort of nervous over it all." Her gaze grows earnest as she watches me. "You really thought I did a good job?" She sounds surprised at my praise. Doesn't she realize her worth, both to the business and . . . to me?

Maybe not.

"You led the group expertly and spoke so highly of the winery. You were perfect." I smile, fighting the urge to touch her.

Relief crosses her face. "Whew. Thank God. I really was worried."

"I don't know why. You were composed and handled yourself well. I honestly don't think you could ever disappoint me," I say before I can stop myself.

Her expression softens, her eyes sparkling with some unknown emotion. Christ, she's gorgeous and sweet and reminding me of that night when I not-so-accidentally kissed her. "Thank you, Matt. That means a lot to me, that you would say that." She pauses, her gaze tearing from mine so she can watch the party unfold before us. "You've done such a fabulous job of putting this all together. Everything looks so beautiful."

"It does look good, doesn't it? And you had plenty to do with putting this together as well, you know." I glance around, pride suffusing me. Everyone definitely looks like they're enjoying themselves. But we still have hours to go.

"Hard to believe the day is almost over," she says, sinking her teeth into her lower lip as she turns her gaze on me once more.

Hell. I want to grab her again. Kiss her until she can't see straight, until *I* can't freaking see straight. Having her here standing by my side, wearing a dress that should probably be illegal is pushing me past my limits.

I want to get her alone. Now.

Really?

Really.

"Do you mind coming with me to my office real quick?" I ask, my brain scrambling for an excuse. I shouldn't do this. Shouldn't ditch the party; the most important night of my life.

A night that could be ruined if my father does show and does something stupid which he's an expert at.

She frowns. "What for?"

"I forgot something in there, and I need your help to find it." Lame as hell, but I don't care. I'm filled with the need to be with her. Alone. Just for a moment.

"Um, okay. Do you think it's smart for the both of us to leave the party at the same time?" Bryn looks unsure, but I can't let that bother me now.

Taking her hand, I lead her toward the office building, savoring how her fingers clasp mine. "It'll only be for a few minutes. Besides, there are other employees out mingling, and Archer loves to keep an eye on everything."

Bryn doesn't reply.

We enter the building, though I don't bother turning on the lights; the countless strands of lights outside illuminate the interior well enough. I take Bryn to my office, letting go of her hand when we enter.

"What exactly are you looking for you so I can help you?" she asks.

Guilt gnaws at me for the ruse, but I push it aside. Fuck it. "I didn't lose anything, Bryn. I just . . . wanted to get you alone."

She parts her lips as she stares at me, but doesn't say a word.

Her silence prompts me to go for it.

Finally.

Bryn

shouldn't do this," Matt says, coming right at me, one determined step after another, and I slowly start to back up, fear and excitement bubbling up inside me, making it hard to think clearly.

"Shouldn't do what?" I lift my chin, my gaze meeting his, and I can see all the turbulent, confusing emotions in his eyes, the grim set of his jaw and usually lush mouth. The man means business—what sort of business I'm not exactly sure, but I can take a guess. Increasing my pace, I take hurried backward steps to get away from all that handsome intensity coming at me until my butt meets the wall.

I'm trapped. And in the best possible place too.

In his office, alone with him and in the dark, right back where we started.

"You've been driving me fucking crazy since the minute you arrived tonight," he practically growls, stopping just in front of me.

I have? I want to ask, but I keep my lips clamped tight. I only just got here and besides, he never seems to notice me, not that I really want him to now. Not after the fiasco that went down a few nights ago.

Or at least, that's what I tell myself.

"I don't understand how I could be, considering I just got here," I say, panic flaring within me when his eyes darken.

Do I want this? I try so hard to earn his respect and I let myself end up in these dangerous situations. I'm beyond confused. I want my boss to value me as an employee, but I also want him to see *me*. Really see me. Not just as the dependable, efficiently organized Miss James who makes his life so much easier.

I want Matt to see me as a woman. A woman he wants.

For one shining moment, he did. It ended disastrously, but here I am, alone with him yet again.

Playing with fire.

The thought floating through my brain is apt, considering the potent heat in Matt's gaze.

"Trust me. You're a distraction I absolutely do not need," he says, his voice low. Sexy.

A tremble moves through me, but I stand my ground. "I've done nothing but work my tail off for you the entire day, so please don't tell me you're suddenly angry with me now," I retort, wincing the moment the words leave me. I blame my mounting frustration over our ridiculous situation. The push and pull is getting old, and I'm not sure I can take it much longer.

I'm tired, I've done nothing but live and breathe this winery reopening for the last few weeks if not months, and I'm ready to go home and crawl into bed when I've only just arrived here. Pull the covers over my head and sleep for a month.

But if a certain someone wanted to join me in my bed, there wouldn't be any sleeping involved—just plenty of nakedness and kissing and hot, delicious sex.

My entire body flushes at the thought.

"And I appreciate you working that pretty tail of yours off for me, Bryn, really I do," he drawls, his gaze dropping low. Like he's actually trying to check out my backside. His flirtatious tone shocks me, rendering me still.

Our relationship isn't like this. Strictly professional is how we've kept it, minus the one incident we haven't really talked about. I can still taste his lips on mine, not that I'd ever bring it up now.

His last remark though was most definitely what I would consider flirting. And the way he's looking at me . . .

Oh. My.

My cheeks warm when he stops directly in front of me. I can feel his body heat, smell his intoxicating scent, and I press my lips together to keep from saying something really stupid.

God, I want you. So bad my entire body aches for your touch.

Yeah. Again I sound like those romance novels. The ones I used to find on my grandma's bedside table when I was young. I always thought those emotions were so exaggerated. No way could that actually occur in real life.

But I'm feeling it. Right now. Again. With Matthew De-Luca. And the way he's looking at me makes me think he's feeling it too.

"So, um, h-how have I been driving you crazy?" I swallow hard. I sound like a stuttering idiot, and I'm trying to calm my racing heart, but it's no use. We're staring at each other in silence, the only sound is our accelerated breathing, and then he reaches out. Rests his fingers against my cheek. Lets them drift along my face.

Slowly I close my eyes and part my lips, sharp pleasure piercing through me at his intimate touch. I curl my fingers against the wall as if I can grab onto it, afraid I might slide to the ground if I don't get a grip and soon.

I can smell him. Feel him. We've been close to each other before, but not like this. Never like this. The first time was an accident and had turned into an opportunity—a rushed opportunity that had ultimately ended in utter disappointment.

I don't want to risk that again. I don't know if I could survive it again.

But I want it. I want him.

"You look so damn beautiful tonight," he whispers, his rough voice sending a scatter of goose bumps across my skin.

"Thank you," I say because I don't know what else to do. I crack my eyes open to find he's moved even closer, one hand braced against the wall, the other still touching my face. Tilting my head back, I meet his gaze, my lids flickering when he strokes his thumb across my lower lip.

"It's taking everything inside of me not to just give in and kiss you," he admits gruffly, his hot eyes roaming over my face, then dropping lower, settling on my chest. I can feel my nipples tighten beneath the silk fabric of my dress and I'm suddenly achingly aware of what little clothing I'm wearing. No bra, no panties . . .

My dress is the only barrier between Matt's hands and my skin.

God, I want that. I do. I want to feel his hands roam all over me. I want his mouth on mine, I want his mouth everywhere. I'm tired of resisting him, especially when he so clearly wants me as much as I want him.

For once, I'm going to be bold. I want to see what he does when I invite him to do exactly what he wants to me.

"What's stopping you? We've already kissed before." I reach out, slip my fingers down the length of his black tie. I can't believe I just said that. I can't believe I'm touching him, though really I'm only caressing his tie. Big deal.

But I can feel all that hot, hard strength beneath his shirt, the beat of his heart, the scent of his skin. Relief floods me. We've been dancing around this attraction, especially the last few days, and it feels like we're finally giving in. Again.

Well, I've been dancing around it. He always seemed mostly oblivious to me.

Maybe he isn't. If his current behavior is any indication, he definitely isn't.

"*I'm* stopping me. Or at least I should be," he says, resting both of his hands on my waist as he steps so close, our legs tangle, our chests brush. I hold my breath, waiting for what I know will be a totally disappointing conclusion to our conversation.

He doesn't say anything at all. Instead, he lowers his head, his mouth settling on mine, softly. Sweetly. His kiss obliterates everything, all of my thoughts and worries and concerns, until I'm consumed by the sound and the feel and the smell of him. He surrounds me, overwhelms me, and when he thrusts his tongue deep inside my mouth, I'm lost.

And only Matt will be able to find me.

When he breaks the kiss to slide his mouth down the length of my neck, his low, sexy growl makes my insides flutter. He sounds like he's barely keeping himself in control, and I reach out, wrapping my arms around his neck, burying my fingers in his hair like I enjoy doing. His hair is so thick and soft, the strands cling to my fingers, and I feel like I can't get enough of him.

The way he's kissing me makes me think he can't get enough of me either. His mouth returns to mine and devours me. The kiss so hot, wet, and deep, I feel completely and utterly consumed.

I love it. I want more. I cling to him, mold my body to his and wish he would slip his hands beneath my dress. I want to witness his discovery that I'm wearing no bra, no panties, no nothing beneath it.

I have a feeling he'd be rather pleased with that revelation.

"Jesus, Bryn, you feel good," he says when we come up for air. His hand is roaming, rising from where it rests on my waist to slide up, over my ribcage to rest just beneath my breast. He pulls away slightly, catching sight of my nipples pebbling painfully beneath the silky fabric of my dress, and he lifts his other hand. Traces the deep V neckline of my dress with his fingertip, his touch featherlight as he brushes my skin, causing skitters to rush across it.

Sighing, I close my eyes, savoring his bold yet delicate

touch. He slips his hand beneath the fabric, covering my right breast with just his fingers and makes a rough sound of pleasure at finding me braless.

His calloused fingers play with my nipple, driving me crazy with need, and I drop my arms from around his neck, arching into his touch as I keep my eyes tightly closed. I'm almost afraid to look at him for fear he'll abandon me once he realizes what we're doing.

And then he's kissing me yet again, his hands moving up to cup my face, holding me still. I want to melt. His thumbs brush across my cheeks, his touch gentle, the way he cups my face almost as if he . . . cherishes me. No man has ever held me like this, kissed me like this before. I wrap my arms around his waist, clinging to him, whispering against his lips *please don't stop, don't ever stop*, when he stills. Lifts his head from mine and cocks his ear toward the window.

"Did you hear that?" he asks, his voice hushed.

Beyond the roaring in my ears brought on by his skilled mouth and my own pleading words, I can't really hear anything. Oh, there's the partygoers outside, their chatter a low hum in the quiet confines of his office. A hint of music coming from the hired band but that's it.

"I swear I heard someone yell my name." He kisses the tip of my nose, one cheek, then the other. "Sounded like my father," he whispers.

"Really?" He kisses my forehead, my temple, my ear, my chin. Sweet, soft little kisses that make my lips tingle in anticipation. "I didn't realize he was coming."

"I forgot to tell you about it." He kisses me this time, his lips lingering on mine for long, delicious moments before he finally breaks it. "I didn't think he'd show up. More like I hoped he wouldn't show up."

I'm surprised that he would even invite him. Last I heard from Ivy, their relationship was strained at best.

And then I hear it. A loud, rough bellow:

"Matthew DeLuca, where the fuck are you, son?"

Matt hears it too—who couldn't? His entire body goes still and he pulls away, leaving me. I'm immediately cold without him near.

"That's him," he says grimly. "I should go."

"I'll go with you. Do you want my help?" I reach for him, but he's still backing up, pulling completely away from my grip.

He's withdrawing into himself right before me, and I hate seeing it, though I can't blame him.

He needs to go subdue his father and quick.

"Just mingle and make sure everyone's having a good time. I need to go and make sure he doesn't make an ass out of himself and me and ruin everything," Matt mutters before he turns tail and flees.

I slump against the wall, my heart thumping wildly, my lips still tingling from his delicious kisses. I need to compose myself. Gather my thoughts and emotions and put on the hostess mask.

I need to help Matt. He's stressed. The last thing he needs to deal with is his volatile father making a scene.

Putting aside my tumultuous emotions and locking my still-wobbly knees, I stand up straight, smooth my hands over my skirt, and head for the courtyard.

Chapter 7

Matt

S on! There you are. I've been looking everywhere for you,"
my father says as he stumbles toward me.

"Well, you found me." I grab hold of my dad's arm to keep
him steady. Smells like someone already hit up a bar before
arriving here and disgust fills me. I'm pissed that he would
show up to one of the most important nights of my life and
my career, drunk as hell.

But what did I expect? Not like he cares about me, or my
reputation; he's such a selfish old bastard.

"Where's the wine?" he asks loudly, drawing the attention
of more than one partygoer. "I want a sample of that shit
you're brewing."

He can't even get the terms right. "I think you should lay
off the booze for a while," I say as I try to steer him toward
the table laden with food. He needs to eat something and
drink some black coffee, anything to soak up all that alcohol
coursing through his system and sober him up somewhat.

"Don't tell me what to do." He jerks his arm out of my hold
and heads toward the table I wanted him to go to in the first
place, grabs a small plate, and starts loading up on endless
appetizers.

I follow after him, keeping close, smiling and chatting

with everyone I recognize or know. I feel like I can't leave my father's side, which is such total bullshit, especially because I had to leave a perfectly willing woman back in my office.

Not that I should've been fooling around with a woman in my office when I had a party going on out here but . . .

My mind drifts to Bryn and how good she'd felt in my arms. I'd had my hand beneath her dress only moments ago, touching her breast, playing with her nipple, and she hadn't protested. No, she'd arched into my touch, little sounds of pleasure escaping her. She looked amazing in that dress, her long hair down, her lips parted as she gasped when I gently pinched.

Hell. I want more. I wanted to take her back to my place, strip her out of that dress, and kiss every inch of her naked skin. Instead, I'm babysitting my drunken dad.

Fuck, life is really unfair sometimes.

"Quite the spread you got here," Dad says, clutching his already overflowing plate. "How much did this cost you anyway?"

Damn it, I want to die of embarrassment, his voice is so loud. "Don't worry, Dad, I have it under control," I reassure him.

"Little snot, won't tell me how much money you're spending on this fancy, good-for-nothing shindig. Not that it matters. I don't care what you do with your money. I already gave you your piece of my pie but that's it. I'm cutting you off. You'll have to earn everything else, fair and square." He lurches toward me, his plate nearly goes flying, and I take it from him, wait while he readjusts himself and stands up straighter.

White hot anger flows through my veins, setting my blood on fire. I want to kill him. Wrap my hands around his neck and squeeze until he's not breathing any longer. Not that I could do such a thing, but every time he acts like this, which is pretty much every time I see him, he makes me hate him more.

It's a lot more complicated than that though, my relationship with my dad. I also love him. Still seek out his approval despite how much trouble he causes.

And Vinnie DeLuca causes an enormous amount of trouble everywhere he goes.

"Let's find you somewhere to sit," I tell my dad, grabbing hold of his arm again and leading him toward the tables where guests sit and eat. He jerks against my hold, muttering a string of curse words in protest, but I ignore him. The old man might be the same size as me, but I'm younger and stronger.

"You're manhandling me like you're gonna kick me out of here, son," he says when I push him into a seat. Thank God this table is empty. I don't need him spouting off to other guests.

"Just trying to help you out, Dad," I say through my clenched teeth. Glancing around, I check to see if anyone is watching, specifically anyone from the media, but for the most part, no one's acknowledging us.

Thank God.

"Mr. DeLuca! It's a pleasure meeting you." Bryn appears in front of the table, an angel in magenta clutching a white coffee mug. The smile on her face is as bright as her eyes, and she shoots me a knowing look before she returns her attention to my father.

"Well, well, who's this pretty young thing?" Dad takes the mug from her and sips, wincing when he discovers what it is. "Coffee?"

"Decaf. And laced with whiskey." She winks at him, then winks at me, and I know she's full of absolute crap, just saying that to make him happy. God, I could hug her for this. Kiss her.

Not that I need an excuse to kiss Bryn. My body is still humming from our shared kisses.

"Thank you," Dad says gratefully as he drinks from the cup, finishing off half of it in a couple of swallows. "It's good."

"Miss James is notorious for making the best cup of coffee around," I say, hoping she can hear the gratitude in my voice.

"You know her, son?"

"She's my assistant." I wave a hand between them. "Dad, this is Bryn James. Bryn, this is Vinnie DeLuca."

"Lovely meeting you." She takes Dad's proffered hand, literally batting her eyelashes at him. I swear I hear a hint of her Texas twang when she speaks.

And it's sexy as hell.

"Likewise." Dad won't let go of her hand, and she has to tug out of his hold as discreetly as possible, not that he notices. "You're a looker, darlin'. Where you from?"

"Why, Cactus, Texas, sir." More batting of the eyelashes, her voice is syrupy thick with the accent. She's flirting with my dad and I don't know if I should be horrified or thankful.

She doesn't really . . . *want* to flirt with him, does she?

"Well, what do you know, I met a hot little thing who lived near Cactus years ago, when I was on one of the farm teams. That was a long, long time ago though." Dad grins, most likely reliving the memory and enjoying the hell out of it.

"I probably know her. Not many people ever leave Cactus," she says.

"Miss James, can I speak with you for a moment? Privately?"

I rest my hand on Dad's shoulder. "You'll be all right alone so you can eat, right, Dad?"

"Of course. Go handle your business with your Miss James." Dad waves a hand, cackling wickedly. "You sure are smart, son, more than I give you credit for, hiring a looker like this one. I bet you chase her around your desk all the damn time, trying to get your hands on that ass. I know I would."

Bryn stiffens, her expression frozen with shock. I see it happen right before my eyes. She looks at me, her gaze a little wild, her chest rising and falling with her accelerated breaths.

I have no idea why his words triggered that strong of a reaction, but, of course, my dad's involved so what else is new? The man offends women—everyone—on a constant basis.

"Dad. Come on. Show the lady some respect," I say, giving his shoulder a firm squeeze.

"Yeah, yeah." Dad starts digging into his food, not bothering to offer her an apology, and I feel like shit.

This night is going from bad to worse at a rapid pace.

Bryn

Matt steers me to a dark corner a few feet away from the packed courtyard so we're standing beneath a mighty oak that actually doesn't have a string of lights wound through the branches. His expression is grim, his gaze contrite as he turns to face me.

"I'm sorry." He runs a hand over his face, looking downright traumatized. "My father is an asshole, and I can't believe he said those things to you."

"It's okay," I say softly, my heart still panging from Vinnie DeLuca's earlier words. They'd cut way too close to the truth, reminding me of my old boss.

And of how I haven't changed a bit, even though I think I have. I fall into the same habits time and again, self-destructive to the point that I'm wondering if I seek this sort of attention out.

Was I so neglected as a child that I prefer any attention, good or bad?

"No, it's not okay. You came sweeping in, handling everything perfectly, and he still treats you like that. He's awful." Matt blows out a frustrated breath and rests his hands on his hips, staring out at the courtyard. The music has picked up the pace, and people are actually dancing. The wine is flowing and being praised; the grounds are still packed with people. The party is a huge success.

And here Matt stands, looking so desolate and sad all I can think about is how much I want to comfort him.

Don't do it, Bryn. Not in public. He'll probably freak.

Ignoring my inner voice's protestations, I step closer to him and rest my hand on his chest. I can feel his heart pumping wildly beneath my palm, and I smile up at him, trying to offer reassurance. "He's an old man stuck in his ways. Do you know how many of those types live in Cactus?"

He smiles. "I did notice you slipped into your Texan accent when you spoke to him."

"I did? I didn't even notice." I smooth my fingers down the length of Matt's tie, loving how firm and solid he feels beneath my touch. I wish I could see him naked. I know he has a body to die for. I've seen him bare-chested and sexy as hell online, but I'd prefer to see the real thing. So I can get my hands all over his hot, hard flesh.

"I appreciate you trying to help me," he says, his voice low and sexy, igniting that flicker of desire that always seems to burn within me when he's near into a full-on flame. "You were great with him. Even when he started insulting you."

A soft huff of laughter escapes me. "I know how to handle guys like your father. I've dealt with them a lot." Too much. It's like I can't ever escape them.

He steps away from me, and I drop my hand, pushing aside the sadness that nips at me. I'm acting like a girlfriend when I need to remember my place. I work for him. I'm his assistant.

That's it.

"I'll ask Archer or Gage to spend time with him for a while and keep him entertained," Matt says, his mouth grim. "They know how to handle him. They have before."

"I can do it," I say, wincing the moment the words leave me. Why did I volunteer myself to sit with Vinnie DeLuca? Am I crazy?

Yes, crazy for your boss and looking for any way to please him.

"No way." He shakes his head, but I can see it in his eyes. He's desperate. And if I can ease his stress by babysitting his dad, then so be it.

Even though I'm totally taking a chance here. From what I could see in just the few minutes I've spent in Vinnie's company, he's beyond obnoxious.

"I can handle your father. I'm a lot tougher than I look," I say, wanting him to agree so I can prove I can handle anything he throws my way.

"I don't know . . ." He rubs his chin, his gaze full of doubt.

"Let me do this for you," I whisper, swallowing hard the moment the words leave me. Why do I want to please him so bad?

Because you like him, silly.

A sigh escapes him and he shakes his head. "Listen, if he's rude to you or gets out of control, find me, and I'll take care of him. I'll keep my eyes on you too and make sure he doesn't try anything crazy." He studies me, just waiting for me to bail on him I'm sure.

But I won't. I'm doing this—for him.

"He'll be fine. And I don't mind. Really." Well, I sort of do, but I'll do anything to ease Matt's burden, especially tonight. "I can sit with him, hopefully sober him up and maybe convince him to leave? Is that what you'd prefer?"

I see the guilt and the worry swirling in the brown depths of his gaze. I get it. My grandma is crazy. I adore her, but I wouldn't want her out in public with me, especially on a night as big as this. She'd embarrass the hell out of me.

"Yeah. Actually, I would. I sound like an ass, wanting to get rid of my dad, but if you can subdue him and somehow convince him he needs to go, that would be perfect," he finally says.

"I'll do what I can." I turn and start to head back to the table where Vinnie is sitting when Matt grabs my hand and tugs me back toward him.

"Thank you." He lifts my hand and presses a soft, damp kiss to the back of it. My knees wobble when I see the glow in Matt's gaze as he studies me. "For everything."

"Y-you're w-welcome," I stutter. I can hardly think when he's touching me, looking like he wants to devour me, let alone talking to me. No man has ever made me feel quite like this before.

"We'll talk in a bit, all right? I need to socialize and schmooze," he says as he slowly releases my hand.

"Fine. Makes sense. I've heard nothing but good things from everyone I've talked to, I promise. DeLuca Winery is a big hit." I offer him a quick smile before I flee, going to the table where Vinnie sits munching on one appetizer after another. He spots me, his eyes lighting up, and he pats the empty chair beside him.

"Come sit by me, girly. Want a glass of wine? Some food?" He pushes his plate toward me like he's going to share it as I sit down next to him.

"No, thank you," I say, laying on the sweetness. May as well play it up and entertain the old booger for a while. The last thing I want to do is drink with the already drunk Vinnie, and I'm not really hungry since nerves are still eating at my stomach.

"How long you work here for Matt?" Vinnie asks amicably.

"Well, I was working for the winery before Matt purchased it. I was the assistant of the other owner. We all thought we'd lost our jobs, but then Matt asked us to attend a staff meeting. When he announced that he wanted to keep us all working for him, we were so grateful. We've been loyal to him ever since," I explain, remembering how big and strong and handsome I thought he looked that day. Sweeping in and making his grand declarations, and better yet? Actually keeping his word. I'd wanted to fall at his feet and weep in gratitude, I'd been so thankful.

And I know I wasn't the only one who felt that way either. Men who'd worked in the vineyard for the previous owner's family for years were incredibly thankful for Matt's generosity as well. It's why we all work so hard for him. He shows us respect, and we show it right back.

"That was a good thing my boy did," Vinnie says with a firm nod. "Keeping you all here working for him. Everyone loves my Matthew. Every once in a while, he has a bit of goodness in his heart."

"He's a good boss," I agree, wondering how his dad can both praise Matt and knock him down all in one sentence.

"Even though he don't know shit about wine," Vinnie mutters, making me stifle a laugh. "What? It's true and you know it, girly. I bet he's been scrambling since he bought this place trying to learn everything he can."

His dad wasn't too far off the mark with that assessment. "What he lacks in knowledge, he makes up for in enthusiasm."

"Now that was a diplomatic answer." Vinnie grins and points at me. "I can see why he kept you on. Not only do you look real good, you sound good too."

"Thank you. I think." I glance around, looking for Matt, and spot him standing with a group of people who seem to be enthusiastically chatting him up.

Good. He doesn't need the stress his dad brings him while worrying if anyone is impressed with the wine. Not that I ever doubted he'd succeed, but he's been on edge for days. Weeks. Months.

Probably why he kissed you. Needed an outlet for all that nervous energy and you were the perfect distraction.

The thought comes upon me so quickly, I go still as I turn it over again and again in my head. Could that really be the reason why he kissed me? A way to unleash all that edgy energy he's been living on for the last few weeks?

God, I hope not.

"So can I ask you a question, pretty lady?"

Vinnie's voice reminds me what I'm supposed to be doing, and I turn to look at him, a tentative smile on my face. "Sure. Go ahead."

"Are you fucking my son?"

Chapter 8

Bryn

My mouth is completely dry as I gape at Matt's father, shocked that he would say such a crude and horrible thing.

They have similar features, Vinnie and Matt. Same dark hair and brown eyes, though Matt's are much kinder than Vinnie's cold, almost mocking glare. His mouth is set in a firm line too, as if he doesn't smile much.

I bet he doesn't. It seems he's got a mean streak in him a mile wide.

"Well? Cat got your tongue or what? I can only take your silence as confirmation that yes, indeedy, you're fucking my son," he says. "The lucky bastard."

Swallowing hard, I search for composure. The very last thing I want him to believe is that Matt and I are having some sort of illicit affair. I wouldn't put it past this man to sell the story to whoever would listen if it brought him any bit of attention.

"Your son is my boss," I finally say, my voice raspy, and I clear my throat. "That's it. There's nothing between us except a working relationship."

He casts a skeptical glance my way. "Uh-huh. That's why

he looks at you like you're his favorite dessert and he's a starving man. I get it. Really I do. I never could keep my dick in my pants, you know, especially when faced with a gorgeous woman such as yourself. And neither can he." Reaching out, he touches me, slides his fingers down my forearm. I yank my arm away, my skin literally crawling from his touch.

"There's nothing going on between us," I say, my voice firm, my insides anything but. I'm a nervous, quaking mess, afraid this man will somehow figure out that Matt and I have at least kissed.

His questions, his blunt wording, are tainting everything I've shared with Matt. Reminding me that I'm just the same ol' girl from Cactus, Texas. The girl everyone chases after and expects sexual favors from, all because she has a pretty face and curvy figure.

That's me. I'm that girl, the one who everyone makes feel like she's a slut. A whore. I've slept with two men in my life. I could count the sexual experiences I've had on one hand. Nothing lasting, nothing good, and I always run before it can turn into anything more. I'm always too scared.

Yet I'm the shameless hussy who's out to fuck around with every man I see. I'm a home-wrecker. A man stealer. A girl who's good for nothing but cock sucking. A pervert's dream. I've been told this time and again.

And I'm being told it right now.

"You keep on saying there's nothing between you two, but soon you'll fall under the DeLuca charm. You all do. We're irresistible. My son and I have both had plenty of women. I know when one's interested. And you, my girl, you are definitely interested." Vinnie puts his hand over mine and holds firm, trapping it on the table. "If my son doesn't take the bait, just know I'm always here waiting whenever you're ready."

Oh my God. Now he thinks they're interchangeable? That I'll just bounce from father to son? "You're disgusting," I say, my voice low as I finally snatch my hand back from beneath his.

He laughs, the sound so loud more than a few people turn and look in our direction, including Matt. He shoots me a look of concern, but I shake my head, offer him a quick smile. The last thing I want is him coming over here and discovering this particular conversation. I can handle this man on my own.

He's not the first to think like this, and I'm guessing he won't be the last.

"Disgusting only because you don't want to hear the truth." He reaches for his cup of coffee and drains it. "Keep doing what you're doing, girly. He'll get you into his bed sooner or later."

That's it. I've had it. The man is a pig, and I need to get him out of here. "How did you get here tonight, Mr. DeLuca?" I ask, using my best, most professional voice. Not a twang or *y'all* in sight.

"Ah, now we're back to the formalities, huh? Well, I got myself a ride. The car and driver are sitting out in the parking lot," he says with a grin.

"Then let's go." I stand and grab hold of his arm, yanking him to his feet. He stares down at me in shock, most likely surprised little ol' me could tug him to his feet like that, but I just smile my best smile and lead him toward the entrance of the winery. "You need to get on home. I know Matt was thrilled you thought of him and wanted to stop by, but I think your time here is through."

"You can't just push me out of here," he mutters, but I ignore him, practically dragging him by the arm toward the valets we hired for this evening. I paste my cordial, I-work-here smile on my face as I stop before them.

"We're looking for Mr. DeLuca's car. Do you happen to know where it is?"

One of them did, enabling me with the pleasure of dumping Vinnie DeLuca off onto some other poor, hapless soul and wiping my hands of him and his antics for the evening.

"Think you can get rid of me that quick, missy?" Vinnie shouts from the open window of his car, but I ignore him. Why engage the crazy?

I head back to the courtyard, wincing when my new stiletto sandals pinch my toes. I'm not used to heels or to walking on graveled pathways and cobbled courtyards *in* heels. I can't wait to soak my feet in the bath when I get home.

Alone.

Because there is no way I can pursue something, anything with Matt. Spending just ten minutes in his father's presence confirmed that. I can't go on pretending we would work out. I'd be seen as the gold-digging slut because I'm the poor girl from Texas dating the rich, billionaire boss and he'd be seen as the ass who couldn't keep it in his pants around his own employee.

Any sort of relationship between the two of us, temporary or serious, could ruin his reputation as a businessman in the area. I refuse to play a part in that. I would never be able to forgive myself.

And what would that do to me? I can't destroy my last

chance here at a great job. If I fail at this, I'm going home. I can't afford to live in this outrageously expensive state while unemployed. Lord knows I'd hightail it out of here if I did end up parting ways with Matt professionally. It's hard enough as it is, finding a job that pays as well as mine in the area.

My footsteps slow, and I stop just at the edge of the courtyard, watching everyone. I see Gage and Marina out on the dance floor swaying in each other's arms as they smile and then laugh. I see Matt talking with another group, all of them men, every one of them reeking with importance.

I hope they can give him the connections he's looking for.

He looks so handsome in his dark suit and wine-colored tie, his hair ruffled by the occasional breeze. His smile flashes white against the tan of his skin and there are slight wrinkles around his eyes, as if he laughs often.

Which I hope he does. I haven't seen him laugh much since he's been so stressed-out since I started working for him, but hopefully that will change once everything settles down. Then he can relax and reap the benefits of all this hard work.

I probably won't be around to witness it though. And that thought alone fills me with such complete and utter sadness, I almost fall to the ground, my legs get so wobbly.

Pushing on, I head toward the crowds opposite of where Matt stands. I find an empty table and collapse in a chair, slipping my hand beneath the heavy weight of my hair, so I can rub my neck. No wonder I don't wear it down very often. It's heavy and thick, making me hot and my neck hurt.

I should just cut it all off and be done with it.

"Are you all right? You look like you're contemplating murder." Ivy pulls out a chair and settles in next to me.

"Only the murder of my hair." At her weird look I explain. "I'm thinking of cutting it all off."

"Don't you dare. It's gorgeous."

I shrug. "Like anyone notices. This has all been for nothing."

"Ah, Matt didn't notice? I know he's busy trying to keep everyone happy tonight," Ivy reminds me.

"Oh, he noticed." He definitely noticed if his mouth fused with mine and his hands roaming all over my body earlier was any indication. "His father came along though and ruined everything."

Ivy's mouth dropped open. "His father came? I never saw him."

"Aren't you lucky?" I mutter.

"Aw. Did he say something awful to you?" Ivy reaches out and grabs my hand, giving it a quick squeeze. "He's terrible—says the most offensive things ever. When I was younger, he used to try and hit on me."

"He doesn't try and hit on you now?"

"Well, I haven't seen him in a while and besides, Archer would kill him. Like tear him apart and murder him with his bare hands if he so much as leered at me, let alone touched me." Ivy smiles, a dreamy look in her eyes. "He's so hot when he gets all possessive like that."

Envy curls through me, gripping me tight. "Must be nice."

"Someday I bet you'll experience the same thing with Matt," Ivy says, full of a confidence I wished I felt even a tenth of.

Instead of making her more curious, I decide to put on a brave face. "Yeah, maybe I will," I say with a false enthusiasm that makes Ivy give me the side eye.

I can't get anything right, I swear.

Matt

I caught sight of Bryn escorting my dad out of here not even twenty minutes ago, and it was like a weight had been lifted off me, making me infinitely lighter. It took everything in me not to fret and worry like a little old lady, my gaze constantly going to where Bryn sat with Dad.

I was afraid he'd say something horrible to her, or worse, touch her in an inappropriate manner. Wouldn't be the first time he's done something like that to some poor, innocent woman.

I just don't want him doing it to *my* woman.

With my dad off the premises, I find my focus and really start to work it. I talk to the local winery owners I invited, who all seemed grudgingly impressed with my wine list. I speak with plenty of local media who want to feature the De-Luca Winery; being a former pro ball player gives my story an extra edge they all want to explore.

I haven't eaten dinner and I'm starved, living on the occasional appetizer I find here and there, taking way too many swigs of wine. My head is spinning—I'm high on tonight's event coming together so perfectly—and I wonder where the hell Bryn is.

Plans to celebrate with her are definitely on my late-night agenda.

"Have you seen Bryn?" I ask Archer when I find him moving through the crowd, clutching two glasses, one full of water. I figure he's on his way back to Ivy.

"She's sitting with Ivy over there." He gestures with one of the glasses. "Ivy asked me to grab her a drink."

I should probably stay and talk with my guests some more, but I'm growing exhausted being on all the time. I need a break. I want to hang out with my people. "Yeah, I'll come with you."

"Uh-huh." Archer flashes me a knowing smile over his shoulder as I fall into step behind him. "Missing your girl, hmm?"

"She's not my girl," I say, though the thought of Bryn with any other man, of her giving another man the right to call her his girl, fills me with a near overwhelming rush of jealousy.

Yeah. That was sort of a lie. I wouldn't mind if Bryn was my girl. But she can't be my girl. I have a bet to win.

Fuck the bet.

"You got what—less than forty days? Then she can be your girl. If you can hold out that long," Archer says, stopping at the table where Ivy and Bryn are sitting, deep in conversation. "Look who I found, ladies," he announces as he sets the glasses in front of the women.

They both glance up, their gazes dark and not necessarily happy when they see me.

Weird.

"Hey, Matt," Ivy says first, grabbing her water glass and taking a big swig. "Looks like tonight was a huge success despite your father showing up."

I frown. Great, did she notice? Or did Bryn tell her? "Yeah, well, thanks to the dependable Miss James, who took care of everything and made sure he didn't cause too much of a scene."

"Yes, thank goodness. You can always count on Miss James. Right, Bryn?" Ivy casts her an unreadable glance, which Bryn returns silently.

The vibe is completely off, though Archer seems oblivious to it. They'd been talking about me. And somehow, someway, I must've pissed Bryn off. But how? She'd been so sweet to me right before she went and took care of my dad. How could it all have fallen apart in that short amount of time? Could Dad have said something to her, and she's keeping it to herself?

Shit.

"Well, listen I'm going to wander around and see if there's anything else that needs to be done," I say, gripping the chair in front of me.

"Off to play the gracious host, huh?" Archer asks, slinging his arm around Ivy's shoulders. She snuggles up closer to him and jealousy fills me, sharp and painful.

I wish I had the right to be as affectionate with Bryn. We're not even close to that comfort level yet. I touch her in front of Gage and Archer and they'll be all over me like white on rice, ready to call the entire bet off.

Not that I care about the million dollars, but damn it, it's the principle. I won that bet fair and square. I want to collect from them and rub it in their faces.

I feel like an immature asshole, but I want to win.

"Gotta do what I must to ensure everyone's having a good time," I say with a smile, glancing at Bryn to find her watching me with those all-seeing, sky-blue eyes.

"Do you need my help?" she asks.

"No, relax. Sit and enjoy the party. You dealt with enough already." I'm trying to communicate with her how much I appreciate her taking care of my dad. That couldn't have been easy. The old man is a grumpy asshole with a mouth that never, ever stops.

"Okay. As long as you're sure." She smiles but it doesn't quite reach her eyes. She looks so beautiful and so incred-

ibly fragile sitting there next to the pregnant Ivy, who's glow-
ing with vitality. Compared to her, Bryn's natural light from
the last week is dimmed. She doesn't need the beige tonight.
Even in magenta she looks subdued.

And I hate that. Knowing I'm the cause of it all.

"Could I talk to you for a moment though?" I suddenly ask.
"Privately?" I need to make sure she's all right.

"Sure." She shrugs those beautiful, bared shoulders and
stands, going round the table so she's next to me. I lead her
away to another table at the far end of the courtyard, ignoring Archer since I can feel him watching me. Just waiting for
me to slip up and somehow touch Bryn inappropriately in
front of him.

Jackass.

"What's going on?" she asks when we stop to talk.

"Did my father say something to you? Did he offend you
or try to put his hands on you?" I ask, cutting right to the
point.

She sighs, hangs her head. "He said a few things. Nothing
that I haven't heard before."

What the hell does she mean by that? "What are you talking about?"

Bryn lifts her head so her gaze meets mine once more. "He
asked if the two of us were—sleeping together yet, though he
phrased it a little more crudely."

I inwardly groan. "What did you tell him?"

"I told him we weren't, of course, which is the truth." She
stresses the last word. "He didn't believe me."

"What a bastard," I mutter, running my hand through my
hair in pure frustration. "How did you get him to leave?"

"Well, he wouldn't stop with the crude remarks and insults
so I finally dragged him to his feet and hauled him out of

here. Turned him over to the guys working valet, and they got him to his car," she explains matter-of-factly.

While I wish I could've been there by her side to defend her, I'm also proud of the fact that she handled herself so calmly. "You're amazing," I say softly, wishing I could touch her. But I can still feel Archer's eyes on me so there's no way I'm going to do it.

"I did what you asked. Don't make it out to be more than it was." She offers me a wan smile. "Is that all you wanted to ask me?"

"Bryn." Unable to help myself, I reach out and touch her arm lightly. Screw it. I don't care what Archer thinks. "Are you okay? You seem upset."

"Nothing like a little dose of reality to bring me back and remind me of what I really am." The smile turns brittle, and she inclines her head toward the rest of the partygoers circling in the courtyard. "You need to go talk to everyone else and make them all happy that they got a chance to speak to the owner of the new and rather impressive DeLuca Winery, don't you think?"

I let my hand drop. "Can I see you? Later tonight?"

She slowly shakes her head. "I don't think that's a good idea, Mr. DeLuca."

And with those last words, she walks away, leaving me in the dust.

Chapter 9

Bryn

The phone has been ringing constantly since I got into work this morning, but I blame that on the aftermath of the party. Everyone's looking for Matt, including me. Though I shouldn't. I'm not sure if I'm quite ready to face him yet.

I stayed home the entire weekend, not daring to go out, barely glancing at my phone. I ignored the calls and texts from Ivy and Marina, ignored the single text from Matt too. It wasn't work related so I figured I was safe. The text had come Saturday afternoon, asking if I'd survived the night okay, and I didn't bother answering.

How could I tell him the night had been a revelation? That I realized exactly who I am and what people saw when they looked at me? Well, specifically what men see, minus the bland outfits and boring hair.

That hurt, though deep down inside, I knew it. That's why I hid, pretending to be something I'm not.

Avoiding Ivy and Marina was tough because I would've loved to confide in them, but what if my confession turned them against me? All the old worries and insecurities swamped me these last few days. It's hard to shake those old habits when they'd been such a part of my life for so long. Men don't respect me, they never have. I didn't have many friends growing up, and I definitely haven't had any since I've come to California.

I'm scared if I tell Ivy and Marina my fears, what happened between Matt and me, what his dad said about me, they'd see me differently. Dumb, I know, since they're the ones who convinced me to go after Matt in the first place, but I can't help it. I'm afraid they'll know what I really am versus what I present. A silly dumb girl who is only thought of for her sexuality, not her brains or her skills.

And I don't know if I could face them, seeing the judgment in their eyes.

Besides, I know they kept reaching out to me because they only wanted to gossip about Friday night's party or analyze what happened between Matt and me. I'd rather not think about it at all. The more I do, the more upset I become, especially when the things his dad said to me come into play.

I bet you chase her around your desk all the damn time, trying to get your hands on that ass. I know I would.

Spending the majority of the weekend in bed watching bad TV and eating junk food didn't do anything to help my mood either. By the time I got my act together and prepared to go into work, I had bags under my eyes, my skin was kind of pale, I felt five pounds heavier, and I had a zit on my chin.

Great.

I showed up right on time though, not wanting to disappoint anyone—specifically Matt. Not wearing any beige or my severe hairstyle either, deciding to give in and go with what's natural for me, not the phony front I've put up since I've arrived here. Clad in the dress I wore last Monday, with the black background and blue and green flower and bird pattern, I leave my hair loose and hanging down my back.

I'm tired of the facade. Of being something I'm not. If I

had my slightly trampy clothes from my time in Hollywood or even my wardrobe from Cactus, I'd be wearing them. Today. Right now.

But I don't have any of those clothes anymore. I burned most of them. It had felt like a cleansing of sorts, one I'd needed to start fresh.

Now I wish I had them. Just to remind me of my roots and who I really am. That reminder would fuel me and keep me strong for what I'm about to do today. Something I need to do.

I need to quit.

But Matt showed up late which made me antsy. He came in just past nine with a harried expression on his face, rushing into the room with the determination of a man on a mission. He'd dressed casually, jeans and a polo shirt that fit him to perfection.

My mouth literally waters when I see him now.

But what else is new?

"Had a meeting with the Napa Valley Vintners this morning," he says, stopping just in front of my desk. His mind is going a mile a minute, I can tell. "I need you to look into flights to New York City in a few weeks. We're going to attend the Savor Wine Guild annual convention. Had no idea it was going down, so I need to make arrangements quick."

I grab a pen and start jotting down notes. "What are the dates?"

"We'd have to leave two weeks from today," he says, whipping out his phone and scrolling through his emails.

My pen stills on the notepad, and I pause for a moment, his words slowly sinking into my dense brain. I glance up to find him watching me carefully. Almost too carefully. "Did you say 'we'?"

"I want you to go with me, Bryn. I'll need your help. It's only for a few days, but it's a busy few days. I'll want your input, and you'll have to keep me on task," he explains.

He wants me to go with him, alone, to New York City. I must be hearing things.

"Are you serious?"

"Serious as a heart attack." His expression is dead serious too. "You're my assistant, right? I can't do this alone, Bryn. There's going to be a two-day forum with business discussions, workshops, and extensive, in-depth wine tastings. I can't be everywhere at once, so I need you to take on some of the workshops and talks or whatever, take notes and get back to me."

"Okay." I take a few more notes then turn to my computer and start searching for flights. "Are you sure you want to bring me though? I mean, really? Won't it be just an extra expense, my flight and hotel room, food and everything else that comes with traveling?"

"I need as many write-offs as I can get," he says dismissively. "And I can afford to bring you, Bryn. That's not an issue, so don't worry about it."

All my plans of giving my notice to Matt fly right out the window at his rapid-fire requests. There's no way I can leave now. He needs me, as ridiculous as it sounds. Despite all the trouble I will no doubt bring him and the expectations he'll have, I need to be there for him.

I can do this. I'll work for the next two weeks, take the trip to New York, run around this convention with him for a few days, come home, and then I'll give my notice. That ought to give me enough time to find a job in Cactus, not that it should be too difficult.

I'd called my grandma last night, asking if I could go back

and live with her in Cactus. She'd agreed readily, her boom-ing voice coming at me over the phone, loud and reminding me why I left my hometown in the first place.

"Of course you can come live with me, girl. I know Wanda down at the Soap-n-Snip needs a new phone girl. Maybe you could get your cosmetics license and make that career happen. It's a good one, you know. Why, that sweet little Becky who's only two years older than you has made herself quite the career working there."

Then she'd launched into a twenty-minute gossip session full of what's been happening in Cactus the last few years. By the time she finished, I knew everything. All of it.

Some stuff I found interesting. Other stuff I couldn't care less about. Typical Cactus talk, all of it.

And soon I'll be back, right in the midst of it all. Working at the Soap-n-Snip, answering the phone, sweeping up hair, and generally miserable with life.

At least I'll be in my element, back in my hometown. Where I can literally let down my hair, be free and be me.

I don't feel like I can be me anywhere else, not even here.

Especially not here.

"I'll find some flights and show you the options," I say, my voice crisp as I go into efficient mode.

"Great. Go to the Savor website and register us too. We'll probably have to pay for late registration, but I don't care. I can't miss this. The people at the Vintners said I must attend this event. We'll find out the latest trends, see both the business and the creative side of winemaking; it's going to be pretty awesome." He smiles and I smile back, unable to stop myself.

He's just so excited, so pumped to do this. I want to be excited for him. Even though I plan on disappointing him completely within the next month.

Matt

You sly dog." Gage shakes his head just before he takes a bite of his cheeseburger. We're at a restaurant in downtown St. Helena, one that makes the best burgers and sandwiches and doesn't have a vegetarian or gluten-free option in sight. This is why the place is filled with mostly men. We've grown weary of the massive health movement that's taken over our area so easily.

"What are you talking about?" I ask, my voice neutral.

"You know. Taking the assistant to New York City where none of us can keep tabs on the two of you. Where you're free to walk around and hold hands, kiss her on the street, and fuck her all night in a hotel room. Smart move, man. Smart. Move." Gage laughs.

I ignore him, digging into my hamburger with gusto. I'm freaking starving, I've been so busy with work for the last three days: hardly taking a break, skipping lunches, staying late. Gage had been giving me endless shit, calling me the last two days saying he wanted to meet for lunch. Finally, after harassing me all morning with nonstop texts, I gave in, telling Bryn I'd be back in an hour and that if I didn't show up at the office by one-thirty, she needed to buzz me and get my ass back there.

When I'm with either Archer or Gage, we usually start talking about all sorts of crap and lose track of time, especially if there are beers involved.

Today, there aren't. I made sure of that.

"Does Archer know you're taking her to New York? I assume he does. I only found out because Marina told me after she spoke with Bryn yesterday. Like you'd ever tell us." Gage laughs some more. "I guarantee at the end of the forty-five days I'm going to find a way out of making this payment to you. Watch me. Why should we pay you when you're off fucking your assistant?"

"You have a dirty mind," I mutter, grabbing a fry and dipping it in ketchup before I point it at him. "Not everything is about fucking, you know. How does Marina put up with your ass day in and day out?"

"Marina loves my ass. And she especially loves my dirty mind." He waggles his brows at me like a pervert. "And listen to you, the former king of groupies, chastising me like a prude. You sure as hell need to get laid and quick so we can cancel this entire bet once and for all. I'm tired of dealing with your insufferable ass."

"Yeah, yeah. Fuck off," I mutter, shaking my head, concentrating on my lunch. "You're the one who wanted to have lunch with me in the first place." He has a point. I'm grumpy as hell because I want Bryn, and she's turned off the signal completely. It's like she barely realizes I exist.

I know why though. It's because of my father. It's because of that kiss. I regret her having to deal with my dad and the things he said to her. I wish I could've protected her from that.

But the kiss? I don't regret that at all.

"I asked you to lunch so I could find out where your head is at." He takes a drink from his soda. "So tell me. Did you plan this so-called business trip on purpose to get her in your hotel room or what?"

"Not even," I scoff, munching on another fry. "We're attending a conference—and not some phony one either, which I'm sure you'll accuse me of. I won't even have time to think about doing anything else except going from workshop to workshop, attend wine tastings and the like. It's all about the business, my friend. Something you've forgotten since you're too enraptured with your new girlfriend."

"Says the man taking his obsession with him to New York City so he can do *business*." Gage rolls his eyes. "Give me a break, man. We know exactly why you're taking Bryn with you. To get in her panties."

Thinking about Bryn in her panties just about gives me a coronary. So many lost opportunities we've had in such a short amount of time. Now she acts like she couldn't give two shits about me.

I hate it. And it's all my fault so I have no one to blame but myself.

"Definitely not," I say firmly. "I think she's over me."

"Ha!" Gage points at me, his gaze bright and full of triumph. "You admit it; you two *are* interested in each other."

"Yeah, well, if she was interested in me, she's definitely not now. She's back to the efficient, no-nonsense Miss James."

"I bet she sure is hot though, when she's the efficient, no-nonsense Miss James," Gage says with a shit-eating grin.

Jealousy flaring, I throw a fry at him, aiming for his face, but he dodges it just in time. "Shut up, dickhead. You're acting like a child." What the hell, I feel like lately we've reverted to college talk—when we were young and dumb and talked crudely to and about everyone, especially each other.

"Who's the child here, throwing food and calling me a dickhead?" Gage shakes his head. "I don't know if any of us are going to survive these new terms. The longer you go without getting some, the grumpier you become. I bet your Miss James lost interest because you've become such a tyrant."

That can't be the reason. Can it? I doubt it. I think it has something to do with Dad. I have no idea what he said to her; she's not talking and neither is he. I called him up a few days ago and flat out accused him of saying something shitty to Bryn, but he didn't give an inch.

Leaving me to conclude that he's guilty as hell.

"The DeLuca Winery is all anyone's talking about around town," Gage says, thankfully changing the subject. "Your re-opening was a huge hit."

"Yeah, it went pretty well, didn't it?" I'm trying to down-play it more for my own sake than anything else. There are still some deals and transactions in the works—trying to get some regional markets to carry the DeLuca brand, pushing out and growing our distribution list. More publicity oppor-tunities too, ones that I'm hopeful will come to fruition and take DeLuca wine to a national level.

Going to Savor will get the DeLuca brand out there even more. I've realized quick, especially after meeting with the local Vintners group, that I need to be constantly push-ing the name, constantly talking to people in the industry. Creating a good wine is key, but networking is a necessity to selling good wine. Growing, learning, taking it all in—especially at conferences where I meet others in the business, so I can bring it back to DeLuca and apply everything I've learned—is important.

Do I really need to take Bryn with me to Savor? Probably not. I would've been exhausted running around that con-ference for two days, and missed a few talks or workshops I wanted to check out, but I could've done it all on my own. It's just so much more fun having her with me. And easier, of course, since she's beyond capable and will keep me on schedule.

Spending time with her on a plane, in the city, at a hotel. It's all ripe with possibilities.

If the woman I'm interested in actually acted interested in me, that is.

Chapter 10

Bryn

Two weeks later
New York City

I sit on my cushy king-size bed with my laptop, glancing over my hand-scribbled notes taken from the endless amount of workshops I went to all day. I have never, in all my life, stayed in a hotel like the W New York at Times Square. Of course, the biggest city I've ever been to before was Los Angeles and that's just a sprawling metropolis with crowded freeways and shopping malls everywhere.

New York City has a completely different vibe. All the buildings are so tall, the sidewalks packed, and everything is open so late. I've never seen anything like it. In my hometown, the sidewalks rolled up and shops closed around eight o'clock, nine on Saturdays.

We arrived last night, and Matt had wanted a slice of pizza at one in the morning. We'd promptly gone out and found a place open—not only open but packed.

It thrilled my small-town-bumpkin-self right down to my toes.

While I attended workshops today, Matt went to a discussion symposium, a special wine tasting, and currently he's at a keynote dinner. He tried to get me to go with him, but I declined, saying I'd rather call for room service and type up the notes I knew I'd have.

He'd reluctantly agreed, telling me I could order whatever I wanted from room service since he was paying for it.

It's funny, considering how hard I've seen him work and how many hours he's put in at the winery, but a lot of the time I forget Matt's wealthy. As in billionaire-wealthy. The guy is loaded, thanks to both his father and Matt earning a bundle from his baseball contract and various endorsements.

And those are just the most recent ones.

It wasn't until we stepped on the plane and sat in first class that I saw how the other half lives. Talk about star treatment. I've flown once in my life and that was when I went to California—on a shitty little crowded plane that made me pay for a soda, for the love of God. I declined, sitting in my cramped little seat between two large, sweaty businessmen who leered at me the entire flight.

I hated it.

But flying first class in the wide comfy seats, being served constantly, and sitting next to Matt? I felt like I'd died and gone to heaven.

That was until I saw the hotel. Oh, my word, it was the prettiest, most modern hotel I've ever seen in my life, not that I've stayed anywhere beyond a Motel 6. I made sure Matt had a two-room suite with a gorgeous city view and since my room was right next to his—which he'd asked for—I had the same.

I didn't even care that I wasn't outside amongst the hustle and bustle of Times Square. I was perfectly content sitting in my suite with the gorgeous white bed and shocking pink comforter. The sleek glass furniture and the blooming hot pink orchids everywhere. Me, the Cactus, Texas-supposed-slut, feels like a real life fairy-tale princess.

All thanks to Matt.

What sucks? I have to give my notice when we return. There's just no way I can continue working for him. I'm pretending to be this certain type of quiet, demure woman when I'm not. My real self is bound to pop out sooner or later, and I don't want to do that in front of Matt. He thinks I'm a good girl.

And I can't seem to let go of my old, bad girl insecurities.

It's bad enough we've kissed a few times. The last thing I want to do is hurt his reputation, so I try my best to avoid him, but it's near impossible. The tension between us is still there, though we never talk about it. I see the way he stares at me when he thinks I'm not looking. I want to return that longing stare. Worse, I want to lock myself away in his office, plop myself on his desk right in front of him, and beg him to kiss me.

I think he'd take me up on the offer. I know he would.

But then I'd become the slut everyone accuses me of being. Sleeping with my boss to get ahead—at least, that's what it would look like. Indulging in a heated affair with the man who signs my paychecks is not smart. Didn't I learn anything after my failed attempt at a minor affair with Brian Fairbanks?

Leaning against the fabric headboard, I stare out the window at the city lights that surround me. I hadn't thought of his actual name since I don't remember when. I prefer to think of him as this faceless, nonentity, otherwise known as my ex-boss. It's just so much easier that way, not thinking of his name.

Now it all comes back to me. Brian would flash that charming smile as he whipped his thin blond hair away from his eyes, his gaze always eating me up. He had this way of making me feel like I was special, despite the ridiculous way he talked to me about titties and ass and how much his palm itched to give me a spanking.

Yes, he said that. He said a whole lot more too, plenty of which I wish to banish from my brain forever.

When I told my grandma what happened with Brian—how it turned out he had a wife and kids—she'd read me the riot act. Chewed me out for what felt like hours, though it probably only equaled about fifteen minutes. Told me if I continued flirting with these men who were in positions of authority, I'd never get ahead unless I had sex with them. That was all they thought of when they looked at me.

A sexpot. She'd called her own granddaughter a sexpot, though now I suppose she said it to warn me. I always heard how I needed to make good choices.

So I tried. I tried and tried and tried and here I sit, in a hotel suite paid for by my boss, and I'm still contemplating how I can get him into my room, so I can have a chance with him at least once before I quit and go back home to Cactus.

Have I lost my mind? I worry so much how others will see me, yet I still want Matt. I can't help it. If people are going to call me a sexpot, a slut, or a tramp, I guess I can go ahead and give them a reason to, right?

Respect yourself. If you don't, no one else will either.

I need to remember that.

My cell phone buzzes and I glance at it to see a text from Matt.

You in your hotel room?

I sure am, typing up notes just for you, I answer.

No reply, and I stare at the screen of my phone, willing something to appear. When nothing happens, I toss it aside and start typing up my notes again, my eyelids growing heavier with the menial task.

It was bad enough I had to sit through those sessions. Now I'm reliving them by rewriting the notes, reminding me exactly how boring they'd been.

Well, boring to me. Matt would probably find it fascinating since he's in the business, but definitely not me.

My phone dings again, and I grab it.

> You should meet me at the Blue Fin Restaurant downstairs in thirty minutes.

> Why?

I chew on my fingernail, waiting for his answer. I already had room service for dinner, ordering a delicious pasta dish with shrimp and a salad on the side the moment I got back to the hotel. I'm not even hungry.

> I want to take you out to dinner.

The Blue Fin is a gorgeous restaurant in the hotel; I keep peeking in there when I walk by. I'm dying to check it out, but not like this.

Staring at my phone's screen, I contemplate how I should answer. The conference is done for the night. We have one more day tomorrow and then it's over. Dinner tonight isn't official business.

It feels personal. Like a date.

> I already ate. Didn't you eat too?

> Have dessert then. And the meal
> they gave us at the keynote was crap.
> I'm still hungry.

A little sigh escapes me, and I stare out the window again, drinking in the beautiful city view. I should decline. I should stay in my pretty hotel room and type up my messy notes and fall asleep in my deliciously soft bed. A good girl would do that. She wouldn't be tempted to do something bad, like go out on a dinner date with her boss.

But I never said I was a good girl.

I want to spend time with Matt. I want to go out to dinner with him and stare at his handsome face from across the table. I want to hear him tell me a story, and then I want to tell him a story and make him laugh. I want him to reach across the table and grab my hand, entwining our fingers.

I want it all, and I want it with Matt.

Grabbing my phone, my fingers hover over the keys for a millisecond before I start typing.

> You said thirty minutes?

Yep, he replies. We on?

A smile curves my lips as I answer him.

> We are definitely on.

Matt

'm exhausted. The jet lag, the running from one session to the next at the conference, the information coming at me from all sides, it's all depleting my energy. I should've just gone to my room, ordered room service, and collapsed into a deep, dreamless sleep.

But none of that matters because here I am, waiting for Bryn at the entrance to the Blue Fin, eagerness at seeing her making my stomach jump like a pond full of hyperactive fish. I've hardly seen her since we arrived in New York City. We've been on separate schedules, meeting up in odd spots, like in the corridor of the event center earlier this afternoon. I'd been rushing by, but I called her name when I noticed her exiting a room.

She'd waved, looking adorable in dark-rinse jeans that fit her sexy legs perfectly, a secretive smile curling those sensual lips.

My cock had literally twitched at seeing her, even for such a fleeting second.

"Hi. Hope I didn't keep you waiting."

I turn at the first sound of her sultry voice, smiling when I see Bryn standing before me. She'd changed and is now wearing a sleek, simple long-sleeved black dress that covers pretty much every available inch of her save her face, hands, calves, and feet. Yet somehow she still manages to be sensual as hell, what with the way the fabric clings lovingly to her body.

"Miss James. I must say you're looking extra beautiful this evening."

Her cheeks color, turning a beautiful shade of pink as she clutches her hands in front of her. "Thank you," she murmurs, her gaze meeting mine for the briefest second before she lets it drop. "You look good too."

I'm still in the black trousers I've worn all day but changed into a white button-down shirt right after I texted her, wanting to dress up a little bit since I figured the Blue Fin had something of a dress code. I'd planned on going to dinner alone. Well, I told myself that. "Thank you. Ready to be seated?"

When she nods, I lead her to the front desk, requesting a table for two. The hostess grabs two menus and leads us up the floating stainless steel staircase to a semi-private alcove, filled with quiet booths that line the wall and overlook the bright lights of Times Square. A small jazz quartet plays along the opposite wall—soothing, soft music that adds to the hushed atmosphere.

"You're not hungry?" I ask after the hostess leaves us, flipping open the menu immediately. "I'm starved. Conference chicken and dry rice pilaf doesn't do much for my appetite."

She laughs, the sweet sound washing over me, making me yearn. For her. "Sounds awful."

"It was." I glance over the entrees, my stomach grumbling at some of the offerings, especially the blue cheese–encrusted filet mignon. "I know what I'm having," I say, shutting the menu.

"So do I," she says, closing hers as well, her sparkling gaze meeting mine. She looks extra pretty in the candlelight, and I can smell her. That intoxicating scent of hers that drives me wild. I don't know if I can withstand it much longer.

"You getting dessert?"

"I think so. I filled up on a pasta dish from room service earlier. It was delicious." She smiles, a mysterious little curve of her lips that makes me want to discover all of her secrets. She has lots of them. I don't know much about her, and I wish I did. Seeing her like this, spending time with her, fills me with greed.

I want more. More of Bryn.

"That's what I should've done rather than listening to that guest speaker. He was boring." I take a sip of my ice water, hoping it'll cool my suddenly heated skin. Just watching her, how the candle flickering on our table casts her face in a golden glow, I'm mesmerized by how beautiful she is, how at ease she seems to be with me tonight. This is a first. We haven't felt this comfortable with each other in weeks.

"We should've ditched the conference altogether today and explored the city," Bryn suggests. "I know we're here to work, but I've never been to New York City before."

"It's kind of crazy, isn't it?"

She nods. "I feel like a total hick coming here. Like I want to stop in the middle of the sidewalk and just stare at everything. All the people, the noise, the lights, the smells—I've truly never seen anything like it. Cactus has nothing on this place."

I like it when she talks about her past, which isn't often enough for my liking. It offers a glimpse into her world that I don't get to see. She's a private person, and I can't blame her, but I'm still curious.

The waiter approaches and we order drinks—water for Bryn and a beer for me—plus a crab cake appetizer that I offer to share but she passes on it.

"I don't really do seafood," she says, wrinkling her nose.

Damn, she's cute. I notice when she gets tired or feels comfortable, the southern accent makes a faint appearance.

"Really? I love it."

"We don't get much seafood in Cactus if you know what I mean. It's terribly dry and flat and not an ocean in sight."

We grew up in completely different worlds. I'd spent my entire life in the Bay Area, bouncing around as my dad moved us from place to place, but never really straying. Growing up by the ocean in such a huge city, I never realized what an effect it had on me. How it made me view the world. For Bryn, growing up in such a small town in the middle of nowhere had profound effects on her too. "What made you leave your hometown?"

"There was nothing there for me." Her expression shutters, and I wonder why. It always feels like there's more behind her reasoning, and she's just not telling me. "It's a small town that's going nowhere. I would've gone nowhere." She tears her gaze from mine, staring off into space. "But sometimes if you have no other choice, you have to settle for nowhere, you know?"

No, I didn't know, but I'd never been one to settle. If there was something I wanted, I went after it until it was mine. I liked a challenge. "Settling for nowhere sounds like a last resort."

"What if you've tried all the resorts and none of them worked out?" she asked, her voice dropping to a low murmur as her gaze meets mine once again, her eyes wide, her expression . . . forlorn.

I immediately want to comfort her. Wrap her in my arms and reassure her everything's going to be all right. I don't even know what I'd be referring to, but I don't care. She brings out a protectiveness in me I didn't even realize I had.

"What are you talking about Bryn?" There's definitely more going on here than what she's saying, and I want to know what it is.

"I left home because I had a bad experience at a job." A funny little smile crosses her lips, and I wonder what sort of bad experience she's talking about. "Then I moved to Los Angeles because I decided to become a model. I'm tall, I have a decent face, and I decided I was going to use my natural assets to get a job. But that was a disaster."

I can only imagine. I've heard plenty of firsthand stories of how Hollywood chews up these pretty, naive girls and spits them out.

Bryn was gorgeous enough that I wouldn't doubt she had a lot of interest. Probably all of it overtly sexual though, since so many of the sleazy photographers and directors that line the Hollywood streets won't do anything for a girl unless she sleeps with them first.

"So the job at the winery was a last ditch effort before I had to go back home for good. I found the job on Craigslist. I loaded up my old Saturn with my few boxes of stuff and drove north to the land of new opportunities. Only to discover the winery was hanging by a thread and eventually we weren't even getting paid properly. Until you walked in and saved us all."

The waiter chooses this moment to show up with our drinks and my appetizer, interrupting Bryn's story. I wait impatiently as he places everything in front of us and takes our dinner orders—well, my dinner order since Bryn chose salted caramel cake for her dessert. He even tries to make conversation, and I finally glare at him until he gets the hint and takes off.

"Matt, that was kind of rude," Bryn chastises the moment

the waiter's gone. "He was just trying to do his job and be nice."

"He interrupted you." I grab my silverware and place my napkin in my lap before I dig into the crab cake. It smells amazing, the sauce that comes with it is delicious and my starving stomach is applauding my choice even as I begin eating. "Go on," I prompt her after I swallow.

"I was pretty much done. You were my savior and now here we sit, in New York City. You showing the country bumpkin how the big city folk live." She props her elbow on the edge of the table and rests her chin on her fist. "You've taught me a lot in a short amount of time, Matt, and for that I'm eternally grateful."

She's speaking with a finality that makes me uneasy. "I'll show you more if you let me," I say, going with the double meaning behind my words. Why pretend any longer? I'm sick of it. I don't know if she is too, considering she's been running pretty hot and cold lately, but I am one who goes after something—or someone—once I realize I want it.

And I want her. Bryn. I'm tired of fighting my attraction for her.

Her arm drops from the table as she leans back in her chair. "What do you mean by that?"

I shrug. "Take from it whatever you want."

She studies me for a long, quiet moment, her gaze roving over my face before she finally reaches for her water glass and drains half of it. "I won't sleep with you, Matt," she says after she sets the glass on the table.

I'm shocked yet pleased at her boldness. "What I'm suggesting won't involve any sleeping, Bryn."

Her lips part as her eyes widen the slightest bit. "We shouldn't."

"Why not?"

"I work for you."

"I know. That little fact does make my attraction for you rather—awkward." There. I said it. And I'm not taking it back either.

"I've tried resisting you." She drops her head, studies her lap, and I want to reach for her. Pull her into my arms and offer her reassurance, let her know she's not alone in this confusing sea of emotions and wants and needs.

I'm right there with her, drowning in the swirling sea, hoping she'll be the one who finally throws me a life preserver and tows me in.

"I've tried resisting you too," I confess in a low murmur. "Clearly it's not working since I still want you."

"Is it a case of wanting what you can't have?" Her head is still bent, her voice so soft I can hardly hear it.

My appetite has fled. I set my fork on the edge of the plate and push it away. All I can think about, all I can want is this woman sitting across from me. "No. It's a case of wanting what I've had a taste of, and needing more of it. More of you."

She slowly lifts her head, her gaze meeting mine. "I got in trouble for doing this before."

I frown, confused by her change of subject. "For doing what?"

"Fooling around with my boss. I was nineteen. It was my first real job. My boss flirted with me and really turned on the charm until he finally wore me down, and I fell under his spell." She pauses, licking her lips. "He literally chased me around his desk all the time. It turned into this . . . game, and I actually liked the chase. Finally I let him catch me."

"What happened?" Dread fills me. I don't think I want to hear her answer.

"I . . . let him kiss me. A lot. And . . . and more. We had sex, right there in his office. He made all of these promises to me, and I believed him. Oh, how I believed him. I thought I'd met the perfect man for me. Older, experienced, and sophisticated. I thought he would take me out and show me the world." She makes this funny little face, rolling her eyes, and smirking like she can't believe how silly she was. "Then I found out he was married and had a child. His wife called me and yelled at me. Told me she found text messages he'd sent me, and I couldn't believe he kept them on his phone. She called me a whore and a slut and a home-wrecker."

"You were young," I say in her defense. "And he tricked you."

"I was dumb. And a home-wrecker just like she said. How could I not know he was married? Cactus is a tiny town. I should've known." She presses her lips together, looking ready to cry.

I reach across the table and grab her arm, lifting it up so I can interlace our fingers, giving her hand a squeeze. "Hey, stop. Don't beat yourself up. You didn't know."

"I was an idiot," she sniffs.

"No you weren't." Her boss was a jackass of the worst kind. Taking advantage of a young, naive girl. Getting her to fall for him all while he was married.

"I had sex with my married boss."

"I'm not that guy. And I'm definitely not married." I reach for her with my other hand, slipping my fingers beneath her chin and lifting her face up. "And I don't have any kids either. You can kiss this boss all you want."'

She smiles in spite of it all, a beautiful, bright, and toothy smile unlike any I think I've ever seen her display. "I like you, Matthew DeLuca. A lot."

"Enough to kiss me again?" I ask, my heart starting to pick up speed.

"We shouldn't."

"There are lots of things we shouldn't do." Leaning in, I hover just above her lips, feel her breath feathering across my own. "Sometimes we just have to do it anyway."

Chapter 11

Bryn

He kisses me after he says that. His mouth touches mine gently before he lifts away from me to flash a quick smile. He dips down and kisses me again, for real this time, with heat and tongue and little moans and rough groans. I lose myself in his taste, in the way he squeezes my fingers in his, how his fingers hold my chin and softly caress my skin.

Right here in a booth in the middle of a restaurant in the middle of Times Square, Matt kisses me like he means it. After he hears bits and pieces of my sordid story, it's like it didn't even affect him. Oh, he showed sympathy in all the right places—shock and horror and disgust—but never at me. It was like he understood what happened.

And kissed me anyway.

Someone clears their throat, and I spring away from Matt to find the waiter standing before our table, holding a tray with our plates on it and a smug smile on his face. Matt scoots away from me reluctantly, letting go of my hand as the waiter scoops up his appetizer, which he'd hardly eaten.

The salted caramel cake is set before me, and my mouth waters at the sight. It's white cake with caramel sauce and berries sprinkled on top, the sticky sweet smell making me breathe deep, a little smile on my face. I glance over in Matt's direction to see he's watching me, his expression hungry, his massive steak sitting in front of him forgotten as he continues to watch me.

"Enjoy your meal," the waiter says before he vacates, and I can't help but think yes, indeed we're going to enjoy our meal.

But what I'm really looking forward to is what we're going to do *after* the meal.

I know Matt feels the same way.

"HAVE YOU SEEN my room?" Matt asks the moment he pulls me into the empty elevator, my hand clasped in his.

I slowly shake my head, loving how close I'm standing next to him. I can see the dark stubble dotting his cheeks, the scar just on the underside of his chin. He glances down at me, smudges of darkness just below his eyes show that he hasn't been sleeping very well. Considering how busy he's been lately, this doesn't surprise me.

"I'm pretty sure we have identical rooms," I say, hoping he realizes I'm teasing.

"Ah, mine is better. I can almost guarantee it." He squeezes my hand and tugs me close, so I'm standing in front of him, my back to his front. Releasing his grip on my hand, he settles his big, warm palms on my shoulders and starts rubbing. "You're tense."

I don't have the heart to tell him he's the one making me tense. All the sexual tension that's swirled between us for the last few weeks and months—it's overwhelmed me.

The elevator doors slide open and Matt gives me a push so I exit with him right behind me. We go to his room, and I wait with jumpy anticipation as he slides the keycard into the slot, the little light above the handle turning green. He opens the door, and I trail behind him inside, a shocked gasp escaping me when he turns and presses me against the door.

His hands rest at my waist as he pins me in place, his head dipping toward mine. Our mouths meet. I exhale against his lips, feel him smile before he takes the kiss deeper, and then there's no time for breathing or thinking or saying a word.

All I can do is savor. Savor the sensation of his mouth on mine, his fingers digging into the fabric of my dress, my skin. The cool metal of the door is shocking against my backside, paired with the pure heat radiating from Matt's big body as he steps in so close to me, he's all I can see and feel and smell. His tongue thrusts, his hands tug at the fabric of my dress, lifting, lifting, until I feel cool air on my thighs and realize he's pulling up my skirt.

I tear my lips from his, desperate for us to slow down. My brain needs to catch up with my body before I do something really crazy and stupid. "I thought you were going to show me your room."

Matt drifts his mouth down the length of my neck, covering it in hot, wet little kisses. I grow slick between my legs with just his mouth pressed against my neck, and I clutch at him for fear I might fall. "I thought you said your room is exactly like mine," he whispers against my skin.

"I'd still like to see it." I press at his shoulders, trying to get him to back off just a little without having to say it. I need the space. I like having him in *my* space, but still . . .

I'm not real good at this sort of thing. As in, I don't have a lot of experience. Especially with a man surely as experienced as Matthew DeLuca—in his previous life as a ball-player, he must've had beautiful women constantly throwing themselves at him.

He lifts his head, his dark gaze meeting mine, and then he

drops his hands from my waist as he steps away. "Come on, then. I'll show you around."

I pull my skirt back into place as I follow him deeper inside the room, my legs still shaking from the potency of his kiss, his touch. The effect he has on me is so powerful, so unbelievably overwhelming, I'm not sure what to think, or how to think.

"So? Is it just like yours?" he asks as we approach the window that overlooks the city.

I glance around, notice the orchids, the bright pink throw across the foot of his bed, the sleek, glass furniture. "Definitely. It's almost identical."

"You must have a really great boss then," he says, a smile playing at the corners of his mouth. God, he's sexy. "Putting you up in a fancy hotel like this."

"He's pretty great," I say, my voice soft. "He's smart, successful, extremely wealthy, but he never throws it around. In fact, I tend to forget he's so well off."

His smile fades and his expression goes serious. "Do you prefer that, Bryn? Does my—financial status intimidate you?"

I shrug, trying to push down my small-town-hick worries so they don't rise to the surface like they always try to do when I talk money and status and wealth. "A little bit," I admit.

It's something I never even realized before. Matt can have anything he wants. Can go out and buy whatever he wants, he has so much money. He's a billionaire, for the love of God, yet I know he doesn't live in a giant mansion, I've never seen him drive an outrageously fancy car beyond his sensible—but gorgeous—Range Rover. He's not flashy, not outrageous, like I can only assume his father can be.

And I find that extremely attractive, how simply he lives. If he'd been such a blatant, wealthy man, like Archer Bancroft, who intimidates the shit out of me every time I'm around him, I don't think I would've been able to handle Matt.

But he's not like that at all. He's gentle and kind and sweet and hardworking and sexy as all get out.

"Don't let it." He comes to me and presses his mouth to mine in a lingering, drugging kiss. "You did forget to mention one thing about me though."

I frown up at him and give in to what I've wanted to do all night. I touch his face, span my fingers across his cheek, so I can feel the slightly rough prickle of his stubble against my palm. "What?"

"My charismatic good looks." He grins, and I laugh, but he muffles my laughter in seconds with his mouth, kissing me so deliciously deep my head is spinning, my legs grow weak, and I slump against him, lost in his taste and the way his arms grip me around my waist.

I pull out of his embrace without a word, and he lets me. I go to the window, desperate to gather my racing thoughts while I stare at the city spread out before me. Pressing my fingers against the cool glass, I gaze down and watch the bright lights of Times Square flash, the seemingly millions of people that fill the sidewalks, the cars, the streets.

"Your view is familiar," I tell him from over my shoulder, smiling when I feel him stop just behind me, just like he did when we were in the elevator. But this time he doesn't touch my shoulders.

He settles his big hands at my hips, giving them a firm squeeze before he lets them wander down across my backside. "Nervous?"

I close my eyes, losing myself in his assured touch, the way he squeezes and massages my skin. Everything inside me melts when he slowly tugs up my skirt, until the fabric is bunched just below my butt, my legs, my thighs completely exposed. "Yes," I admit on a whisper.

"Don't be. I'll go slow," he promises, and I believe him. "Christ, you've got the sexiest legs I've ever seen." He grips my hips and pulls me toward him slightly, so I'm bent at the waist, my butt thrust out.

It's overtly sexual, the way he has me positioned. And when he steps closer, my backside brushing against the front of his jeans, I bite my lip to keep a moan from spilling out.

"Move closer to the window," he commands, and I do so, keeping in position as best I can. His hands slip beneath the bunched fabric, touching my hips, and his fingers curl around the skimpy waistband of my panties. He pulls them down, over my butt, down my thighs, and then I'm helping him, kicking them off while they get tangled around my shoes. I go to pull those off as well but his dark command stops me.

"Keep the shoes on."

Oh. My.

Matt

Her panties are solid white lace, a scrap of fabric that probably barely covered her, not that I'll ever know now, since we tugged them off and they're lying discarded on the floor nearby.

Not that I'm protesting.

She's a contradiction. Innocent yet sexy, with the face of an angel and a body made for sin. One minute she's shy and acts inexperienced, the next she's a laughing, sultry mistress who looks like she wants to devour me in one swallow.

I like it. I fucking love it and want to discover more about her, everything that she holds within, everything that makes her who she is. But she holds out on me. She told me bits and pieces of her past earlier at dinner. She's a woman who's run from her problems. She acts like she might run from me.

But I won't let her. After tonight, she'll know who she belongs to.

Me.

I've waited for this moment for far too long to prolong it further, so I grip her by her hips and grind against her, let her feel my hard cock against her lush ass. She hangs her head down and moans, the agonized sound going straight to my dick and hell, I want to thrust in her now. Just fill her with my cock and know what it's like to finally be a part of her.

That's what I seek. That connection—the union of our bodies and minds and souls. I want it, I fucking need it, and I grasp hold of the ends of her thick, dark hair, pulling gently until she lifts up, turns her head so I can kiss her with everything I have inside of me.

She gasps against my mouth, her arm curving around my head, keeping me close as our tongues thrust against one another, our bodies doing the same. I want to take her just like this. I know it's not the most romantic position in the world, but at the moment, I'm not feeling very romantic.

I feel possessive. Like I want to mark her and let her know she's mine. I break our kiss, help her tear off her dress, and then she's standing before me in a matching white lace bra, those sexy black heels, and nothing else.

Damn, she's gorgeous. I can see her pink nipples, hard

and thrusting against the innocent white lace, her breasts so full they threaten to spill out over her bra. "Take it off," I say gruffly, pointing at her chest.

She does so without hesitation, her hands going behind her to undo the clasp and then the bra is gone, fluttering to the floor to join her panties. She's standing before me completely naked save for the shoes while I'm still fully dressed.

Fuck me, that it. I'm done for.

The million dollar bet be damned. I couldn't give a shit if Archer or Gage find out I've been with Bryn. What's done is done.

I have to have her.

Reaching behind me, I grab my wallet and flip it open, pulling out a condom I keep nestled inside. I haven't been with a woman in months. I'm fucking afraid I'll come the moment I slide inside Bryn's body, but I close my eyes, breathe deep to try and keep my libido in check.

But it's going to be so fucking hard.

"I want to fuck you right here," I whisper as I step into her space, her naked body pressed against the cool glass, my body pressed close to hers. "From behind, with you looking down at the view. Wondering if anyone can see us."

She releases a trembling breath. "A-all right."

"Does that bother you? Us having sex like this for the first time?" I kiss the top of her ear, the spot just behind it. Push her heavy hair aside so I can brush my mouth against her nape, along her shoulder. Her skin is soft, fragrant with the unique scent that drives me fucking wild, and I lean into her for a long, lingering moment, overwhelmed at what she does to me, how she makes me feel.

"No," she says softly as she circles her hips, her ass brushing against my denim-covered erection. "I-I think I like it."

I close my eyes, relieved that she's given her permission. I don't want to push, she's fragile, I can tell, and no way am I going to screw up tonight.

I grasp her face with one hand and she turns toward me, our mouths colliding, tongues sliding against each other. With my other hand I fumble with my belt buckle, desperate to get it undone so I can unsnap my jeans and pull my cock out. Roll the condom on and thrust inside her nice and slow, watching as I enter her body for the first time.

A full shiver moves through me and I break the kiss, trying to gain some control. "Brace your hands on the window," I tell her, and she does, spreading her legs, and I step back, checking out the view of her pretty pink depths.

Groaning, I touch her there, sliding two fingers between her legs. She's drenched, soaking wet, and I finish undoing my belt buckle, then tear open the button fly of my jeans. She's thrusting against my fingers, subtle lifts of her hips, and I brush against her clit, hear her gasp and moan.

My quest to get out of my jeans momentarily forgotten, I stroke her deeper, thrusting my fingers inside her velvety hot channel, driving us both crazy with lust. I want to get her off with my fingers, want to watch her fall apart by my hand, and I start whispering dirty words in her ear. How much I want to fuck her, how wet she is, how good she feels. She tilts her head back, her eyes closed, her mouth open as she pants frantic little breaths, and then she's coming all over my fingers, her inner walls trembling, her entire body wracked with shudders.

I have to get inside her. Now.

Within seconds I have the condom on, and I slowly enter her still-trembling body, sliding deep, groaning as I fill her completely. She relaxes into me as I hold myself still, letting her get used to me being inside her, around her, holding her. Her back is covered in a light sheen of sweat, her fragrance even stronger as it fills my senses, and I slowly start to move.

In and out, my movements are shallow, teasing as I draw the moment out. Her hips start to move with my every thrust, and soon I'm increasing my pace, Bryn keeping up with me as she pushes back every time I push forward, taking me deep, deeper, until I can go no farther. I'm completely embedded in her.

I am hers. And she is mine.

"Harder," she gasps when I slow down, that familiar tingling sensation at the base of my spine telling me I'm about to come and it's going to be a big one.

"Baby, I go any harder, and I'm coming right now," I confess through clenched teeth.

"That's okay," she whispers, turning her head to glance at me over her shoulder. Her expression is one of wonder and pure, unadulterated pleasure. "Please, Matt."

She doesn't need to beg. I grip her hips and begin to move within her in earnest. Again and again, harder and harder until I'm coming, her name falling from my lips as I erupt again and again, my orgasm strong as I go still above her, unable to move, only able to revel in the exquisite sensation of coming inside Bryn for the first time.

Chapter 12

Matt

I am on top of the fucking world. I fell asleep with Bryn in my arms, her naked body wrapped all around mine, her fragrant hair in my face. We woke up twice in the middle of the night, coming together easily, so easily, both times. The first was by my initiative, when I started kissing down the length of her body, between her legs, until I had her writhing and coming apart beneath my lips and tongue.

She returned the favor, sucking me so deep inside her mouth I groaned loud enough to probably wake up the entire floor of the hotel. She made me come in an embarrassingly short amount of time.

The second time, she woke me up. It was her turn to rain kisses all over my body, driving me crazy with her lush, wet mouth. She finally grabbed a condom, slipped it on me, and then rode me into oblivion, making herself come by grinding against my cock.

That had been hot. So hot I gripped her body and flipped her over so she was pinned beneath me and I drove myself inside her again and again, coming until I was a gasping, exhausted mess.

We collapsed in each other's arms, slept the rest of the

night away until the alarm on my cell phone woke us up, reminding us of our sole purpose for being here.

The Savor conference.

We took a shower together before she slipped into a robe and snuck into her room, where she continued to get ready. We then took a taxi together to the conference since the weather was shit.

I held her hand the entire ride over, our fingers linked casually together, a representation of our relationship and how I was feeling. Usually that sort of shit scares me to death, but not this time. Not with Bryn. I want her in my life. I don't care that she works for me. Hell, she can become my partner, helping me run the winery, making decisions—everything she already does.

I love the idea so much I know I'm going to mention it to her later tonight when we meet up again after the day's activities at the conference are over. She might balk and say she doesn't deserve the position, and that's one thing I've realized since I've started working with her: Bryn doesn't believe in herself very much.

She should though. She's talented and smart and keeps me on track like no one else. She offers thoughtful opinions and is always, always thinking ahead when it comes to the business. DeLuca Winery is always at the forefront of her thoughts and she's exactly what I need.

Bryn is all I need.

I move through the day like a giddy asshole in love, which is sort of how I feel. I can't concentrate, can't focus on what the speaker is saying at a very important, highly anticipated keynote I'm sitting in on. Instead I bounce my foot against the floor, thinking of last night. How Bryn felt in my arms. The taste of her nipples. The sounds she makes and what she looks like when she comes. That satisfied little smile that curled her lips this morning when I rolled her over and told her she should join me in the shower.

Yeah, I can't let any of that go. I don't want to let any of it go. I really think Bryn and I could make this happen.

First I need to confirm that she's interested in taking it further than a simple affair while we're out of town.

When I finally make it back to the hotel, I know she's already there since she texted me about an hour ago. I'm eager, ready to tell her my grand ideas about our personal and business future together, planned when I should've been listening to the state of the future of wine making.

Ah well, fuck it. I'd rather think about Bryn.

But the moment I enter my hotel room I can sense the mood has changed. She's sitting on the edge of the bed—I gave her a key before we left earlier—her head bent as she scans through something on her phone. Her shoulders are slumped, her hair falling forward and shielding her face. There's something wrong.

I can feel it in the air.

"Hey," I say, letting the door shut softly behind me. "You all right?"

She lifts her head, her watery gaze meeting mine, and my heart lurches in my chest. She's been crying. Why? Over me?

God, I hope not.

"What's wrong?" I ask as I rush toward her, and she holds out her phone, averting her head so she doesn't have to look at me.

"Read this," she says, her voice rough with unshed tears.

I take the phone from her, see that she's brought up an article from a prominent gossip site. There's a hazy photo of Bryn and me at the window, her skirt bunched around her waist, white panties on brief display. You'd have to be an idiot not to realize what we're doing. I'm standing behind her, my hands resting on her hips.

The headline alone makes my heart drop into my toes:

Former Baseball Player Matt DeLuca Rounds the Bases with His Secretary!

"Shit," I say aloud as I sit heavily on the edge of the mattress right next to her, skimming the article. It goes on about Bryn and me, how she's worked for me since I took over the winery, and we've been having a heated affair for months. The unidentified source talks about our supposed affair and how it will be the eventual demise of my new business venture if I don't watch it.

The final nail in the coffin? The source goes on to say I'm just like my father, who's been embroiled with one scandal after another ever since the beginning of his career with the Oakland A's:

"Like father, like son, the apple doesn't fall far from the tree. Though at least the dad always seems to land on his feet. We'll see if his son can do the same."

"Who the fuck could've done this?" I ask grimly, thrusting the phone back toward her. I have my suspicions. I just don't want to say them out loud yet. "We need to figure out who's behind every word of this stupid, deceitful article."

Her head is still bent, like she can't stand to look at me. "It's not lies. It's the truth."

"It wasn't the truth until last night and that doesn't count," I tell her as I pull out my own phone to find a few text messages from Archer and Gage, both of them asking what the hell is going on with the article being blasted all over the place.

Oh, and I have a voicemail from my father. Interesting.

I refuse to listen to it. Not now, in front of Bryn. I need to keep my emotions under control before I lose it completely.

I think he might have had a hand in this. The tone of the entire article makes me think he's behind it. That the article actually mentioned my father multiple times when he hasn't been in the spotlight in years makes me suspect him.

"Doesn't count?" She lifts her head, her angry eyes meeting mine. "Are you saying what happened between us last night doesn't count?"

"No. Of course not." I slowly shake my head, amazed at all the emotion I see blazing in her gaze. "I think—shit, I think my dad could be behind this. God knows when he could've tried to first sell this article, probably right after the opening, when you so kindly pushed him out and sent him on his merry way."

"I didn't kindly push him out," she admits. "He said horrible things and basically accused me of being a slut and sleeping with his son. Oh, and when I grew sick of you, he said I could come and have sex with him any time I wanted. You know, because the two of you are so similar and all." She lets out an angry little sound that's a cross between a growl and a squeal. "The man is a pig."

Fuck. Tell me all about it. The worst part? He's my father. And supposedly I'm just like him.

"He said that to you?" I ask weakly, wincing when she stands to glare down at me, her expression one of pure fury.

"Yes! He made me feel like the cheap hussy everyone else seems to think I am. And look, we proved him right by having sex." She throws her arms up in the air. "I'm exactly what everybody says I am. A stupid whore who sleeps her way around, who just falls into bed with her boss because she's too dumb to know better."

I stand, grabbing hold of her shoulders and giving her a little shake. "No. Stop calling yourself such horrible names. You're nothing like that. We've been fighting this and trying to do the right thing for months, Bryn. Months. You didn't just fall into bed with your boss because you're too dumb to know better. I hope you came into my bed because you care for me as much as I care for you."

Bryn

I stare into Matt's eyes, shocked by his words, by his easy defense of me. I . . . I don't know what to say. I'm overwhelmed, upset, embarrassed. At least my name isn't in the article, though it doesn't need to be. There's the photo as proof it's me. Everyone at the winery will see the article and the picture, and I'll become a mockery. People in the community will hear the rumors and know I'm the one who's supposedly having a torrid affair with my boss.

It's the type of humiliation I've been trying to run from since Brian Fairbanks chased me around his office. I'd kept myself above it all, all these years. Running just ahead so that it never touched me.

But look at me now, neck deep in a huge scandal, and I have no one to blame but myself.

"Say something." Matt gives me another little shake, rattling me out of my thoughts. "I need to know if you're as invested in this as I am."

"Invested in what?" I ask, feeling like I'm in a daze.

"Invested in us," he says, his mouth grim, his eyes dark, fathomless. "Tell me. I need to hear you say it."

"I-I don't know how I feel, Matt," I say truthfully, horrified when I see the devastation cross his face.

God. I can't get this sort of thing right no matter how hard I try.

"So you don't want to be with me," he says, his voice dull as he releases his hold on me.

"I never said that." I watch as he turns his back on me and runs his hand through his hair, an exasperated little sound escaping him.

My heart, my entire body aches to go to him. Offer him comfort and let him know we won't let this stumbling block break us. We can survive this.

But I don't know if that's the truth.

"I don't know what I want," I say when he doesn't speak. "Last night was . . . it was amazing. One of the best nights of my life, but after seeing this article today and the photo, I don't know what to think of it. Of us being together. Will we be dealing with this sort of thing for the rest of our relationship? Can we survive this type of scrutiny?" I'm scared not only of the media but of what others might think of us together. His friends, his peers in the industry. I don't want to bring him down.

I don't want to embarrass him.

He turns to face me, his expression full of confusion and anger and frustration. I feel terrible. I'm the one who's doing this to him, who's putting him through all this. "This is a fluke, Bryn. I'm pretty much out of the public eye and have been for over a year. No one cares that I have a winery in the Napa Valley, except for people in the freaking Napa Valley. Otherwise, I'm long forgotten. Some new young ball-player has taken my place, and I'm fine with it. I've moved on. But my dad? He hates that I'm out of the public eye.

Hates that he is too. He's fed the media stories about me for years."

"You really think he's behind this?" I ask incredulously. My grandma may drive me crazy and has heaped on plenty of helpings of tough love, but she would never blatantly sabotage me or spread such lies.

He grabs his phone, punches a button and holds it to his ear, his expression grim, eyes blazing with anger. He must be listening to his voicemail or something. I wait nervously, wrapping my arms around my middle, my mind racing.

What if the photographer took more pictures? What if they release more to the media over the next few days? God, what will that do to us?

"He left me a message asking if I'd seen the article, sounding like a smug asshole," Matt says, knocking me from my thoughts. "And hell yes, I do, especially after what you just told me. If he said those kind of things to you, then he could definitely be behind this. I mean, no one else would mention my dad and he just happens to appear in this stupid article. He's our unidentified source." He exhales loudly and pushes his fingers through his hair. "Wonder how much the asshole got paid for spreading these lies. I wonder who he got to follow us."

"Right. And who knows if any more pictures will show up? I will die if that happens, I swear. I can't live like this," I say, my voice soft yet steely while inside my nerves are in absolute chaos. "I can't do it, Matt."

"What are you talking about?" he asks, and I close my eyes, afraid to look at him, scared to see the sadness in his gaze.

"Having to deal with this sort of thing will wreck my self-esteem, and it's already pretty wrecked." I crack open my eyes to find him staring at me, shock written all over his handsome face. "I'll never be able to escape the shadow of being the home-wrecker, the easy girl. The dumb slut who sleeps with her boss because she thinks that's what she's supposed to do."

"But that's not what we have, Bryn. Can't you see it? This has nothing to do with me being your boss and you being my assistant. What we have, what we shared last night, is about us being a man and a woman who are attracted to each other." He pauses, staring at me. "Right?"

I can only look at him, not sure what to say, how to defend my feelings. They are what they are, and I have no explanation for them. They're just there. And they're not about to go away anytime soon. It's not that easy.

But I don't tell him any of that. He wouldn't understand. He's wealthy and established and confident in going after what he wants, be it a new career, a new woman—a new whatever.

Me, on the other hand, I lack confidence. I'm young and broke and striving to make myself better, but every time I think I've pushed myself into a better place, I fuck it up somehow and end up taking about forty steps backward.

Until I'm right back where I started.

"I don't know," I admit softly. "I'm not sure if this can work out."

"Bryn." His voice breaks on my name and the sound breaks my heart. "Don't do this. Don't say that."

"I was going to give my notice when we returned home," I blurt out, wanting him to know the truth. "I was going to give you two weeks. Then I was going to pack up all my stuff in boxes, shove it into the back of my Saturn, and drive home to Cactus. My grandma said I can stay with her until I get back on my feet and find a job."

Now he looks good and pissed. "You were going to give

your notice so you can go back to Cactus? Have you lost your mind?"

I shrug, angry that he would be so insulting. "I have nothing else holding me here." It's a lie. He could hold me here, but I know it wouldn't work out. And it wouldn't be what's best for me. I'd just end up making another mistake and making us both look bad.

He's better off without me. And I don't know if this is true, but I'm probably better off without him too.

"You have nothing else." His voice is monotone, the look in his eyes blank. "So what happened last night *doesn't* matter."

"Not when it'll end up hurting us, which it will undoubtedly do." I approach him, but he takes a step back, like he doesn't want to be near me. "I'm not sure if we're good for each other," I admit.

He stares at me, his mouth set in a grim line. "So you still want to give your notice?"

Slowly, I nod, ignoring the wave of panic that threatens to consume me at my silent confirmation.

"Then I accept your notice. You don't even need to give me two weeks. We're done." His voice, his expression, is final, and I swear I want to burst into great, heaving sobs.

But I don't. I remain quiet, composed. How, I'm not sure.

"I think you should try to call and change your flight so you can head home tonight," he suggests, his voice clipped. "I'll reimburse you for the change fee which I'm sure will be huge."

"Fine. I'll leave tonight." I lift my chin, refusing to let him see me down. This was what I wanted after all.

Wasn't it?

Chapter 13

Matt

Two weeks later

You answered." I rub my jaw, the rasp of stubble prickling across my palm. I haven't shaved in days, and I've slept like shit.

"You keep calling my damn phone so yeah, I answered," Dad says, sounding downright hostile. "Whatcha want, son?"

I want Bryn. I miss her. I hate what happened between us, how easily our tentative relationship was destroyed. Just by a slightly scandalous photo and a few choice words on a bunch of crappy gossip websites.

Hell, it was a very scandalous photo, leaving Bryn feeling beyond embarrassed. Vulnerable. I'm used to those gossipy sites saying a bunch of lies and spreading rumors. Bryn isn't.

I'd been angry when I left New York. Now I'm just . . . miserable. She left. I'm not exactly sure to where, but I know she couldn't handle being near me another minute longer. Not that I handled our last conversation in New York particularly well. The moment we discovered the article and photo, it all went to hell.

The most amazing night of my life with the most amazing woman I've ever met, ruined. Just like that.

"I want to know why," I finally say, then pause. Waiting for the answer I'm sure will never really come.

"Why what?" Oh, doesn't he sound innocent?

"You know." I take a deep breath, trying to keep my anger under control. "Why did you blab to the media? How much did they pay you? Was it worth it? Having those photos of my innocent assistant spread across the internet?"

"She didn't look so innocent in that picture." Dad has the nerve to chuckle, the bastard.

I close my eyes, count to five. He's pushing every one of my buttons, and I'm sure the jackass knows it. "I'm used to this sort of treatment. You can drag my name through the mud. I don't care. But you don't bring Bryn into this. She didn't deserve that sort of public humiliation and you know it."

"She humiliated me at your fancy winery party," he says, his voice full of venom. "Believe what you want, but you'll see what I did was right for you in the long run. You don't need that silly little tramp dragging you down."

His casual confession makes me sick to my stomach. I knew he'd done it. Finally hearing him say it reaffirms I'm about to do the right thing. "Bryn James is the best fucking thing that's ever happened to me and you ruined it. Ruined it with your blabbing to the media. I hope they paid you enough to make this all worth it."

"Son, it was completely worth it because it got your name in the public eye again. I bet you've seen an uptick in business with the winery, am I right? You don't want people forgetting you. You're still important, you know. A hero to many. Just like I am too," Dad says smugly.

"You're nobody's hero, you fucking asshole. I never want to see or talk to you again." I'm seething. I literally see red, and I pull the phone away from my ear, ready to end the call when I hear his voice.

"Don't cut me off too quick, Matt. I'm the last thing you've got in this world. And you know it."

Not true. I have my friends. Archer and Gage. Ivy and Marina. And if I'm lucky enough, I'll have Bryn back in my life.

"I don't need you," I murmur into the phone, then end the call.

I don't need Vinnie DeLuca at all.

I definitely need my friends though. And more than anything, I need Bryn.

But first, I need to find her.

"IF I THOUGHT you were bad before, you've turned into a complete sullen little girl lately," Archer says with a shake of his head as I stop at the table he's sharing with Gage. "I don't know if this forty-five-days idea was such a good one after all."

"It wasn't. Fuck the forty-five days." The last thing I'm thinking of is the stupid bet. I settle heavily into a chair, barely looking at the scantily dressed waitress that appears at our table. "Double vodka, straight up. Make it Grey Goose," I mutter.

"Anything else for you guys?" The waitress's voice is bright and cheery. I chance a glance at her, taking in her short skirt, the belly-revealing top that clings to her enormous breasts. I don't bother looking at her face. From the way she's dressed, clearly that's not her intent anyway.

We're at a local sports bar known for its spectacularly gorgeous waitstaff, Archer demanding via text I meet him and Gage there for drinks after work. So here I am, miserable and ready to drown my sorrows in booze.

They're probably somehow trying to tempt me by having us come here. With the bet extension still on, I'm sure they're looking for any way to get me to break it. The waitress is mega hot.

I couldn't give two shits about her. All I want is Bryn.

"We're good right now, thanks," Archer says. His beer bottle is full, as is Gage's. They're both looking at me as if I've lost my mind. I can feel their eyes on me, but I stare at the table, tapping my fingers against the edge of the wood.

"Lack of sex has made you grumpy," Gage starts and I lift my head to glare at him. He shuts up.

"And angry," Archer adds. "What gives?"

Should I tell them? My mood has nothing to do with lack of sex and everything to do with having the best sex of my life with the most beautiful woman I've ever known. The very same woman who exited my life almost two weeks ago.

The woman I'm in love with but was such a wimp I couldn't even tell her.

"You saw the article on the gossip site, right?" I say, figuring I may as well start at the beginning. And come on, have they forgotten already? I know they're wrapped up in their own thing since they're both busy, occupied with work and the women they love.

Lucky bastards.

Plus I've avoided them for fear they'd want to talk about it. Call me out on everything. I've been alone with my misery and finally they forced me to crawl out of my hole.

"Yeah, and the picture. You insisted nothing happened between you two." Archer sends me one of those skeptical, raised eyebrow looks he's so good at. "Not sure if I believe you though. What with Bryn's, uh, panties on display."

"You shouldn't believe me," I say, offering the waitress

a grim smile when she sets my drink in front of me, her cleavage practically in my face. Ignoring her boobs, I grab the glass, slam back the vodka with one long swallow, and hand it back to her. "Another one, please."

"Right away," she says with a nod before she leaves.

"Damn, dude. Slow down," Gage says. "I don't want to be the one driving your drunk ass home."

I wave a hand. "I'll take a cab."

"No, you won't," Archer says firmly. "Tell us what happened, Matt. Where's Bryn? Ivy says she left. As in left town. Seems sort of extreme."

"She did leave. The article and photo proved too much for her. She quit. Moved back home." I hate my dad for making this happen. Hate even more how he thought he'd been doing me a favor.

I'd been too much for her too, though. She said she'd planned on giving her notice before that stupid article came out. Before we even left for New York. She was going to leave me. After everything that had happened between us, before she would've given me another chance, she would've walked.

Great. I got my chance, and she still bailed. My heart literally fucking hurts at not having her around.

"Where's the waitress with my drink?" I mutter, glaring at Archer and Gage. They both visibly recoil, not that I give a damn. I'm always the nice one. The easygoing guy who doesn't give anyone much shit.

Lately, I am the furthest thing from nice and easygoing. They're all lucky I'm holding it together because I feel like at any moment I could totally lose it.

"Hey." Gage's firm voice makes me meet his gaze. "What happened with you and your dad?"

I shrug. They know Vinnie was behind this; I told them

when I came home. I just haven't talked about it since. I've been too busy wallowing in my misery. "I called and confronted him right after we got back."

"And?"

"And he denied he did it at first. Kept asking why he would do something like that to his own son, but I kept throwing it back in his face. I never once believed him. I finally broke him down."

I shook my head, offering a whisper of thanks when the waitress returned with a fresh drink. Archer waved her off when she lingered, and I held the glass up to them as if in salute. "He admitted he tipped off the reporter. They spotted Bryn and me at a restaurant in the hotel and took some pictures there. But then they somehow caught sight of us in the hotel room window and decided those were the better photos to put on the site." I drained my glass and set it on the table.

"So your dad is responsible," Gage says, shock in his voice. The look of disgust on my friend's face says it all.

"Yeah. The asshole," I mutter, sadness filling me despite my anger. That my dad could be so heartless and do something like this to me.

It sucks. Our relationship is beyond repair. At least for now. I can't even fathom talking to him again, sharing anything personal with him, even speaking to him casually. Hell, I wouldn't send the man a fucking Christmas card. He's ruined everything.

He'll have to grovel on his hands and knees before I'd consider talking to him again.

"And Bryn left," Gage says.

"She did." I nod, my head a little dizzy. I can feel the alcohol coursing through my blood and I wait for the numbness. I welcome the fucking numbness. "We can call off the bet, you know."

"Wait . . . what?" The confused expression on Archer's face could almost be laughable if I wasn't drowning in my misery.

"Call it off. I won't collect. I can't." I pick up my glass, remember it's empty, and set it down again with an irritated growl. "Bryn and I had sex. Amazing, fantastic, never-to-be-had-again sex."

"You sly, lying dog," Gage starts, but Archer shoots him a look. Gage shuts up.

"And she left you anyway. That's tough, bro. I'm sorry," Archer says cautiously. Funny how knowing he's about to be a father makes a man suddenly turn compassionate. The Archer of old would've given me endless crap about this.

The new Archer who's madly in love with Ivy and excited about becoming a dad has become . . . considerate of my feelings.

Yes. I'm having a total *Oprah* moment. I blame the vodka.

"Tough doesn't come close to what it is." I smile, but it feels like my face is cracking in two. "Do you know that stupid site ran the article and then they said nothing else? Some other sites picked it up, but then another scandal broke out, I can't even remember what. Rendering me and Bryn long forgotten. That's how much of a nonentity I've become. And you know what? I love that. I don't miss the fans and the photographers and the crap. I miss playing ball. I'll always miss that, but otherwise, yeah. I'm over it. I have a new life. A new career that I love and I found a woman I could love too. Instead she leaves me."

Damn, I sound pitiful and morose even to my own ears.

"All right. We're calling off the bet," Archer says, his expression full of worry. "But—"

"You're going to let her go, huh?" Gage asks, interrupting Archer. "Just let her walk away and forget all about her?"

I glare at them both. "What do you mean?" The waitress delivers another shot glass in front of me, much to the disgust of my friends, and I smile gratefully up at her, actually looking in her eyes versus her tits. I wonder if she appreciates that.

Probably not.

"Go after her," Gage urges. "Go to her hometown and tell her you want her back."

I grimace, finish off the contents in my shot glass, and then grimace again as the vodka slides down my throat. "You make it sound so easy."

"That's because it is," Gage says with a slight smirk. I'd like to wipe it off his face with my fist. Must be the vodka still talking. "Just hop on a plane and go to that little Podunk town of hers and find her. Can't be that hard to figure out where she lives, her address. When you see her, tell her how you feel."

I let his words sink in and swirl around in my brain along with a heavy dose of vodka. I could do that. Maybe. "What if she rejects me?"

"Then at least you tried," Archer adds. "Then you won't have any regrets or what-ifs. Those what-ifs will kill you, man. Trust me."

Huh. He's right. I wonder how I would even get to Cactus, Texas. Fly into somewhere and rent a car, I assume. I don't know her grandma's name. But I bet everyone would know who Bryn James is. The most beautiful, sweetest, kindest, sexiest woman ever.

"I'll do it." I curl my hand into a fist and pound it on the table, making my shot glasses and the now-empty beer bottles on top of it rattle. "I'll go make flight arrangements right now." I start to stand, but both Archer and Gage wave their arms at me like they're trying to flag my ass down or something.

"Slow your roll, my friend," Gage says, shaking his head with a chuckle as I fall back into my chair, my head spinning. "You need to sober up first. Look at you, three shots of double vodka and you're done for."

"Whatever," I mutter, my mind filled with images of Bryn. Smiling Bryn. Beige Bryn. Naked Bryn. Sad Bryn.

I frown. I never want to see sad Bryn again. I need to find her.

I need to go make that woman mine once and for all.

Chapter 14

Bryn

Girl, you better clean out that chicken coop and something quick! That rooster looks ready to tear into his girlfriends. He sure don't like walking in shit!"

Sighing, I toss my phone—the very iPhone Matt let me keep despite having purchased it for work purposes—onto my mattress and exit my bedroom to see what my grandma is hollering about now.

She's standing at the kitchen sink washing dishes. I wish we could afford a dishwasher, but that's so not happening. Staring out the window, she's watching the chicken coop in the backyard, a fragile-looking structure one of the neighbor boys built for her a few years ago.

"What did you ask me to do?" I sound resigned. Of course I am, when the only job I can seem to find in this godforsaken town is doing odds and ends for my grandma around the house. I didn't get that job at the Soap-n-Snip, answering the phone and sweeping up hair. Stacy Jo Nesbitt got that job. She graduated two years after I did, and she already has two babies to take care of.

She deserves the job far more than I do.

"The chicken coop, baby doll. It's a shit storm of epic proportions and that snotty, mean-as-hell rooster hates it when the crap piles up." Grandma cackles again. She loves saying crazy things, shocking people. As she gets older, it gets worse and usually I ignore it or laugh with her.

But today, the very last thing I want to do is laugh. It's hot outside, and I don't want to be out there scooping up chicken crap.

"You want me to clean it out now?" I ask, my shoulders slumping.

"I sure do. Look at that cock." Another cackle. "He's gonna peck the head of every chicken out there if you don't take care of it and quick."

I go to stand next to my grandma and see that she's not exaggerating. The rooster is strutting around in the small fenced-off chicken yard, pecking the head of every poor innocent chicken that approaches him.

Typical male. That rooster is a complete asshole.

"Fine," I say with a sigh. "I'll go clean it."

"Don't forget your waders," she calls to me as I head toward the garage. "And a bucket and a shovel so you can scoop up all that crap!"

I grab the bucket and the shovel she uses special for the chicken coop then slip on the old rubber boots I bought at Walmart years ago that I'd wear when it rained or snowed—which is rare, but still. They're white and hideous, scuffed up after years of wear, but I don't care. I'm wearing an old ratty tank top and a pair of denim cutoffs along with them. The people of the great Napa Valley would probably shit themselves if they saw me, but I'm out here in my grandma's backyard with no one around for miles.

I've got nobody to impress.

Rounding the side of the house, I head for the chicken coop and open the gate, thrusting the shovel out to hold back the rooster, who's a mean old jerk that would love nothing more than to jump me from behind and spur me with his claws. He's done it to me before, and I nearly had a heart attack, he scared me so bad.

But this time I'm prepared. You can't turn your back on him or he'll sneak attack you, like your worst enemy.

God, if I really thought about it, I could learn a lot of life lessons out here cleaning up the damn chicken coop. I laugh and shake my head as I start scooping up the chicken poop, which has somehow piled up into little mountains along the inside of their caged area.

It's really freaking disgusting.

It's been a month since I left New York City and went back to St. Helena. I went to the winery early the next morning and cleaned all my personal belongings out of my desk. Gave my notice at my apartment, not caring that I had to pay another month's rent for breaking the lease, even though I was leaving at that very moment.

I just wanted the hell out of there.

It took me a few days to pack up all my stuff, finalize some things, and get everything prepared for the move. But when I was finally ready to take off, all packed up and headed to the gas station before I went roaring off into the sunset, I decided to check my mail one last time. And found a check from DeLuca Winery—three months' wages. Severance pay, it said on the notes line.

That check both burned my ass and thrilled me down to the bone. I didn't want to take his pity pay, but I also wasn't about to look a gift horse in the mouth, as my grandma would say.

I never did quite get that phrase, but whatever. It fit.

So I went to the bank, deposited all that money, and then hit the road. It took me six days, but I finally made it only to find myself with no prospects, no energy, and sadder than I've ever been in my life.

I miss Matt. I was dumb, running away from him and my feelings. He'd been so willing to face the troubles beside me head-on, and I walked away. Let him go, let him slip right through my fingers like he didn't matter.

God, I'd been such an idiot—I could tear up right now just thinking about it.

But crying over our lost relationship isn't going to bring him back or bring me peace. I messed up, and I need to face facts. Chalk it up to a mistake made and a lesson learned.

Don't let a good man go, is what my grandma told me when I explained to her what happened a few nights ago. I'd held onto my story, my blow up with Matt, for weeks until my grandma finally found me crying on the back porch and point-blank asked what the hell was wrong with me.

That had been her one sentence of advice when I finished.

Don't let a good man go.

Too late, Grandma.

Sighing, I rub at my forehead with the heel of my hand before I start scooping up more crap. I should've worn gloves, but I forgot. At least I'm not touching the poop directly, thanks to the shovel.

God, what a transformation I've undergone. One month ago, I was in New York City staying at the most beautiful hotel I've ever seen in my life, and now I'm digging out chicken shit.

Oh, how the mighty have fallen.

I fill up practically the entire bucket with chicken poo, constantly thrusting the shovel in the rooster's direction when he comes at me, always on the defensive around that guy. I'm starting to sweat, I probably stink, and my feet feel all squishy and disgusting in the rubber boots.

I'll need a shower as soon as I'm done with this horrendous chore. No wonder my grandma doesn't want to deal with it.

"Bryn?"

I still, turning my head to the left. I swear I just heard Matt's voice call my name. Great. Now I'm going crazy and hearing things.

"Lousy men," I mutter, shaking my head and pointing the shovel at the rooster, who looks ready to jump me at any minute. "You're all alike. Ready to jump on a woman and tear her apart before she can put herself back together again."

"Bryn, what the hell are you doing, talking to a chicken?"

Standing completely straight, I turn slowly, the sun suddenly shining in my eyes. I cover them with my hand to find—

Oh my God, to find Matthew DeLuca standing in my grandma's backyard, on the other side of the chicken coop, looking gorgeous in a pair of khaki shorts and a wine-colored polo shirt.

"I'm not talking to a chicken," I explain, my voice weak. "I'm talking to a rooster."

"Same difference?" Matt asks, a hint of a smile curving his lips.

"Don't tell that to the rooster. You'll only piss him off," I mutter, turning and pointing my shovel at the very creature

I'm talking about, who'd gotten closer to me what with my distracted state.

My heart is racing, and I can't believe Matt's standing here. With me.

But why?

"You, uh, look good, Bryn."

He's a liar. I look crazy, and I know it. Turning more fully to face him, I kick out one foot, showing off the boots. "You like them?"

"They're interesting. I prefer seeing you in those tiny denim shorts though." He whistles low, a rush of pleasure flowing through me at the sound. "Your legs look mighty long in 'em."

Giddiness courses through me at having him here, with me, in Cactus, Texas, checking out my legs and telling me I look good. If anyone looks good it's him, all sexy and handsome in the shorts and the polo, his dark hair a haphazard mess, his face covered with a shadow of stubble.

If I wasn't dressed like a fool and standing amongst chickens and their crap, I'd run over and throw myself at him.

"Shit!" I yell when a sharp pinch digs into the back of my knees. I turn and swat at the rooster who attacked me. Turn my back on him for a second too long and look at how he treats me. "Goddamn asshole!" I screech, swinging the shovel at him. Thankfully he struts away, and I snatch up the bucket, backing out of the coop until I feel the gate directly behind me. I unlatch it in a hurry and slam it shut, leaning against the chicken wire for a brief, relieved moment as I try to calm my racing heart.

Only to turn around and find Matt laughing at me so hard, I'm afraid he's going to double over and collapse onto the ground.

Matt

I shouldn't laugh. Bryn just about got the scare of her life, if the expression on her face was any indication. I hadn't any chance to warn her, and it had been quite shocking to see that rooster fly in the air so fast. One minute we'd been flirting and chatting, the next a wild, puffed-out red rooster came at her, his legs extended and his claws digging right into the back of her legs.

That had been horrifying. The funny part? The curse words flying out of Bryn's mouth, made even more humorous by her thick accent. She'd been pissed. Furious that the rooster jumped her and tried to take a hunk of flesh out of her legs.

"That wasn't funny, you know," she says as she approaches, which launches me into a fresh round of laughter.

"Oh yes, it was," I say between breaths.

She stops directly in front of me, dropping the bucket by her booted feet. I look at her, really look at her as the laughter dies in my throat. Despite the crazy outfit, she looks hot as hell. The tank top is torn and bleach-stained, clinging to her breasts, and those denim shorts should be illegal they're so damn short. I can't help but wonder if she's even wearing any panties underneath because if she is, they're pretty damn tiny.

But those white rubber boots are the finishing touch. I've never seen Bryn look like this.

I kinda like it.

"What are you doing here, Matt?" she asks, sticking the shovel into the ground, her fingers still gripping the handle.

"I came looking for you." My mouth goes dry the longer I stare at her. A faint sheen of sweat covers her skin, and I can smell that addictive-as-hell scent of hers wafting all around me, despite the bucket of chicken shit sitting at her feet.

"Why?" Her voice is so soft, so full of doubt I wish I could pull her in and hold her close.

But I don't. Not yet. I might have to wait until she takes a shower or at the very least washes her hands, but I will be holding this woman very soon in my arms, I promise.

"I want you to come back with me, Bryn," I tell her, keeping it simple. "I miss you."

Her lips part, and she grips the shovel handle so tight, her knuckles go white. "What?"

"I miss you. Have you missed me too?" I step closer to her, notice the way her eyes widen, her tongue sneaking out for a quick swipe of her lips. Damn, I want to kiss her. "After being without you, I realized I need you."

"As your assistant?"

Ah, my silly Bryn. She just can't believe someone would actually want her, can she? Wouldn't she be surprised, knowing I have been a complete wreck while she has been gone? "Not as my assistant. I need you in my life. I want you by my side, helping me run the winery."

"Working for you," she says, her voice flat.

"I'll pay you, yes, since technically you'll be my employee, but not as my assistant. You'll be my partner." I smile gently and take another step toward her, until I'm standing directly in front of her, reaching out my hand to settle it over hers still gripping the shovel handle. "I'm in love with you, Bryn. And I don't want to live without you anymore."

"Matt," she starts, but I squeeze her hand, silencing her.

"Don't protest or tell me you don't want to bring me down

or whatever other crazy excuse you came up with the last time we talked. I don't want to hear it." With my free hand I reach for her, cupping her cheek, savoring her soft, soft skin. "I want you in my life. I want you living with me in California and working with me. I want us to be partners and grow De-Luca Winery together. What do you think?"

She smiles, her blue eyes bright with tears. "I think you're crazy."

"You're right." Unable to resist any longer, I lean in and press a soft kiss to her tempting lips. "I'm crazy for you, Bryn. Now say that'll you give up scooping chicken shit for the rest of your life and come work with me."

Bryn laughs, the tears flowing freely now. "I don't know. Let me think about it."

"Stubborn woman," I murmur just before I kiss her again, this one deeper, hotter, full of plenty of tongue and sweet, low murmurs of pleasure coming from my woman.

My woman. Mine. That's the only way I've thought of Bryn since she left me. It just took me this long to work up the courage to finally go after the woman I want.

"What about . . . what will everyone say?" she asks when she pulls away. "They'll talk about us. About how you're screwing your assistant."

I'm completely offended she would simplify our relationship like that. "I'm not screwing you. I want to be with you. I want you as my partner. In business, in life, in everything. I want you. Fuck anyone who questions that."

She gapes at me like she can't believe what I said. Clearing her throat, she murmurs, "I've been so worried how all of this will affect me. Being with you. I've not had the best luck with men, you know."

"I know," I say softly, my heart breaking for her. She looks scared. Nervous. The very last things I want her to feel. "I would be proud to call you my partner in all aspects of my life, Bryn. You're smart and strong. I need you in my life. More than you can even imagine."

Her eyes shine with unshed tears. "Really?" she asks incredulously.

I dip my head, my mouth hovering above hers. "Really. I love you," I whisper against her lips, as I thrust my fingers into her thick, beautiful hair. "Come home with me, Bryn. Be with me. I need you."

She smiles, a tremulous laugh escaping her before she nods. "I love you too, Matt. I missed you so much. I—I couldn't stand being without you."

"I missed you too, baby. And trust me, I'll never make you scoop up chicken shit at my house. It's one hundred percent chicken shit free." I kiss her again because I can't resist and we both release our grip on the shovel handle at the same time, grabbing hold of each other, our bodies colliding. She feels so damn good next to me, her sexy little body barely covered, looking like my every dream come to life.

Even in the crazy white rubber boots.

"Are you saying you're my own personal savior again? Coming in to rescue me from a life of scooping chicken crap?" She blinks up at me, and I smile, nuzzle my nose against hers.

"Yeah, that's exactly what I'm saying. Only when you call me your savior, I gotta say, you've become mine too." I lower my head and kiss her, wanting her to know how ready I am to take her out of Cactus and bring her home with me for good.

Where she belongs.

Intoxicated

Chapter 1

Archer

"I'm going to have a baby," Ivy declares as she stops directly in front of me. Well, her belly stopped directly in front of me, the rest of her soon followed.

Yes, indeed, my wife is definitely going to have a baby. Soon.

I'm getting ready—staring at the mirror as I mess with my tie, making sure it's perfect—when she approaches me. I shoot her a grin, feeling good, feeling on top of my game. Life couldn't get any better, you know? We're celebrating today and with good reason.

"I know, sexy mama." I turn away from the mirror and wink at her. "Trust me, I haven't forgotten that I'm the one who knocked you up."

She stares at me, no reaction to my wink or my words. She usually slaps my ass and kisses me. Says something sarcastic at the very least. But I'm getting nothing. And it's kind of disconcerting. "Archer. I'm dead serious. I'm going to have the baby."

"I know, babe. And I can't freaking wait." I study her, noticing that she looks a little pale and her pupils are dilated. Hmm. "You feeling okay?"

Rolling her eyes, she rests her hand on top of her

protruding stomach, rubbing it absently. Then, not so absently. As in, she's clutching her belly like she's in pain. "I'm in"—she sucks in a harsh breath, holding it for a few seconds—"labor, damn it."

"Oh, Christ!" I lurch toward her, both of my hands landing on her stomach. The baby kicks at that precise moment, and I feel the hit against my palm and start to laugh. "Seems like she's ready to make her escape."

We have no idea what we're having. Ivy wanted it to be a surprise and I went along with her plan, but deep down, not knowing is driving me crazy. I'm dying to meet this little booger of mine and find out if I have a son or a daughter.

My guess is it's a girl who'll look just like my wife.

Ivy shoots imaginary daggers at me with her eyes. "This is the worst possible time for me to go into labor. You do realize this, right?"

I shrug, rubbing her belly. I can't resist it. My wife is fucking sexy when she's pregnant. Even when she's big and miserable, like she is now. Knowing that her body is working hard, growing a child within her, *my* child . . . I can't help it. It turns me on.

She's told me more than once I'm a sick fuck, but whatever. I'm allowed to find Ivy sexy when she's pregnant. She's my wife, after all.

"Your brother will understand." And he will. Because Gage's about to become an uncle, and I know he's pretty excited by it, though he would never admit that to anyone.

"But it's his wedding day," Ivy stresses. "You're Gage's best man. I'm Marina's matron of honor. This is not good, Archer. She's going to kill us."

"Bridezilla needs to take a chill pill." I reluctantly release Ivy and go to the closet where her suitcase for the hospital has been packed and waiting for the last two weeks. My girl is efficient, I gotta give her that. "We need to go now, babe. Let me change out of my monkey suit and then we'll head to the hospital." I pull the suitcase out and set it on top of the bed. Nerves bubble up inside me, but I ignore them. I need to be the steady one. I made that promise to my wife weeks ago. I don't want her to panic or freak out while she's in labor, so one of us has to keep their cool.

Ivy tilts her head, contemplating me. She's still in her silky white robe that now barely wraps around her front. She can hardly fit into her dress for the wedding, so she should be glad she doesn't have to make an appearance. "Marina is going to be furious."

"She'll get over it. She's hours away from being part of our family for good. We can disappoint her, make her mad, whatever, but there's nothing she can do about it because we're family. So don't worry." I tug the tie that I'd been patiently working on only moments ago from my neck, letting it fall onto the floor, then start unbuttoning my shirt with one hand as I grab my cell and quick-dial Gage with the other. I keep an eye on my wife as she moves about the room, her hand going to her stomach every few seconds, as if she's in pain. Which she probably is.

Worry seeps into me, thick and sluggish. What if something goes wrong? What if there are complications and something happens to the baby? Or worse, what if something happens to . . .

Yeah. Can't go there.

"You are the last person I want to hear from at this moment," Gage says when he answers, sounding amused. And slightly irritated—but more amused, thank God; the news I'm about to deliver might not go over so well if he's in a bad mood. "Your ass better be on its way over here. This wedding has to start on time or Marina's gonna flip."

I frown, let my hand fall from my now unbuttoned shirt. "My ass is nowhere near where you're at."

"Why the hell not? You better get over to the winery stat." Gage and Marina are having their wedding at our friend Matt's winery, which he's considering opening up to various private events, thanks to the idea from his girlfriend, Bryn. We're the first to use the facility. "The ceremony is in a little over an hour. Shit is going down, man. This is *it*." At least he doesn't sound like he's being led to his doom.

"Yeah, about that . . ." I pause, listening to someone chat him up for a brief moment. "Something's come up."

There's an uneasy quiet over the line for a beat too long before Gage explodes. "What the hell do you mean, something's come up? What could be more important than your best friend and brother-in-law getting married, asshole?"

"Your niece or nephew finally making its way into the world?"

Again I'm greeted with more silence, which is really starting to get on my nerves. "I don't get it," Gage finally says.

I start to laugh and that earns me a stern look from my wife, who's slowly changing into regular clothes, an oversized sweater and black leggings. I immediately sober up. She's moving like an old woman and that isn't her usual style. "Your little sister has gone into labor. We're leaving for the hospital now."

"Wait a minute. Now? How long has she been in labor? You're not at the hospital yet?" Gage asks, going all concerned big brother on me.

"No, she only just told me she was actually in labor. We're leaving now. But you realize what this means, right?" I pause, feeling guilty but knowing there's nothing I can do about it. "We're going to miss the wedding."

Thankfully, Gage doesn't even hesitate with his answer. "That's okay. We completely understand," he says, excitement lacing his voice. Just as I'd hoped, Gage is fine with our not making the wedding. How could he hold this against us? A baby was being born, for Christ's sake. *My* baby. His sister's baby. His future niece or nephew. This is a big freaking deal, as is his marriage to Marina. And it's all going to happen on the same day. "Just make sure to call and keep us updated."

"We will, but via text," I say. "Don't want to interrupt the ceremony, right?"

"Right," Gage confirms. "Good luck, man. Tell my sister I love her."

"I will. Promise." I end the call and contemplate what's about to happen.

Our lives are changing completely. It won't just be Ivy and me anymore. We'll have someone to take care of—someone who solely depends on us.

Scary.

"Oh, Archer," Ivy says, pulling me from my thoughts.

Turning to face her, I see that her eyes are filling with tears and her face looks ready to crumple. I go to her, grabbing hold of her hands and giving them a squeeze. "What's wrong, baby?"

"I feel bad." A little sob escapes her as she shakes her head. I tug her in as close as I can, slinging my arm around her waist. "I'm going to ruin Gage's wedding."

"No you're not. It's going to be one of the most memorable weddings ever. No one will forget this day," I say, smoothing my hand over her hair. I want her reassured, not worrying about wedding plans. Everything we know is going to change in mere hours.

"Exactly. It's supposed to be Gage and Marina's day and instead it's going to turn into our day. Our *child's* day. How selfish are we?"

"We're not selfish. We can't help it if you're going into labor right now. It's not like we did it on purpose." I shed the rest of my clothes quickly, throwing on a pair of jeans and a T-shirt. "Speaking of labor, we need to get going. Are you ready? Get some shoes on, babe." I give her a gentle push out of my embrace and toward the closet door across our bedroom.

"*We*? Who's the one who's about to give birth?" Ivy mutters as she shuffles toward the closet. A little snort escapes her. "*You* won't have anything to do with this labor stuff, Archer. This is all on me."

"And I think you're going to do an amazing job. You're the strongest women I know," I say.

At those words, my wife promptly bursts into tears.

Gage

You're not going to believe this," I say into the phone. I'm pacing the room, distracted by the news my best friend just gave me.

My sister is hours away from becoming a mom. I'm both excited and . . . nervous. She's my little sister, and I've always protected her. What if something happens? It's a helpless feeling, and I don't envy what Archer is experiencing at this very moment. He's expressed his worries before, but always glossed over them quickly, like they were no big deal.

They linger though. I know it.

"What's going on now?" Marina sounds anxious, but that's nothing new. My fiancé has been on edge for weeks. Months even. I'm more than ready to get married and get this whole ceremony thing over with.

Moving on to the honeymoon is what *I'm* looking forward to. I haven't touched my almost-wife sexually—her choice, not mine—in weeks. I'm dying here.

"Archer called. Ivy went into labor." I keep my voice calm, but deep inside I'm a bundle of nerves. I'll admit it to no one. Not even Marina. This is the first baby in the family and even Archer's coldhearted parents are excited. Ivy won't tell us whether she's having a boy or a girl and it's making me nuts. It's making everyone nuts. "They're on their way to the hospital."

"WHAT? Are you serious? Oh my God! This is going to ruin everything," Marina practically screeched.

I'm offended. I can't help it. The way Marina's been acting these last few weeks, she's become unrecognizable. I blame the wedding planning. It's stressing her the hell out which, in turn, is stressing *me* the hell out. "Are *you* serious? We knew this could happen. What's the big deal? Didn't you put a plan B into place or whatever?"

"You really expected me to have a secret plan B? Gage, I work full time and I've been planning this wedding. I'm barely keeping it together as it is." Marina blows out an exasperated breath.

"We'll figure something out." My wife-to-be is at the hotel Archer owns, getting ready. I'm already at the winery, in a private room Matt arranged for me to get dressed in. Our wedding is in approximately ninety minutes.

Marina is probably on her way to legitimately freaking out.

"The ceremony is almost here." Her voice lowers to a harsh whisper. "What are we going to do? Who's going to replace them? This is bad, Gage. Super bad. My mom is going to lose it."

"Why?" I'm incredulous. Her mom likes to lose it over a lot of things. It's the Italian in her. They can be sort of . . . dramatic. Marina too.

"It's bad luck when things don't go right on the most important day of your life." Marina blows out an irritated breath. "No, I'm not ready for my hair to be curled yet. Hold on," she tells someone else. Some poor, innocent soul whose job it is to take care of her today.

Good luck with that.

"We create our own luck," I say, going for positive. "Come on, baby. It's our wedding day. Don't worry about the small stuff. I'll talk to Matt. You should talk to Bryn. I bet they would step in for Archer and Ivy since they're already a part of the wedding party."

Marina remains quiet, but I know she's still on the line. I can hear the soft murmuring of voices in the background, all of them female. I'd guess that hotel room is full of women getting their hair done, makeup done . . . whatever. Sounds like my worst nightmare.

Glad I'm all alone in this quiet room, though I know Matt will show up any minute.

"What do you think?" I prompt when she still hasn't said anything.

"You're right. I can't let this get me down. I mean, Ivy is

having a baby. We should be excited. I shouldn't act like such a selfish bitch worrying who's going to be my maid of honor." Marina sniffs, and I immediately feel like shit.

"Come on, babe. Stop being so hard on yourself. We're getting married. I know you're emotional with everything going on today, but focus on the positives. You're going to be my wife." I lower my voice, desperate to make her laugh. "And I can't wait to violate my wife tonight."

She laughs softly, and I smile, relief flooding me. I can't stand the thought of Marina upset. But I also can't wait for this wedding to be over. So we can focus on living our lives.

Together.

Matt

I knock on the door and enter as I hear Gage say, "Come in." He finishes up a phone call and slips his cell into his front pocket, smiling at me. But the smile looks forced. Not the sort of thing a man should be doing on his wedding day. "What's up?" I ask. "Everything okay?"

"Naw, it's cool. I'm thankful you let me get ready here, man. A lot simpler than being at the hotel with my future wife worried that I might see her someway, somehow. She'd freak out. Bad luck and all, the groom seeing the bride before the wedding," Gage says, waving a hand.

Marina had been on a tear the last few weeks. Wedding stress was spilling over like a pot of water on full boil and making the bride turn a bit . . . angry.

I'm trying to be kind here. Gage is my best friend. And I like Marina. Bryn's grown incredibly close to her. Planning a big wedding is stressful. I know this. I also know my woman wouldn't act like this when planning *our* wedding.

Because that's going to happen. I'm determined to make that woman mine in the most official way. Soon.

"It's almost over, man." I clap Gage on the shoulder, letting him know he has my sympathy. He's been good, never really complaining about Marina, but both Archer and I know Gage is ready for the wedding to be over so his almost-wife will return to her normal self.

"Yeah." Gage rubs a hand across his jaw, then drops his head, staring straight at me. "So get this. Archer called me. Ivy's gone into labor."

"No shit?" I grin. Finally, that baby is going to be here. I have a bet going with a few others over what they're going to have, a boy or a girl.

My bet is a boy. And I hope like hell I'm right since five hundred dollars is riding on this.

Yes, I've turned into a cheapskate, considering the million dollar bet I made with Archer and Gage. A bet that still doesn't have a true winner.

But we all know it's me. After all, I was the last bachelor standing. Those two fell for their respective women like a house of cards. I just lucked out that their relationships happened before mine.

"No shit. This throws off the wedding though. Marina almost lost it when I told her." Gage is still watching me closely, and I almost want to squirm. I feel like I've done something wrong.

"Yeah, I bet." I wouldn't want to be in this guy's shoes right now. Despite how ready I am to make the permanent move with Bryn, I know that for us, we don't want a big elaborate wedding like Gage and Marina are having. Her giant Italian family, which must make up half of the Napa Valley, is part of the problem. I don't have a big family and neither does Bryn. We could run away to Vegas and get married without offending a soul.

Well, maybe her grandma would get mad. She might sick her mean rooster on me. She's a woman I don't necessarily want to mess with. But I'm willing to take the chance.

"Want to step in and be my best man?" Gage asks suddenly.

I glance up and see that my friend is dead serious. "Of course," I say automatically. I was never offended that Gage chose Archer over me. They've known each other longer so it made sense. "I'd be honored, man." And I mean it.

"Great. Okay." Gage nods, smoothing a hand along his jaw, a contemplative look on his face. "You paid attention at the rehearsal last night? I don't need to tell you what to do as best man, do I?"

"I think I can handle it," I drawl, laying the sarcasm on thick. "What do I need to do? Hand over the ring? That's about it."

"You're going to need to give a speech at the reception," Gage points out.

Ah, shit. I'm not big on giving speeches, but I hold my own when I have to. "No problem."

"Marina's going to ask Bryn to be her maid of honor."

"So we'll be a matched set."

"Yep." Gage nods. "You cool with this, bro? We're having to change it all up at the last minute, and it's not like you two are second choice, but . . ."

"We're second choice," I finish for him. "And I'm not offended. I'm sure Bryn won't be either."

My cell dings at that very moment punctuating my sentence, and I pull it out to see it's a text from Bryn.

Maid of honor now. Are you the best man?

Smiling, I type her a response.

You know it.

Nervous?

Not with you by my side, I answer.
And that's the truth.

Chapter 2

Bryn

I've seen Matt in jeans and a T-shirt, a suit, shirtless in a pair of sweats, and I've seen him naked. A lot.

But I have never seen him in a tux before, and oh my God, he's gorgeous. He only wore a suit to Ivy and Archer's wedding, so I didn't get to see him in his full tux glory. And he is just flat-out glorious.

My heart is tripping over itself as I make my way toward him. I struggle to keep the giddy smile off my face, but it's no use. I'm full-on grinning by the time we reach each other.

"You're beautiful," he says before I can even get a word out. His eyes practically smolder as he drinks me in.

My cheeks heat up. It's so ridiculous, but I'm still not used to Matt's praise; that a man like him would be interested in a woman like me. Silly but true.

"You look amazing." I barely get the words out before Matt's dipping his head, his mouth brushing against mine. We're in a small building on the property that Matt's assigned as wedding headquarters for the day. This is the first wedding we've held at the winery, and I told Matt if it's a huge success, we should consider putting together some advertising and marketing plans so we can rent the winery out to the public for events. Aside from this wedding and happenings for the winery, so far, we've only put together small parties for people we know.

He said he wasn't sure he's ready to go big, but I'm excited at the thought. I could become a wedding planner. I love putting together events, and I'm always doing that sort of thing for Matt's winery business anyway, trying to draw attention to the DeLuca Vineyard.

"You're pretty damn amazing yourself," he says once we break apart. He grabs hold of my hand and gives it a squeeze. "Love that dress on you."

I glance down. The dress is pale yellow and strapless, with a snug bodice and a flowing skirt that hits me just above the knee. I love it. "I like it too, which surprises me. I'm not a fan of yellow."

"I'm a fan of anything on you." Matt tugs me close and drops another kiss on my lips, but I put my free hand on his chest, giving him a little push.

"Stop," I say without much force—like I'd deny this man *anything*, especially affection. I love it when he kisses me. Touches me. I'd pretty much let him do whatever he wants to me.

I'm that far gone over him.

"We need to focus on our new tasks and keep the bride and groom calm," I remind him. I sent him a text when I arrived along with the rest of the bridal party and he immediately asked me to meet with him for a few minutes. So here we are.

Figures he tried to cop a feel. Not that I stopped him.

"Gage is fine," Matt says, still gripping my hand. "He's more worried about Marina. How is our bride?"

"She's better." Once she'd calmed down about the whole

Ivy-going-into-labor situation, Marina seemed good. Calmer, which she needs to be in order to get through this day. She's been amped with the wedding plans, but I know she's waiting for it all to be said and done. Not that she won't enjoy her wedding, but . . .

I think she's really looking forward to their tropical honeymoon where she can relax. And get wrapped up in her husband.

"Wait until you see her. She's a gorgeous bride," I say dreamily. Marina is the quintessential bride all little girls dream of being. Her gown is something straight out of a fairy tale, with the full skirt, a sparkly bodice, and feathers.

Yes, white feathers. The dress is hand beaded and ruched, made of tulle and silk, and the look is completed with a tiny tiara on her head. Marina will probably make everyone's jaw hit the floor the moment they see her walk down the aisle. I could almost cry just thinking about it.

"You'll be a gorgeous bride someday too, you know." Matt lifts our linked hands to his mouth and kisses my knuckles.

Panic rises within me, but I bat it down. He's been talking so seriously lately. We've been together for only a short time, but I know what he wants. Me. Us. Together.

Forever.

Am I ready for that sort of commitment? I know I can't do much better than Matthew DeLuca. That sounds cold, but it's true. We're madly in love with each other. Not only does he treat me like the woman he worships and loves, but he also respects my mind and work ethic. He values my opinion. We work well together at the winery. We have an amazing relationship. I'm a lucky girl.

It all still feels unreal, us being together. And this scares the crap out of me.

Marina

I sit in front of the mirror and take a deep breath, shrugging off Mom as she tries to hug me. Again. She's been a regular waterworks the entire morning, but now that I'm in full makeup, I refuse to shed another tear until the actual ceremony.

"You look so beautiful," Mom says on a wistful sigh. "I can't believe my baby girl is getting married."

She's said *that* multiple times this morning too. I understand she's feeling nostalgic, but her tears and trembling voice are doing me in. I'm an emotional, exhausted wreck. Wedding planning is hard, and I've been such a control freak, I hardly let the planner Mom and Dad hired for the wedding make a move without consulting me first.

The room Matt provided for the bridal party to wait in right before the ceremony is perfect. Bryn had a hand in putting it all together, and I can tell. I really love that girl. So glad we've become such good friends.

"I hope everything goes smoothly," I murmur to myself, but the way Mom just straightened, I know she heard me.

"It will be perfect. I just know it. You've already had your one flub for the day. Everything else will be fine," Mom says with a steely voice that tells me she's not in the mood for contradictions.

Now it's my turn to straighten. I meet her gaze in the mirror. "What do you mean, 'your one flub'?"

"Ivy and Archer having to back out." Mom waves a hand, dismissing our friends just like that. "I understand we can't predict when a baby will decide when he or she is ready to make their way into the world. It threw us off a little, but Matt and Bryn have stepped in and everything's going to be just fine."

As if she heard her name mentioned, Bryn glides into the room, quietly closing the door behind her. Her lipstick is completely smudged, so that means she must've snuck off and met with Matt.

A spark of jealousy lights inside of me. I wish I could secretly meet Gage and let him kiss *my* lipstick off.

But I can't. We're getting married in a matter of minutes. I'm going to be Mrs. Marina Emerson. I'm excited. More than ready to be Gage's wife. After all—the stress from planning will fade away like a bad dream.

"Hey."

I blink and shake my head, realizing that it's Bryn standing behind me now instead of Mom. She has her hands on my shoulders, a reassuring smile on her face. If she wasn't such a good friend, I could almost hate Bryn for how beautiful she is. She's gorgeous—her face and body such flawless perfection, she could be a movie star.

The bridesmaid's dress looks amazing on her. It's going to be a beautiful wedding. Everything has been planned, down to the finest detail. So why do I feel like such a wreck inside?

"What's up?" I say, offering Bryn a quick smile. "You snuck off and met Matt, didn't you?"

"Yeah. How could you tell?" Bryn looks embarrassed, which is cute.

"You walked out with lipstick and came back with none. That's a dead giveaway," I say.

She rolls her eyes, her cheeks turning the faintest shade of pink. "I think he wants to ask me to marry me soon."

"Wow. Really?" I'm surprised, yet not. If any of those guys

were a not-so-secret romantic, it'd be Matt. He's never tried to hide it either, but his worshipful side has come out big time since Bryn came into his life. "That's wonderful."

"Yes." Bryn shrugs, her expression turning miserable. "It is."

I stand up and peer at her, noting the way she tilts her head so her gaze is cast downward. Like she doesn't want to look me in the eye. "What's wrong?"

Bryn shakes her head. "Nothing. Let's focus on you. It's your wedding day. You don't need to worry about my insecurities."

Beautiful Bryn has insecurities? "You're worried about your relationship with Matt and whether he loves you or not? I don't think you should be concerned. That man is so gaga over you it's sort of disgusting." Matt is always shooting Bryn moony looks, like he can't believe she's with him. "He's madly in love with you."

"And I'm madly in love with him, but . . . I'm scared." Bryn whispers the last two words and lifts her head so I can see the tears welling up in her eyes. "So stupid. I know we have a great relationship, but it's moving so fast. We haven't been together that long, but all of a sudden he wants to marry me? How can he be sure? Does he even know the real me? Do I even know the real him?"

"Oh, Bryn." I give her an awkward hug because I don't want to wrinkle our dresses or mess up our hair. "Don't worry about the what-ifs or how fast your relationship has moved. You love Matt. He loves you. Be happy that he's so willing to commit to you."

"I know. You're right. I should be happy." Bryn fans her hands in front of her eyes, like that's going to stop her from crying. I can feel my own eyes answering the call to cry with her, but I try my best to ignore it. I do *not* want to ruin my makeup. "And it's your wedding day, which means I need to shut the hell up and quit whining."

I start to laugh and shake my head. "I think weddings make everyone emotional. You're not the first person to fall apart on me. Still"—I wag my finger at her, my voice turning stern—"you need to stop crying before you ruin your makeup. The ceremony is going to start soon and the only one allowed to hold it up is me."

"Okay. Right. You're so right." Bryn sniffs and wipes delicately beneath her eyes with the tips of her fingers. "I'll touch it up and pretend we never had this conversation."

"No." I shake my head and take her hands, squeezing them gently. "We'll resume this conversation later, all right? I'm here for you. You've been such a support to me through all of this. I'm not about to ignore you during your time of need."

Bryn smiles. "You and Ivy are the best friends ever, you know that?"

I smile in return. "Right back at you, sweetie." My smile fades. "I miss Ivy though. We need to call her. I hope she's okay."

Ivy

Get it out! Oh my God." I let my head fall back against the pillows. My entire body aches, especially my back. My water broke about twenty minutes ago and the nurse said I'm transitioning, whatever the hell that means. I can't pay attention; that's Archer's job. I'm too busy birthing his baby.

"Babe. You need to calm down. Reserve your energy." He's right by my side, smoothing my hair away from my forehead, offering me water or ice chips from a little paper cup the nurse brought by earlier. What I'd really like is a sandwich, but they're not giving me anything to eat until after the baby comes.

Ugh. I'm starving.

Shivers move through me to the point where I can't seem to stop shaking, and I have no idea what's wrong with me. "Y-you're r-right," I say through chattering teeth. Archer slips his arm around my shoulders, and I lean against him, my forehead pressing into his jaw as he comforts me. He's been sitting on the edge of the hospital bed since we arrived, always with an encouraging word or a kiss on the forehead.

I really, really love this man. And I would really, really love to have this baby. Now.

"You cold?" He rubs my shoulder and tugs me even closer which makes me wince. I don't want to protest since I love nothing more than being in my husband's arms, but I am incredibly uncomfortable. In pain. I feel like I'm about to drop a two ton brick from my vagina—not that I would ever repeat that to Archer—and I'm tired. I didn't sleep well last night, and now I think I know why.

I was in labor. Duh.

"No." I shake my head, my teeth chattering so bad I clamp them shut and try to get myself under control. "I'm actually pretty hot."

"Yeah, you are," he murmurs with a soft laugh. I laugh too because he's always saying things like that.

"Considering that I feel the farthest thing from hot and sexy, I appreciate the compliment," I say as the door opens and we both glance toward it.

A nurse comes in, a pleasant smile on her face. She takes

one look at me and the smile fades as she rushes toward the bed. "Ooh, I think we should check you."

"Why?" Archer asks as he stands. Worry radiates off him, and I love that he's always my knight, standing up for me no matter what. "Is she okay?"

"She's probably close." By my side, the nurse's voice is gentle as she asks me to lie back. I spread my legs, and she peeks under my gown, a little sound escaping her before she pops her head back up. "I think we're ready to call the doctor in. Do you feel the urge to push?"

"Sorta," I say just as another contraction grips me. My voice fades, but a groan escapes as I hold my belly with one hand. Since monitors are attached to my belly, the steady thump of our baby's heartbeat fills the room, and I concentrate on the sound, which reassures me that he or she is trying to get out.

"Let me go fetch the doctor. I'll be right back." The nurse hurries out of the room, leaving Archer and me alone once more. He takes my hand the moment she's gone, interlacing his fingers with mine.

"You ready?" he asks. "Feeling okay?"

"I'm . . . f-fine." I'm overcome with shivers again, and I press my lips together, trying to keep it all under control. I feel like I'm having an out-of-body experience, I swear. Like this isn't really happening to me, though it so totally is. "D-do you think Marina and G-Gage are mad at us?"

Archer's jaw sets in that way it does when he's being stubborn. "I don't care if they're mad or not. You're about to give birth, Ivy. It's not like we said, 'hey, let's fuck up Gage and Marina's wedding day on purpose.'"

"I know, I know." I sigh and lean my head against the pillow. I stare up at the pale green ceiling and wonder how many other women have been in this very room doing the same thing I'm about to do. "I can't help the twinge of guilt I'm feeling though."

"Hey, they understand. I know they do. Gage told me to tell you that they're thinking of you and can't wait to meet the baby."

"I hope they can stop by before they leave for their honeymoon. If the baby will even be born by then," I say with an exasperated sigh.

"The baby will be here by then," Archer says assuredly, leaning over so he's looking me directly in the eyes. "Have faith, babe. It's all going to come together. Trust me."

As I stare into my husband's eyes, I know I trust him one hundred percent. I'm just tired and scared and eager. Eager for all of this to be over with, so I can hold my child in my arms and welcome him or her into this world.

"Hello." The obstetrician strides into the room, the tails of his white coat flying behind him as he approaches the bed. "I hear you're about to have a baby. You ready?"

"As I'll ever be," I answer, offering a smile in Archer's direction.

He smiles in return, handsome despite the circles ringing his eyes and his messy hair. "Me too, babe," he says, not even looking at the doctor. No, my husband's gaze is only for me. "Me too."

Chapter 3

Gage

'm nervous. I didn't think this would happen. I've been the cool, easygoing eye of the storm that has been my poor stressed-out fiancée. But now that the moment has come, and I'm standing with Matt by my side, in front of our guests, as we all wait for Marina to make her appearance, I feel like I might faint.

Yeah. Not good.

Locking my knees, I swallow hard and try not to fidget as the music plays. A crisp breeze washes over us, cooling my sweat-dampened forehead, and I give it a subtle swipe, noting that my palms are clammy.

I'm a freaking mess.

"Calm down, dude," Matt whispers out of the side of his mouth. We're standing so close our shoulders are practically touching. Wonder if he'd catch me if I fall. "You look like you're gonna drop."

"I *feel* like I'm gonna drop," I tell him, feeling like an idiot, but not really caring. He's my new best man, so I need him to step it up. If I pass out, it's on him.

"Your girl is going to make her appearance at any minute." Matt nods toward the beginning of the aisle where no one stands. Where are the girls? We already made our walk down the aisle, Matt walking Marina's mom to her seat, me walking my mother.

"Hope she shows up soon," I mutter, meaning it. I feel antsy. My suit is too tight. My throat is dry. I'm dying for a drink. Preferably booze.

Probably not a good idea.

The flower girl suddenly struts down the aisle, cute as can be in a white lacy gown. Louisa is one of Marina's cousins. She has about a bazillion of them.

Almost all of them are sitting in the crowd, watching me. Probably pissed because Marina and I both agreed that we didn't want a huge, ridiculous wedding party. We blew their chance to wear bridesmaids' gowns.

Then Bryn appears, a freaking vision in pale yellow. She walks down the aisle slowly, a coy smile on her face as she shoots me a glance, then trains her gaze on Matt. As her smile disappears, her eyes widen, and I look at Matt, who's staring at Bryn like she's the most beautiful creature he's ever seen in his life.

Poor dude is straight up in love with Bryn. Like a complete and total goner. I get what he's feeling.

The music fades and a new song starts—a low, melodic tune played to perfection by the small group of musicians set up off to the right. I straighten my spine, clasp my hands behind my back as I wait for my bride to make her appearance.

And then . . . there she is. Her arm curls around her father's, who looks respectably intimidating in his tuxedo. A frothy veil covers her face, and the skirt of her gown is wide, nearly as wide as the aisle they're walking down.

Tears threaten, and I blink once. Hard. Damn it, I'm not going to cry. I'm happy, not sad. But I'm also overwhelmed, filled with love for this woman who's about to become my partner in life.

They approach and stop just before us, turning to each other so her father can lift the veil, revealing her face to me for the first time. He leans in and kisses her cheek as the minister asks who gives this woman to this man, just as we rehearsed yesterday. Her father says "I do," his deep voice a little shaky, and my sympathy goes out to him.

I'm still feeling pretty shaky myself.

Marina steps up to stand beside me, and I take her hand, unable to stop from leaning in and brushing a quick kiss against her cheek. "You look beautiful," I murmur, my voice just as shaky as her dad's.

But I don't care. I have no shame. I'm getting married, damn it. I'm allowed to cry. To smile. To laugh. I'm making this woman mine.

Forever.

Marina

We stop at the beginning of the aisle, waiting for the cue from the music. Dad lays his hand over mine and gives it a squeeze. "You look beautiful, Marina. Your mom and I are so proud of you."

I nod, not trusting my voice. I'm afraid I'll start crying, and I don't want to do that. Not yet.

"I'm going to have a talk with Gage. Tell him he better treat you right or he'll have to answer to me," Dad continues.

"Oh, Daddy." My voice cracks, and I press my lips together

for a brief moment to keep the sob in. Once I have it under control, I whisper, "He loves me. I know he does."

"I know he does too, princess." Dad pats my hand just as the music gets louder. "That's our sign, sweetheart. Let's do this."

I let Dad lead me down the aisle toward Gage. He looks so handsome, the sun shining down on him, making his dark hair glint. He smiles when our eyes meet, though I know he can hardly see me through the veil.

That was the plan. I wanted to draw it out. Make him anticipate me.

When Dad lifts the veil and kisses me, I see the way Gage's eyes widen, the sheen of tears in their depths. Oh God, if he's going to cry, I'm definitely going to cry, and I don't know if I can take this.

Dad hands me over to Gage, and I take my place beside him, surprised when he drops a kiss on my cheek.

"You look beautiful," he murmurs, his voice trembling. My heart skips at his words and the sincerity behind them, the love shining in his eyes.

"So do you," I say, because he does. My groom is gorgeous in his tux, his hair perfect, his expression nervous. "I love you."

"I love you too." He brings our clutched hands to his mouth and kisses my knuckles, earning a disapproving noise from the minister that makes us both smile.

The ceremony starts with words of love and commitment, the sanctity of marriage, the importance of sticking together through the good times and the bad. We turn to face each other to recite our vows, and I'm overwhelmed with love for Gage as I repeat the words the minister says to me. I mean every single thing I say to Gage, and I know he feels the same way.

Matt hands over the ring, and Gage slips it on my finger, a breathtaking diamond band he chose for me months ago. Then it's my turn, and I take the simple platinum band from Bryn and slip it on Gage's shaking finger. He's still nervous. Excited. I feel the same.

"I now declare you husband and wife. Gage, you may kiss your bride," the minister says.

There's a roaring in my ears as Gage pulls me into his arms, his face, his scent so familiar, so dear to me. I tilt my head back and close my eyes, sucking in a harsh breath when his lips light upon mine. The touch is faint and damp, a simple brush before he presses harder, deepening the kiss with a quick and eager swipe of his tongue.

I cling to him, ignoring the hoots and hollers from the crowd because, oh my God, I know we're putting on a show. But I don't care. Neither does Gage. I want to remember this moment forever. Want to make this one of the most memorable days of my life—of his too.

"You're mine now, baby," he says once we finally withdraw. I smile because he's grinning at me, looking almost as if he's in a daze. "It's official and everything."

I burst out laughing and throw my arms around his neck, giving him a sound kiss on the lips. "Whether I like it or not?" I whisper against his mouth.

"Oh, you're going to like it." He kisses me one more time and then steps away, my hands still clutched in his. "I'll definitely make it worth your while."

"Promise?" I tease.

Just then, the minister yells, "Introducing Mr. and Mrs. Gage Emerson!"

"For you, baby? Anything."

Chapter 4

Archer

My wife has been pushing for the last hour and a half and it's killing me that I can't help her. That I can't solve this problem she's having, that I can't be the one having the baby for her. I wish I could take on her pain, take on her exhaustion, take on her every burden so she doesn't have to suffer.

I hate that I have to witness this. Not the birth of my child, oh no. I'm beyond ready to meet that baby of mine. My poor wife though?

She's suffering, my Ivy. Hunched over, her face is red, her forehead sweaty, and long wisps of hair are matted to her skin. Her eyes are wild with a mixture of anticipation and exhaustion and they go out of focus every few minutes. Like she's here, but not.

Her feet are in stirrups, her knees bent as the doctor and nurse hover at the end of the bed, checking her between the legs. She freaked out a little bit when they laid her down on the birthing table. Panicked. She's been saying for weeks that she wants the baby out, but now that we're at the final moment, I think she's having regrets about the entire child-birthing process, though I know that's just nerves talking.

Anyway, too late now. There's no going back. She knows this but . . . pregnant women can be a little irrational sometimes. Not that I would ever, *ever* admit that to Ivy. Or any other woman who's given birth.

The only thing that reassures me in the midst of the chaos and the worry is the sound of my child's steady heartbeat coming from the monitor, filling the room with a relentless beat that tells me they're doing just fine.

Wish I could say the same about Ivy. She's worn out.

"You okay?" I ask her, tracing my fingers down her forearm, drawing her attention. "You've almost got this, baby. You're doing so good."

"I'm okay." She nods, but her voice wavers, and I wonder how okay she really feels. "I just want this to be over with. I'm so tired."

"Maybe . . ." I let my voice trail off, not sure if I should say what I want to say to her or not. I clear my throat. "You've been going at this for hours. Maybe you should consider a C-section? I know we discussed natural childbirth, and you didn't want to have a cesarean, but—"

"I've only been pushing for two hours, if that. The baby isn't stressed. I'm not a quitter, Archer." She sits up straighter, her expression determined. "I've got this."

Aw, man. She's set out to prove me wrong now.

This is usually my cue to give up the fight but, damn it, I'm scared out of my mind something could happen to Ivy. And I'm not about to lose her. I can't even fathom the thought.

My phone starts ringing, and I see it's Matt calling. I walk over to the farthest corner of the room so I can answer it and talk without Ivy hearing me.

"What's up, man? Don't tell me you bailed on Gage and Marina too."

Matt chuckles. "You a father yet or what? Everyone's dying to know what's going on. How's Ivy? Is she okay?"

"The baby's not here yet," I say, glancing over at Ivy's bed. She's got her hand resting low on her belly and her chin is tilted down. I swear her lips are moving, and I think she might be either talking to herself or the baby. Probably telling the baby that they're going to prove Daddy wrong and make an appearance sooner rather than later—which would be fine with me. "She's been pushing for almost two hours," I say, my voice lowering. "I'm worried about her."

"She'll be fine," Matt says. "Women have babies all the time. Your girl is tough."

I know what Matt's saying is true, but I still worry about Ivy. She's my life. I want what's best for her and never want to see her in pain. I had no idea watching her in labor would be so difficult. I need to change the subject for a bit and focus on something else. "So how was the wedding?"

"Great. Everything went off without a hitch and Marina was a beautiful bride. I swear, Gage cried when he first saw her."

"Get the hell out." Gage was turning into a regular sap.

No big deal considering I was too. So was Matt. I blame the women folk.

"Hand to God, dude. I wanted to tear up when I saw Bryn coming at me down the aisle in her bridesmaid dress, she looked so beautiful clutching her bouquet," Matt says, his voice soft.

What a goner he is. He's madly in love with that former assistant of his, not that I can blame him. I would never admit this to Ivy, but Bryn is pretty damn hot, plus she's so nice.

Christ, she'd tear my head off if she knew I even thought that.

"You've turned into a complete pussy," I mutter just to get under Matt's skin.

It works. "Fuck you," he replies cheerily. "Mister I'm-so-worried-about-my-wife-as-she-gives-birth-to-my-baby, though

I get it, man. I get it." Matt pauses for a brief moment, and I hear a cheer in the background. Sounds like they're all having fun, and I wish Ivy and I could've been there to celebrate with everyone. But our baby had different plans. "What do you think you're having anyway? Boy or girl?"

I want to roll my eyes. How many times have I answered this question? Hell, how many times has Matt himself asked me? "It doesn't matter as long as the baby is healthy," I say.

"That's such a bullshit answer. You can tell me the truth. I won't reveal it to anyone. What do you think you're having? What do you *want*?"

"I really don't care dude, okay?" I glance over at Ivy, who's glaring at me. Damn, she looks pissed.

I swallow hard, prepared for the verbal blow I'm about to get.

"Archer," she practically hisses. Her eyes are narrowed, but she looks scared too. And so, so, tired. "I need you."

"I gotta go," I tell Matt. "Pray for my wife," I say before I end the call. I rush toward Ivy, who lets out a long groan as she clutches her belly with both hands.

We're going to need all the help we can get.

Matt

The reception is in full swing, and I can finally relax. During the ceremony, I stood by Gage's side and handed over the ring. I gave a rousing speech during the dinner that made practically every female in attendance cry. And now I'm slow dancing with my girlfriend, holding her close in my arms as we sway to the music.

Since when did my life get so perfect?

Since the first time you saw Bryn.

Right. Exactly.

"They look so happy," Bryn murmurs, breaking through my thoughts.

I glance down at her to see she's watching Gage and Marina dance nearby. Their gazes are locked, arms wrapped around each other as they float slowly about the dance floor, surrounded by other couples. But they aren't paying attention to anyone else, acting as if they're the only two people in this room. They look that lost in each other.

"That's what love does to you," I say because I can relate. I feel the same way. Completely and totally lost in Bryn and what we share. It just flat out doesn't get much better than this, and I'm finding that I count my lucky stars more and more often the longer I'm with Bryn.

I want to make this relationship permanent. We belong together. I know it. She knows it. So why aren't we facing facts and taking our relationship to the next logical step?

"You're right." Bryn smiles up at me, the sight of her pretty face momentarily stealing my breath. "Love makes you do crazy things."

"It does." I nod and swallow hard. This is it. I want to say the words, but they're lodged in my throat like I've turned into some sort of coward. When have I ever hesitated to ask for what I want? I'm a go-getter, and I always have been. If I've learned anything from my pain-in-the-ass dad, it's that you've gotta make shit happen for yourself, not wait for it to happen to you.

Sound advice. Even in relationships.

"You did an amazing job with the best man speech," Bryn continues, smoothing her hand along my shoulder. My skin tingles at her touch, even through the layers of clothing. "Did you even plan what you were going to say? Or was it completely unrehearsed?"

"Considering I had less than two hours to prepare for that speech, and most of that time I was doing other stuff— yeah, completely unrehearsed," I say. I'm not the best when it comes to speaking in public, but I held my own. Unlike now, when I'm losing my nerve just trying to talk to my own girlfriend.

It's only the most important question of my life. What's the big deal?

I break out into a cold sweat. Jesus, this is a huge fucking deal.

"Well, you did great. And you look good too," she says appreciatively. "Though I think I've told you that about a thousand times already."

I raise a brow. "Only *good*?" Looks like I can still flirt at least. That's good because I feel like I'm losing my grip and fast.

"Better than good." She grins. "Hot. Mega hot."

"That's better." Leaning in, I drop a quick kiss on her forehead.

"I love you," she whispers, and my heart cracks with her words. Rarely does she say it first; it's almost like she's scared to confess she may have more feelings than I do at any given moment.

I've lived most of my life always trying to be on top, but this relationship isn't a competition. We're two equals, Bryn and me, and I wish she could realize that. When it comes to relationships and love, I know she hasn't had the best examples in life, but I want her to be confident knowing that I love her.

"I love you too," I say, my voice—and my courage—growing stronger. "Bryn."

"What?"

I stare into her eyes, memorizing the way she looks at this very moment. Happy, beautiful. Perfect. "Will you marry me? Be my bride?"

She stops dancing and so do I, my heart racing a million miles a minute. She's gaping at me, her eyes wide, lips parted, staring at me like I have two heads. Then she takes a step back, her hands dropping away from me as she slowly shakes her head.

"I-I'm sorry. I can't," she whispers, just before she turns on her heel and runs away from me as fast as she can.

Leaving me standing in the middle of the dance floor. Alone and devastated.

Hell. What just happened?

Gage

G age?"

My wife's sweet voice rings through me, and I glance down at her, offering her a soft smile. "Yeah?"

"I love you." Marina smiles at me, radiantly beautiful. I want to fucking cry all over again just looking at her. When I saw her poised at the end of the aisle on her father's arm, ready to walk toward me and begin this journey called marriage, tears sprang to my eyes. The dress she wore was stunning. Her hair, her smile, the way she clutched her bouquet so tightly the flowers trembled—she did me in.

Flat-out wrecked me.

All the stress and joy and arguments and worry and anxiety in planning this wedding had proven worth it in that one single moment.

"I love you too," I whisper, bending down so I can kiss her, even slip her a little tongue which she responds to eagerly. Hey, this is our day. If anyone wants to give us grief for tongue kissing on the dance floor at our wedding reception, well, they can suck the big one.

She breaks the kiss first, her smile wobbly, her eyes a little dazed. "Thank you."

"For what?" I laugh and shake my head. "Kissing you?"

"For putting up with me these last few months." Her smile turns immediately into a frown. "I've been a complete bitch. I don't know how you put up with me."

"You're not a bitch." I kiss the tip of her nose. "You might've been a bit . . . touchy, but hey, you've been under a lot of stress. Planning a wedding isn't easy."

"Planning a wedding for a demanding bunch of Italians all expecting the party of the century is definitely not easy," she says, her voice tinged with sarcasm.

I laugh. There's something about her boisterous Italian family that I love. Even her dad, who still sometimes treats me like I'm scum on the bottom of his shoe. I love that guy. I love her mom too. I love her whole damn family and I know my family embraces her fully, especially my sister.

Shit. My sister. She's having a baby right now, and I haven't contacted her. Our parents already left and headed to the hospital so they could be with her and Archer. I should do the same. We should leave right now and check up on her. We have time before we have to get to the hotel. Hell, we're not even flying out to the Caribbean until tomorrow morning.

"I texted Archer a few minutes ago," Marina says like she can read my mind or something.

Which she probably can. I used to think that crap was scary. Now I just roll with it.

"What did he say? How's my sister?" I hear the panic in my own voice, and I tell myself to calm down. If something crazy were going down, they would've contacted us. Otherwise, they're leaving us alone—those were Archer's exact words to me via text right before the ceremony. They want us to enjoy our wedding, not worry about Ivy the entire time.

I appreciated the gesture, and of course I was able to get wrapped up in the ceremony and reception, but still, I'm thinking of my sister and hoping like hell she's all right.

"She's good. Still in labor. Archer's worried about her," Marina says.

"Should I be worried about her too?"

"No. It's normal. I spoke to your mom a few minutes ago. She called right before you dragged me out onto the dance floor," Marina says, laughing when I scowl at her. "They'd just arrived at the hospital and said Ivy was looking good. Well, she was looking tired and a little grumpy and more than ready to give birth, but still good. There are no complications, and the baby should make his or her appearance soon."

"Good." I'm thankful to hear my sister is okay. The timing on all of this wasn't the best, but hey, it's definitely going to be memorable. Especially if the baby is born today of all days. Talk about a celebration. A wedding anniversary *and* a birthday for the family—you can't beat that.

"I was wondering." Marina sinks her teeth into her glossy lower lip. Damn, she's sexy when she does that. It's been a while since I've had her naked and beneath me. Not only because of stress, but because she actually wanted us to keep our hands off each other for a while.

It'll make the wedding night that much better, she'd insisted.

Whatever. I went along with it, but we're done with that. I'm eager to take her back to the hotel room and strip that dress off her. And whatever else she's got going on beneath it, because I know it must be complicated.

I'm more than up to the challenge.

"Wondering what?" I ask.

"Maybe before we go to the hotel, we can stop by the hospital to see Ivy and hopefully the baby? We won't be leaving here for another few hours, and I'm guessing the baby will be born by then," Marina says.

"Another few hours?" Shit. How long is this reception supposed to last?

"Well, we haven't cut the cake yet, and I haven't tossed my bouquet. And you need to throw the garter. So yes. A few more hours to go at least," she stresses.

At least. Well, that sucks. I'm ready to bail. "But I'm ready to get you alone *now*," I whisper, squeezing her hand as I step in closer to her. So close our chests brush and our legs momentarily tangle.

Her smile turns sultry. "I know. Trust me, I want to get you alone too, but just a few more hours here. I promise. Then we'll go to the hospital, then the hotel. They probably won't let us stay long at the hospital anyway. We'll be lucky to see Ivy, what with visiting hours and all that."

Yeah. I need to do the right thing and try and see my sister. At the very least, hopefully see the baby and Archer.

"You're right." I glance around and notice that no one is

really paying any attention to us. Lowering my voice, I say, "Let's sneak off for a quickie."

Her jaw drops open. "Are you serious?"

"As a heart attack." Just thinking about it has me hard. "I want you, Marina. It's been too long. I don't know if I can wait another two or three hours or whatever it is before I get you naked in bed."

She glances down at herself, then up at me. "It'll take twenty minutes just to get me out of everything I'm wearing."

I can only imagine what she's wearing. I bet every bit of it is sexy as fuck. "Can't I just toss up your skirt?"

Her cheeks go the faintest shade of pink. "God, Gage you're awful."

"You love it. It's why you married me." I kiss her, letting my lips linger on hers. She needs to know how much I want her. A quick grope and fumble will at least take the edge off. "Come on, baby. Let's sneak off somewhere. We'll disappear for ten minutes tops. No one will notice we're gone."

"You're only giving me ten minutes?" Her eyebrows rise.

I laugh. "So greedy. How about you get five, and I get five."

"Now only five?"

Lowering my voice, I brush my lips against her ear. "I can make you come in less than five and you know it."

She shivers and I smile. "You're awfully confident in *my* skills then, giving me only five minutes." Still, she doesn't deny that I can make her come in less than five because she knows it's true.

"I'm already half-cocked. Emphasis on the word *cock*," I whisper, making her laugh.

"Fine," she says, but she doesn't sound put out. She's just as excited as I am. "Let's go."

"Where?" I let Marina take my hand and pull me off the dance floor. The music changes, a fast song comes on and three quarters of the crowd stands, ready to flood the dance floor. Perfect.

"There's a room just down the hall. The room where we all waited for the ceremony to start," she tells me as we walk side by side, nodding and smiling at guests as we pass. Her family is nowhere in sight, and my parents already left to be with Ivy and Archer, so I think we're in the clear.

"Ah, I got ready just down the hall too," I say. "Let's go there. Less chance of someone trying to bust in, don't you think?"

"There's a lock on the door, Gage." She rolls her eyes and smiles at me. "There's no way I would fool around with you at our freaking wedding reception without a locked door."

We both laugh over that, not paying attention to where we're walking until I bump right into someone.

A visibly upset, teary-eyed Bryn.

"Sorry," she mutters when I reach out to steady her after sending her stumbling back.

"Bryn." I give her shoulders a little shake, forcing her to look up at me. "Are you okay?"

She sniffs and flashes me the fakest smile I've ever seen. "I'm fine. Great. Sorry to run into you. I'll let you guys go." She extracts herself from my grip, looking ready to dash away when Marina reaches out and grabs her arm.

"Bryn, what happened?" Marina shoots me a look, one that says she has to find out what's going on, and I feel my erection deflate just like that.

Damn. But hey, I get it. I give her a brief nod and take a step back, letting the two women walk away from me as Marina asks Bryn more questions, trying to get information out of her.

Guess I should go in search of Matt, so I can find out what's up.

Chapter 5

Bryn

The last thing I want to do is dump all of my misery and problems on the bride, but Marina's the one interrogating me. Gage stepped away and gave us some privacy, which blew my mind. I protested when Marina took me over to an empty table in a dark corner so she can question me further, but he waved us off. I'm so lucky to have such great friends.

"Okay." Marina sits across from me, her expression serious, her gaze imploring. "Tell me what happened to make you so upset."

I press my lips together. She's going to tell me I'm the biggest idiot ever when I confess what I did to Matt. I just know it. "I said something stupid."

Marina offers me a little smile. "Don't we all? I say stupid stuff all the time."

"I said something stupid to Matt."

"I always say something stupid to Gage, so no worries there." She's trying to tell me that whatever happened has to be no big deal, but I know the truth.

It's a very big deal.

"Matt asked me to marry him, and I said no," I blurt out, figuring it's best to just get it over with because, oh my God.

It feels really good to tell my friend what I did.

And I must hand it to Marina—she hardly bats an eye-lash. "Give me exact details. Well, whatever details you want to give, that is."

I sigh and launch into the story, not bringing up the fear that has hung over me like a dark cloud since last night's rehearsal dinner. Matt's always had a romantic streak, but he's seemed extra loving since he witnessed the mock ceremony between Gage and Marina. "I think—no, I know—seeing you guys rehearse your ceremony and the vows and all that put ideas in his head. Ideas that he wants to marry me," I say, finishing my explanation.

Marina reaches out and clutches my hand tightly. "And what's wrong with that? You two seem so good together."

"We are. Definitely," I say, nodding. "But don't you think it's happening too fast? We haven't been together that long. Not even a year. And he's already asking me to marry him?"

"When you know, you know," Marina says gently. "Gage and I had been together only a little while before we knew we wanted to get married."

"See that's the thing. I don't know if I want to ever get married," I confess, hanging my head. I feel terrible admitting such a thing, but it's true. I've had terrible examples when it comes to relationships. My mom ditched me, and though I've come to terms with it, the abandonment hurt. I don't really know my father, but whatever. I have no siblings. And I know my grandma loves me, but she's always so gruff. My grandpa died before I was born, and she's rarely had a man since, so I haven't seen her in romantic relationships much.

Matt is the first good thing to happen to me. The most loving, extraordinary man I've ever met. He treats me like a queen.

And like a complete idiot, I told him no. I didn't want to marry him.

What's wrong with me?

I don't even realize I'm crying again until I feel a tear drop on the skirt of my dress. Swiping at my eyes with shaky fingers, I sniff loudly, wishing I had a tissue.

Marina shoves a cloth napkin at me, and I take it, dabbing at my eyes. My girlfriends are the second best thing to happen to me since I moved to the Napa Valley. What would I do without Marina and Ivy? These girls take care of me no matter what, no questions asked. They laugh and cry and get mad when I do, and I do the same for them. They're like family.

"You're scared," Marina says. "And it's understandable. If anyone should understand, it's Matt. He lost his mom. His dad is a complete jerk. Gage told me Matt used to be kind of a jerk too, when he was playing pro ball. But then he got injured and it changed him completely. Like, altered his life both in his career and the way he thought and behaved. He quit being such a womanizer and focused on bettering himself. Then he found you." She smiles. "You helped change him too. You changed each other."

"So as a thank you, I reject him and ruin my chances with him completely. That's just great," I wail, feeling like a complete idiot.

"You didn't ruin your chance," a familiar male voice says from behind me.

I freeze, recognizing that voice anywhere. Closing my eyes, I breathe deep, searching for courage. I need to be brave and face him. He came back for me. Maybe he's telling the truth, and I didn't blow it after all.

Slowly I turn in my chair to find Matt standing there, an

unsure smile on his face as he watches me. "What are you do-ing here?" I whisper, earning a shove from Marina, undoubt-edly for yet another stupid question.

"Go to him," she whispers, and I do. I stand and walk to-ward him as if I'm in a trance, everything fading away until it feels like it's just him and me in the room and not another three hundred or so people.

"I'm so sorry, Matt," I say, shocked when he takes my hands in his and holds them between us. "I shouldn't have run away."

"I shouldn't have asked you that question yet," he says, his voice serious, his gaze searching. "You're not ready. I should've realized that."

"It's not your fault. It's mine. Going so fast . . . it sometimes scares me. We've moved at an accelerated pace, you know," I tell him, entwining my fingers with his. "Like Marina, I feel like I've been on edge with this whole wedding thing. Then you dropped that question on me, and I panicked."

"I know." He sighs harshly and shakes his head. "I'm the type of guy who goes after what he wants. And I know what I want, Bryn." He steps closer and dips his head so our fore-heads press together. "You."

"I want you too," I whisper. "I love you. I'm sorry."

"I'm sorry too." He kisses me. Soft and warm and so lovingly I want to weep all over again, but not because I'm sad.

But because I'm so incredibly happy that my man didn't let me walk away from him without a fight.

"I'll ask you again," he whispers against my ear once we end our kiss. "Later. When you're not so scared anymore. But I'm warning you now; I'm determined to make you mine in the most official way possible."

A deep sigh moves through me, and I close my eyes, press-ing my face in the crook of his neck where he's warm and smells so good. "That sounds perfect," I murmur against his skin.

Marina

I feel good leaving Bryn with Matt because if anyone can work this out, it's those two. They're so in love with each other it's sort of disgusting.

But I feel that way about Archer and Ivy too. Even me and Gage.

Put all six of us together and we're all like . . . super disgusting.

Laughing quietly to myself, I leave the reception and sneak down the hall to the room where Gage told me to meet him via text not five minutes ago. Anticipation curls through me when I slowly open the door to find the room dark and seemingly empty.

I know it's not though. I can smell him. Sharp and clean and so deliciously Gage. Closing the door behind me, I lean against it, my sight adjusting to the darkness until I finally make out his silhouette. He's coming toward me, his strides animal-like, his gaze penetrating as it settles over me. "You made it," he says, the timbre of his deep voice seemingly vibrating through me. "I missed you."

"I was gone maybe ten minutes?" He slips his arms around my waist as I stepped in close, eagerly going into his arms. "I had to help Bryn."

"I know," he murmurs against my forehead, his lips tickling my skin. "Is everything okay?"

"Nothing that can't be fixed." I had faith it would be too.

Matt understands Bryn, maybe even better than she understands herself. She needs to put more trust in him and their relationship.

"You're a good friend." Gage's hands are wandering. Along my arms, to my waist, slipping down to my hips. The gown I'm wearing has a fitted bodice, but the skirt is huge. Like fairy-tale-princess, layers-of-tulle-and-silk-and-lace, Cinderella-at-the-ball giant. I fell in love with it the moment I saw it.

My husband—God, just thinking that word gives me a serious thrill—probably hates it.

"Where's my wife?" I glance up to find him grinning down at me, his hands getting lost in the voluminous skirt. "I can't find her underneath all the fabric."

"I don't know if he ever will," I say with a dramatic sigh, hoping it will spur him on. "Especially when he only has five minutes to find her."

That comment kicks him into action. He's down on his knees in front of me, lifting the layers of my skirt until he's buried beneath them. His hands go to my thighs and I giggle, his touch tickling me.

"Nice garters," he murmurs, his voice muffled as he traces them. His fingers skim the exposed skin of my thighs and I'm thankful he somehow positioned us so I'm close to the wall. I lean against it, a soft sigh escaping me when his fingers explore upward, along my thighs, tracing the seam of my very lacy, very white panties.

I may not be a virgin, but I can certainly pretend to be one on my wedding day.

"Sexy." His voice deepens right when his fingers slip beneath the lace, touching my bare, heated skin. I close my eyes and spread my legs a little, already lost in his touch when I feel him trace my soaked folds. "Baby, you're wet."

"I want my husband," I say, wanting to both laugh and moan because, oh my God, what a picture we must make: me braced against the wall, my husband underneath my wedding gown, hurriedly trying to get me off with a few strokes of his fingers.

"Well, you're getting him. Any way you can have him," he says just as he circles my clit with his finger. I'm already primed and eager, ready for him to push me right over the edge and send me straight into an orgasm. Hopefully it will ease the incessant neediness that's been raging within me for the last few days. Weeks.

I hate how distant we've been lately. But I'm going to rectify that too, with one incredible wedding night and an amazing honeymoon.

Gage touches me in a particular way that I love and a gasp escapes me. That familiar sweet sharpness echoes through my body, telling me I'm close, and I clutch the wall behind me as his touch becomes faster, a little rougher, his lips pressed hard against the inside of my thigh.

And then his mouth is on me, his fingers buried deep. I shriek and he pinches my thigh to remind me where we're at, I'm sure. So I place my hand over my mouth to stop from yelling as the orgasm sweeps over me, leaving me a trembling, panting mess as I'm left slumped against the wall.

The man is good. I will give him that.

Within seconds he's out from under my skirts, his face flushed, his lips damp. He's smiling at me, looking mighty pleased with himself, and I can't help but return the grin.

"My turn," he declares happily, and I laugh as he stands so he's looming over me. He takes me into his arms and kisses me senseless, the taste of me on his lips and tongue.

I don't care. I eagerly accept his kiss, my knees shaky as his tongue plunders my mouth and when he breaks the kiss first, I follow him, my mouth still seeking his.

"Feel this," he tells me as he takes my hand and places it over the very firm erection straining against his black trousers. I stroke him slowly, from base to tip, can feel almost every blessed inch and nuance of his flesh, and I smile up at him when I see the blissed-out expression already crossing his face.

"I think my husband wants me," I murmur as I stroke him again. A little quicker this time.

"You're damn right he does."

"Think I can get on my knees in this getup?" I kick out my foot, making my skirt flare, and Gage chuckles.

"Are you serious?"

Oh, that's a challenge if I've ever heard one. That's one thing Gage and I like to do—constantly challenge each other. "Watch me," I say as I gather my skirt in one hand and get down on my knees in front of my now very shocked husband.

Without hesitation I reach for him and unzip his fly, impressed by his thick cock straining against the damp cotton of his underwear.

"Five minutes, baby?" he asks, his fingers sliding into my hair and pulling me closer to his erection. "Think you can do it?"

"I know I can," I murmur just before I wrap my lips around the tip of his cock, his low hum of pleasure sending a shot of arousal through me. Just like that, I'm turned on again.

And just like that, I make my husband come in less than five minutes with only my mouth. On our wedding day, down the hall from where our reception still rages on.

Yeah. Life can't get much better than this, can it?

Ivy

B aby. Baby, baby, baby, baby."

I let my head flop against the pillow, my chest aching with the ragged breaths I've been struggling to take. This pushing-a-baby-out-of-my-vagina business is fucking hard. Why didn't my mom ever tell me this?

Probably because she knew I'd refuse to do it if I understood the truth.

"Are you talking to me or your future son or daughter?" I ask Archer when I finally find my breath once again. My mouth is dry. My skin is soaked with sweat, and I feel like I'm going to collapse, which is sort of funny considering I'm lying down. Well, half lying down, since I bend forward every few minutes to try and push the baby out.

"You. I'm talking to you, babe. Trying to encourage you." Archer takes my hand and gives it a squeeze. God, I love this man. I really hope with the next few pushes I can produce that baby he's so eagerly awaiting. "You've got this, babe. You've been working so hard."

"I know," I whisper, closing my eyes when I hear the doctor start talking. He keeps saying all the right things, but those things are irritating the crap out of me right now. The only one I want to focus on is my husband. That's it.

No one else.

"One more push, Ivy, and you could be holding your baby in your arms within minutes," the doctor says, making me want to punch him.

He's a guy. He has no comprehension just how damn hard this entire endeavor is.

"Ivy." Archer squeezes my hand again and my eyes pop open to find him watching me, an encouraging expression on his handsome, albeit tired face. "Let's do this, baby. One more push. You're so damn close. I can see our baby's head. So much dark hair and a little scrunched up face." He was just down there with the doctor, checking me out in all my naked, pushing-a-baby-out-of-my-vagina glory and at any other moment, I might've been slightly freaked out.

But not now. I just flat-out don't care. I want the baby out. I'm done. I'm tired and worn out and burned out and done, done, done.

"One more giant push, and we're a family of three," Archer continues. "Isn't that what you want? Your mom and dad are waiting in the lobby, and they can't wait to meet their grand-child. Gage texted me and said he and Marina are going to stop by before they head to the hotel. Let's go, babe. You ready?"

Archer knows exactly what to say to pump me up. That my parents are waiting, that Gage and Marina are going to stop by in the hopes that they see the baby, spurs me on. "Yes." I struggle to sit up and he helps me. I'm bent forward, my knees pointed toward the sky, my legs spread wide for God and everyone to see, and I close my eyes, take a deep breath, and push with all my might.

This is it. I gotta make this happen. I'm tired, and my baby needs to be in my arms.

Within seconds I feel the baby spill out of me. That's what it feels like at least. A baby just slipped right out of my body and ended up in the doctor's hands.

"It's a boy," he declares just as a piercing cry fills the room.

"I knew it," I mumble as I watch Archer look at his son for the first time.

"Cut the cord," the doctor encourages, and Archer does,

looking like he's in a daze as the doctor hands me my baby. I'm crying, cuddling the baby close to my bare skin. I bend over him and sniff his damp head, feel his little face root against my chest like he's looking for a nipple already.

Greedy little thing. Just like his father.

"A boy." Archer settles his hand over our son's head, his palm covering it entirely. His tone, his expression is full of awe and disbelief. He lifts his head, his gaze meeting mine. I see tears glimmer there and that spurs my tears on, until the both of us are smiling and crying and cuddling our baby close.

"He's beautiful," I say.

"Like his mama," Archer agrees, solemnly. "Thank you, Ivy."

"For what?"

"For giving me a son."

"You had a hand in it too." I smile and stroke our son's downy soft hair. The nurse will take him soon to clean him up, so I need to cherish this moment for as long as I can.

"What are we naming him?" Archer asks.

I tilt my head, contemplating him. "Didn't we talk about this already?"

"Well, yeah." Archer shrugs, his gaze dropping to our baby once more. "But a woman is allowed to change her mind."

"You mean that? Okay, I want to name him Oscar then," I suggest.

Archer grimaces. "Hell. No."

"Pauly."

"Gimme a break."

"Jeffrey."

"That name is just . . . no." Archer shakes his head.

"Fine." I roll my eyes, cradling my son close as I stare down at him with wonder. My fingers drift across his cheek, caressing his tiny little rosebud lips as I murmur, "Welcome to the world, Jackson."

We've been discussing names for months, arguing back and forth. One of us would come up with a suggestion we loved just as the other would shoot it down with both barrels. It became a point of contention, made worse because we didn't know what we were having, but I wouldn't budge on finding out early.

It was kind of fun, keeping it a surprise, though deep down inside I knew Jackson was a he. We kept going round and round with girl names but looks like that didn't matter. A few weeks ago, we agreed on Jackson as a name if he was a boy, and I loved the choice.

So did my husband.

Jackson Archer Bancroft has a nice ring to it.

Archer scoots closer to us, sitting on the edge of the bed as he reaches out and strokes the baby's cheek just like I did only moments ago. "Welcome, little man. We're glad to finally meet you."

Turning, I lean in and kiss my husband's cheek, overwhelmed with love for both of these men in my life. "I love you," I whisper. "So much."

"Love you too, babe. More than you'll ever know," he murmurs.

I feel exactly the same way.

Chapter 6

Gage

One week since the wedding

I don't want to go home. Can't we just live here forever?" My wife crosses her arms in front of her bare chest and pouts, looking sexy as hell wearing a skimpy little white bikini bottom and nothing else. Her skin is golden from the sun, her blonde hair piled up on top of her head in a messy knot. Giant sunglasses obscure her eyes and a thin gold chain hangs from her neck. The wedding band on her ring finger is the only other piece of jewelry she's wearing.

She's bare and simple and so freaking gorgeous it almost hurts to look at her.

Almost.

"I would love to live here forever," I agree, looking around at the view of the crystal blue ocean spread before us. We're staying at an exclusive resort in a three-room suite with a giant balcony that has the best view of the ocean I've ever seen. "Maybe I'll move my business over here. I can sell luxurious vacation homes to the rich."

"Ooh, are you serious?" The excitement in her voice makes me smile. She lifts her glasses and peers at me, as if to see if I'm for real or not. "And I can open a bakery here. But I won't call it Autumn Harvest. How about Tropical Harvest instead?"

"Sure. Whatever. It all sounds good as long as I have you with me." I lean back against my lounge chair and slip my glasses down so the intense sun doesn't blind me. We haven't done anything our entire honeymoon besides eat, swim, have sex, lounge around, lay on the beach, have sex, eat—

Yeah. It's been great. Relaxing. My stressed-out bride-to-be has completely disappeared and in her place is my relaxed, happy wife. I don't want to go home either.

But the reality is we're flying back tomorrow. Another reality? I'll be glad to see everyone. Happy to see baby Jackson and watch my sister and best friend lose their minds over one tiny human being.

"I wonder if Jackson's changed at all," Marina muses, reading my mind as usual.

"It's been a week," I say. "He'll be what? Eight days old by the time we see him again? Nine? I'm sure he hasn't changed much since we met him at the hospital." We'd lucked out when we were finally able to stop by. Along with the baby, we got to see Archer and a very exhausted Ivy. Marina had held the baby and cried along with Ivy, which had moved me because I'd had a sudden image of Marina holding our baby someday.

Crazy.

"I've heard they can almost double their weight in the first week. He'll be a completely different baby." I glance over to see more pouting from my wife. "He won't even recognize us I bet."

I bark out a surprised laugh. "You gotta be kidding me. He didn't recognize us before."

"He heard my voice a lot when he was in the womb. I know

he knows me. I'll be his favorite aunt." She drops her arms to her sides and relaxes against the overstuffed lounger cushion, her glasses once more in place over her eyes, her smooth skin glistening beneath the sun.

"You'll be his only aunt," I say, my mouth going dry as I study her. Seeing her like this, wearing the tiny white bikini bottom and nothing else, is making my cock rise to the occasion. You think I'd be exhausted from all the sex, or at the very least, somewhat immune to seeing my wife half naked.

Guess not.

"Do you want a baby right away, Gage?" she asks suddenly.

And there goes my erection. "Uh . . . not really. Unless you do," I add quickly, though I kind of, sort of, don't mean it. We only just got married. We have lots of time before we need to start making babies and creating a family.

We can definitely practice all the time, but actual babies? Not yet. For now, I'll leave that up to my sister.

"I don't," she says as she tilts her face up to the sun. Damn, she's pretty. "I mean, I do want them someday, but not yet. We have plenty of time. If I get baby fever, I'll just find Jackson. I bet he'd let me cuddle him all I want."

"I'm sure he would," I drawl, my gaze locked on her breasts. She has no tan lines on her upper body. It's all golden skin and hard pink nipples. My mouth starts to water just thinking about sucking on them.

She looks over at me, raising her sunglasses to the top of her head once more. "Are you checking me out?"

"Always," I say with a grin. I'm not going to be ashamed by my appreciation of my wife. She's a work of art. Beautiful and sweet and so giving. I lucked out and I know it.

"You going to do something about that?" She waves her hand at the vicinity of my swim trunks.

Glancing down, I look at my erection and then her. "Are *you* going to do something about it?" I ask pointedly.

Marina can barely hide the grin on her face. "What would you like, O husband of mine?"

"Hmm, I don't know." I settle my hand over my cock and give it a firm stroke, my gaze cutting to hers. She's watching me closely, her eyes locked on my hand, her lips parted seemingly in fascination. That we haven't grown tired of constantly having sex kind of blows my mind.

But I am definitely not tired of her. And I'm pretty sure she's not tired of me either.

"Would you like me to come over there and join you?" she asks as she stands, tossing her sunglasses on the chair before she takes the few steps and stops at the edge of my lounger. "You're looking lonely."

"I am lonely." I grunt in surprise when she settles right on top of me, warm and soft as she straddles my hips, her bent knees on either side. "I'm not so lonely anymore though," I murmur.

She rests her hands on the top of the lounge chair, her breasts right in my face. Tilting my head up, I capture one nipple with my lips and suck, earning a gasp for my efforts.

A warm breeze washes over us, doing nothing to cool the incessant sexual fever raging within me as I place my hand on the center of her back and bring her chest closer to my lips.

This is our last day. I need to make the most of this experience. Getting naked outside, the ocean waves crashing in the distance, I need to revel in this.

And so does Marina.

Marina

My husband has the best mouth ever. A talented mouth too, which he's currently using on me quite perfectly. I'm grinding against his hard cock as those talented lips suck and lick my nipples. If he keeps this up, I'll be coming in seconds, no joke.

Our Caribbean honeymoon has far exceeded my expectations. I'd been secretly afraid of arriving an exhausted mess, wanting only to sleep the days away while Gage's typical workaholism kicked in.

But no. We've excessively indulged in each other sexually, we've relaxed, we've hung out at the pool and the beach, and we've eaten fine cuisine on a nightly basis.

The sex, though . . . has been amazing. I feel more connected to this man than ever before. That Gage is my husband, the constant in my life, is both overwhelming and exhilarating.

"Mmm, you taste good," he murmurs against my skin, his lips moving over the tops of my breasts, licking and kissing my skin.

I shiver when his fingers skim down my back so that his hand settles at the waistband of my bikini bottoms. "You feel good," I whisper, a little sigh escaping me when he slips first one hand then the other beneath my bottoms and touches my naked flesh. He squeezes my backside and tugs me against him, his erection rubbing between my legs, driving me crazy. Unable to control myself, I lean forward, crashing my mouth on top of his.

Our kiss is wild, frantic. Our tongues tangling as he works

my bottoms off. I help him out, contorting my body in all sorts of awkward positions before I finally fling the skimpy fabric onto the deck. I love that we can make love so freely outside without worrying that others can see us. The suite offers us plenty of privacy, and Gage and I indulge outside every chance we can get.

"You need to get naked," I whisper once he breaks away from me to scatter damp kisses along my neck.

"Help me out, wife," he says, his voice rough with want.

I comply, standing so I can tug his swim trunks off and tossing them close to where my bottoms lay. I sprawl out onto the lounger once more, lying between his legs, my lips right at his cock. Slowly I draw him deep between my lips, my gaze never leaving his as he watches me suck and lick him. His lids grow heavy and he reaches out, his fingers cradling my cheek.

I could do this for hours. I get off getting *him* off, I swear. Never before have I received so much pleasure when I'm giving it to someone else. Only for Gage.

He's my everything.

My everything is also incredibly impatient. He pushes me off him within minutes, growling about coming too fast, before hauling me into his arms as if I don't weigh a thing. I'm back in the same position I was originally, only this time there's no clothing separating us. I can feel him, thick and insistent, brushing against me, and I shift my lower body, reaching down so I can grab hold of him by the base and guide him inside me.

"Hold on," he says, stopping me. "You touch me, and I'm afraid I'll go off like a rocket."

I lean back so I can look him in the eyes. He's dead serious. "Really?"

"Really," he says firmly as he wraps his fingers around his cock and brushes the head against my damp folds. I stifle a groan by biting my lips, and he stops the movement, depriving me.

"Don't stop," I whisper, and he presses his fingers against my mouth.

"Don't hold back then," he says just before he resumes stroking me with his cock. Driving me crazy.

A moan falls from my lips and finally he adjusts, so I can lower myself onto him. Slowly I take him inside, until he's filling me completely, every inch of him inside of my body. Thick and pulsing, I close my eyes and wrap my arms around his neck, my hands buried in his hair as I clutch him close.

He feels so unbelievably good. I'm afraid to move for fear my body will start convulsing, and I'll come too before we've even started.

"You're so damn beautiful with the sun shining on your skin," he says as he leans back against the cushions to watch me. I start to move at a languid pace, as if we have all the time in the world. My breasts sway with my every movement and he reaches out, circling his thumb around one nipple, then the other.

Gage lets me have my way with him like he's my plaything. Up and down, slow. Slower. Then I increase my pace, going fast. Faster. Until I'm practically bouncing in his lap, riding his cock as I strive toward my orgasm that hovers so close yet is still out of reach.

"So . . . close . . ." I say as I move faster, leaning forward to get that friction I so desperately want that will help me come.

Gage reaches between us, his fingers settling on my clit as he deftly circles it again and again. "Like that, baby?"

I toss my head back as his fingers stroke me, his mouth on my skin, my breasts. The first waves of my orgasm threaten to wash over me. A whimper escapes and then I'm coming, my entire body trembling around Gage's as he lifts his hips and thrusts deep inside. He shouts as he erupts, my name falling from his lips as he holds me so close I almost can't breathe.

"I love you," I whisper into his hair as he slowly relaxes his hold on me. "I can't believe our honeymoon is almost over."

"Baby." He slips his fingers into my hair and tugs, forcing me to look at him. I stare into his eyes and can't help but smile in response to the grin that's on his handsome face. I press my forehead to his. "It's only just begun."

Chapter 7

Matt

Two weeks since Gage and Marina's wedding

"Hey."

I'm glancing at my phone, but the sound of Bryn's voice makes me stop short. My eyes widen in surprise when I find her in my office, sitting behind my desk in full-on assistant mode.

Not that I think of her as my assistant anymore. No way. She's my business partner and she knows it. She has her own office and manages the administrative assistant plus organizes the winery's social events.

But at this very moment, having her back in my office, looking like she does, it's taking me right back to when she worked under me. How bad I wanted to keep her under me . . . but not to work. Oh, no.

More like keep her under me in bed. Naked.

I let my gaze wander all over her, drinking her in slowly. She's got her hair pulled back into a long braid, wispy dark strands frame her face, reminding me of the way she wore her hair the first time I saw her after the famous Ivy-and-Marina makeover. She's wearing a sleeveless black dress that emphasizes the lush curve of her breasts and leaves her long slender arms exposed, a delicate silver bracelet around her wrist.

She looks . . . stunning.

"What are you doing sitting behind my desk, Miss James?" I shut the door behind me and turn the lock, ensuring no one will bust in on us. I can't remember the last time we fooled around at work, especially once we moved in together and it was no longer really necessary.

Not that it was ever really necessary to get it on at work but . . . yeah. It sure as hell was a lot of fun. So I like the direction Bryn is going now.

A lot.

"Why, I have good news, Mr. DeLuca. Tremendous news, in fact. I couldn't wait to share, so I thought I'd wait in your office for your return from the vineyards. You don't mind, do you?" She folds her hands on top of my desk and smiles at me, again reminding me strongly of those first few agonizing months I worked with her. How badly I wanted her.

How I deprived myself of her since I knew our relationship would be viewed as inappropriate. I was her freaking boss.

Yet here I am, now her freaking boyfriend. Glad I pushed past my worries. Then I wouldn't have this amazing woman in my life.

"Of course I don't mind." Like I would. And she knows it. "So what's the good news?" I ask as I approach my desk.

I stop by her side, and she turns in the chair so she's still facing me. The skirt of her dress is short, hitting her about mid-thigh and offering me a glimpse of slender flesh. My gaze locks there for a bit too long, and she clears her throat, drawing my attention back to her face.

"Well, we have four weddings lined up so far," she says, beaming at me.

Ah, yes. I relented the night of Gage's reception, finally giving in to her request that we advertise our event facility.

Within twenty-four hours of agreeing, she showed me a few mockups of print advertising, which just went to show me that she was bound and determined to make it happen, no matter what it took.

That's one of my favorite things about Bryn. All that steely determination in such a sexy package.

"Four already, huh?" I smile at her, loving how pleased she looks. "That's great."

"It is. And I collected deposits from all four of them too," she says, her expression going the slightest bit cocky. "This is going to be an excellent source of extra income, you know."

"I know." I lean over her, resting my hands on the arms of the chair, blocking her in. "It's going to be a huge success, I'm sure."

She smirks. "I'm sure too."

I brush my face against her hair, breathing in her distinct floral scent. A little hum of pleasure escapes her when I nuzzle her cheek with my nose, then press my lips against her cheek. "Why are you so incredibly smart?" I ask.

"I've been hanging out with you too long," she replies.

Jerking away, I stare at her, hating that she puts herself down. Why does she still do that? "This has nothing to do with me and everything to do with you, Bryn. You don't give yourself enough credit."

Her smile fades and her gaze dims. She offers up a little shrug. "You know how I am."

"Yeah, I do," I say vehemently. "You're too humble. You act like all the great things you do are by accident or whatever. You accomplish so much." I shake the chair arms, startling her. "You're amazing, Bryn. I wish you could actually see that."

She licks her lips and gives me a tremulous smile. "You make me feel amazing," she admits softly.

"You do the same for me." I grip the chair arms and brace myself as I move in to kiss her, again and again. Simple little brushes of my mouth against hers. "I love you," I whisper against her lips. "So damn much. And I believe in you. I wish you could believe in yourself just as much." I want to reassure her. Convince her how fucking unbelievable she is. Try to make her see how much I love her, how much she means to me.

How much I need her.

Bryn

'm completely surrounded by Matt, and I love it. He looks so good in his white button-down shirt and dark jeans, smelling of the outdoors, his hair a little mussed, his skin burnished from the sun. His mouth is on mine, firm and insistent as he continues to kiss me. I part my lips, his tongue delving inside, meeting mine, and a little moan escapes me at first contact, a riot of butterflies seeming to flutter just beneath my skin.

"I love you too," I say when we break apart. Our breathing is accelerated, and I stare at his mouth, wishing it was back on mine. He reaches for me, his hands gripping my waist as he plucks me from the chair and places me on the edge of the desk.

He settles in his chair directly in front of me and reaches beneath my skirt, his hands gently gripping the inside of my knees as he slowly spreads my legs apart. "Remember that time I fucked you on my desk?" he asks, his eyes full of wicked intent.

A shiver moves through me at his choice of words and the memories. There have been plenty of times when we've messed around in his office. We've always been so hot for each other, especially at the beginning of our relationship . . .

We'd just started dating and he'd pulled me into the office, locking the door behind us. I'd been facing the desk, and Matt had pushed me forward over it, taking me from behind. I quickly discovered he liked it that way, which was unbelievably hot. But he likes sex pretty much any way, as long as the two of us are involved.

He's done amazing things, that Matthew DeLuca. Always making me feel wanted and boosting my ego.

"From what I remember, you've fucked me on your desk a couple of times." I reach out and trace my fingers down the front of his shirt, along the row of buttons. I slip the top one undone, and then the next, my gaze locked on his chest as his skin is slowly revealed behind every button that comes free. "You did lock the door, right?"

Matt chuckles, massaging my inner thighs with the tips of his fingers. "Oh yeah. Because I definitely plan on fucking you on this desk again."

I finish unbuttoning his shirt and push it off his shoulders. He takes over, shaking it off so it lands on the floor, and I'm confronted with a wall of solid masculine flesh. I love how he's built. All broad shoulders and firm muscle, the faintest amount of hair at the center of his chest—he's beautiful. Warmth radiates from his skin, and his scent wraps all around me as I inhale deeply, breathing him in.

He's addictive. Intoxicating. I can't get enough of this man.

"We need to hurry," I whisper before I press my lips to his chest, just above his right pectoral. "I have a meeting in fifteen minutes."

"I'm afraid you're going to miss it," Matt says as he pushes the fabric of my skirt up until my thighs are completely exposed. "Or at the very least, you'll be late. I'm sure your business partner won't mind though."

"My partner is supposed to be in this meeting too so we can't miss it. And we really shouldn't be late." I reach for the waistband of his jeans and slowly undo his fly. "The people meeting with us are known to be very punctual."

"Damn," Matt mutters, shaking his head. He stands, grabs hold of my waist, and pulls me to the very edge of the desk so my ass is half hanging off. "Guess I'll have to make it quick then."

His mouth returns to mine before I can say another word, his punishing kiss deep and hot and wet. I wrap my arms around his neck, gasping when he reaches for my panties. We make quick work of each other's clothes, hands and mouths everywhere, and his erection probing at my entry within seconds.

"Please," I whimper, spreading my legs as wide as I can. "Matt. I need you." I feel greedy. Empty without him inside me.

He doesn't answer. He doesn't have to. Matt pulls me forward as he thrusts, his cock imbedding deep. I lean back and rest my hands on the desk, wishing I was completely naked, wishing I could feel every blessed inch of him against me.

But this is going to be quick. Fast and easy and delicious and wicked. I watch him as he starts to move, his expression pained, his movements deliberate. He always puts such care into what we do, and I love it. I love him. I'm overwhelmed with the emotion that I have for this man, and I close my eyes. Losing myself in the way he rocks against me over and over, filling me completely, his hands everywhere at once.

"So beautiful," he murmurs, his voice deep and thick with tension like it usually is just before he climaxes. "I love you so much, Bryn. I can't get enough of you."

"Yes," I whisper, cracking my eyes open to find him watching me. "I love you too, Matt."

"I wanna make you come," he mutters as he starts to move faster, his breathing choppy as he hovers above me.

"Make me come, Matt. Touch me," I whisper, urging him on, loving the appreciative growl he gives in response to my provoking words.

He touches my clit, circles it with his thumb before he presses hard. I concentrate on the way he moves inside of me, how thick he feels, the friction that's created between us like we're trying to spark a fire. I feel like we really could almost light a blaze, the attraction is so strong.

Murmuring encouragement, he circles my clit harder as he increases his pace. I move with him, desperate to find that delicious feeling again. Matt is the only one who can make me feel so good, so right. So completely, utterly myself.

I was never comfortable in my own skin; not until I met Matt.

"Don't stop," I say, my breath hitching when he touches me in a particular way, in a particular spot. "Just like that," I encourage, whimpering with every stroke of his fingers, every stroke of his tongue. "Oh God, Matt. Please . . ."

"Come for me, Bryn," he commands as if he knows just how close I am. I explode, my entire body wracking with shudders as the orgasm takes me completely over. I shudder and shake in his arms lifting away from the desk, so I can grip him and hold him close. He lets me but never slows his pace, pushing again and again until he's the one who's shouting and coming inside of me so hard, I swear at one point I'm afraid he's going to collapse on top of me, and I won't be able to move ever again.

"Well," he says a few minutes later. "That was . . . good."

I start to laugh. "More than good."

"We're good for each other," he says softly, his fingers threading through my already mussed-up hair. "Don't you think?"

"I don't think, I know." I smile and snuggle close to him, loving how cherished he makes me feel, how much he loves me. "I love you, Matt. I'm glad you crossed the line and decided to pursue me."

Now it's his turn to laugh. "I love you too. And I'm real fucking glad I decided to cross that line. I owe a lot of my pursuit to Ivy and Marina."

"I know. The makeover and all that." Those girls worked their hardest to put the two of us together and for that, I'll be forever grateful to them.

"Not just that. They talked you up before the makeover," he says, shocking me. "Once they nabbed their men, they decided I needed someone too. Which means I'm the one who won that damn bet, and I intend to finally collect."

Oh God, the bet. How could I forget? I assume Archer and Gage wish Matt would forget about it. "When are you going to collect? And how?"

"I already put in a call to both of those jackasses and made my request." When I remain quiet, he sighs. "I asked them to donate the amount to their favorite charity and be done with it."

"Awww." I kiss him, loving how thoughtful he is. Someday I am definitely going to marry this man. "You're the best, you know that?"

"No, you are. Seriously." He rests his hand against my cheek, forcing me to stare into his eyes. "You're the best thing that's ever happened to me, Bryn. You helped me turn my life around. Helped me find love. I owe it all to you."

"Matt." My voice trembles and we kiss, his lips lingering on mine. "I love you." I can't say it enough.

"I love you too. You're mine, Bryn. You're stuck with me." He grins. "I hope you don't mind."

I wouldn't have it any other way.

Chapter 8

Archer

One month since Jackson's birth

I walk into the living room to find my wife curled up on the couch, little Jackson nestled in her arms as she feeds him. When I realize she hasn't noticed me yet, I stop short and watch them for a quiet moment.

She looks good, still carrying a little extra weight, but I think those curves are sexy. Her hair is loose, falling far past her shoulders, and she's wearing an oversized pale blue T-shirt and black leggings. The shirt is yanked up over her chest and Jackson's dark head is pressed close to her breast. She's staring down at him, cooing unintelligible sounds as she strokes his hair and face.

Love overwhelms me and sticks in my throat, making it impossible for me to speak. I'm damn lucky to have these two in my life. I don't know what I did to earn this.

But I'm not questioning it. I'm eternally thankful for my Ivy and my Jackson.

"Why, Daddy . . . are you spying on us?" Ivy asks, her quiet voice interrupting my thoughts.

Chuckling, I settle on the couch beside her. "What if I am?"

"I might call you a creeper." She shrugs with a little smile just as Jackson falls off her nipple to blink up at me with wide, fathomless, blue eyes.

"You don't think I'm a creeper, do you, Jackson?" I reach out and touch his lips, then trace his chubby little cheek. He's a beautiful baby—though I'm probably biased—and he's fairly easy. Though when he's mad or upset, he definitely lets us know. The kid has a set of lungs on him that won't quit.

I try my best to help, which still kind of blows my mind since I didn't have a good fatherly example growing up. My dad was never around, but I'm determined to be the complete opposite of him. He acts like I'm a nuisance most of the time, even now, though he does dote on his grandchild. Somehow, Jackson has brought my family closer together.

Jackson has also brought Ivy and me closer. I'm stunned at how much I love my wife, how much my love grows for her day in and day out. She's a wonderful mother, a great wife—my passion for her is at an all-time high.

Yet I haven't touched her in weeks. I can't. It's been over a month—since before Jackson's birth. I miss feeling her naked skin against mine, miss burying myself inside of her.

The doctor said six weeks, and I don't want to hurt her or put her at risk. It can't be easy, pushing an eight-pound baby out of your body. She moved like an old woman those first few weeks when she came home from the hospital, but now she's acting so much more like her pre-baby, normal self, that I'm hopeful.

But I won't push. I'll wait the six weeks. It's the right thing to do, no matter how much it's slowly killing me.

"Jackson loves his daddy." Ivy hooks her nursing bra back together and pulls her shirt down, then lifts the baby up so she can burp him. Jackson's struggling to lift his head already and look at me. A surge of love flows through me, and I touch his head, stroking his soft dark hair as Ivy pats his back repeatedly. A huge burp escapes him, making me laugh, and Ivy grimaces at me.

"Don't encourage him," she murmurs. "He'll turn into such a guy."

"Babe, I'm afraid he *is* a guy." I take Jackson from her and hold him close, breathing in his sweet baby scent, loving the way his head knocks into my jaw as he struggles. Little noises escape him, snorts and coos and funny sounds that make me smile.

Man, I love this kid. I can't believe Ivy and I created him, that he's a part of me. I hope only the good parts.

"You're going to teach him all your bad habits, aren't you?"

"Nah." I shake my head. "I don't want him to be anything like me." Well, the bad me. The old me. I'm not that man anymore. Ivy changed me. More like, she made me want to change so I'd be a better man for her.

"What? You don't want him to be sweet and funny and hardworking?"

I turn my head to look at her. "You think that about me?"

She rolls her eyes. "Duh. Why do you think I married you? You're smart and sexy and thoughtful. You're a good husband and father. Why wouldn't you want your boy to be just like you?"

My chest swells with pride. "I like hearing you say that," I admit. "I feel the same way about you."

"You think I'm a good husband and father? Gee, thanks." She punches me in the arm, making me laugh.

"You know what I mean." I kiss Jackson's forehead, then his cheeks. I can't stop kissing my baby. Matt and Gage make fun of my ass, but I don't care. "You're a good wife and mother. You amaze me every day, what you do for me and for Jackson."

"Aw." She leans in and goes to kiss my cheek, but I turn my head at the last minute so she kisses my lips instead. "You are too sweet. And speaking of doing something for someone else . . . did you make that donation yet?"

"Yeah." Gage and I finally conceded that Matt won the million dollar bet. Arrogant fucker really rubbed it in our faces too. But then he came up with the brilliant idea that we donate our share to a charity of our choice. "I received the official letter of thanks from the organization in the mail a few days ago." I contributed to a local charity that assists pregnant women in need. Gage chose a local low income housing project.

"That's wonderful, honey." She kisses me again on the lips, this time on purpose. "I'm so proud of you for turning your stupid bet into something for good."

I laugh. Leave it to my wife to put it so succinctly. "Yeah, well, Matt showed us both up and looks like a total hero."

"How?"

"He made donations too. Two hundred fifty thousand to each of the charities Gage and I chose." Smug asshole. I think this jokingly because while he made us look like chumps and himself look like a hero, yeah, I've gotta give it to him.

Matt did the right thing. He has a good heart, my friend.

"Matt is so amazing." Ivy shakes her head, a dreamy expression on her face. Not good. I want to be the only one who puts that look on her. "I just adore him."

"As much as you adore me?" I ask like a jealous idiot.

"I adore you so much, it's kind of ridiculous." Another kiss, this one longer, a little sweeter, a lot hotter. "But you already know this," she murmurs against my lips.

Jackson struggles between us, giving a single cry like he's saying "pay attention to me" in baby language. I withdraw from Ivy reluctantly and stand, holding Jackson to my chest. "Want me to put him down? He's due for a nap, right?"

"Right." She stands and flashes me a sultry smile. "You should meet me in our bedroom." Taking a step closer to me, she presses her hands against my chest, her fingers caressing lightly. Her gaze is full of intent. "I miss my husband."

Hope lights up inside of me, but I tamp it down. "Aren't you still recovering?"

"I feel good. Perfect, in fact." Her fingers curl into my T-shirt and give it a little tug. "Don't you want to rendezvous with your wife in the bedroom?"

Her choice of words makes me laugh—and sweat. "I'd love nothing more, but aren't we supposed to wait at least six weeks?"

"It's up to you; do you trust your wife or a doctor who has no idea how she's feeling physically?" She releases her hold on my T-shirt and backs up a little. "See you in a bit?"

Hell. "Okay," I say lightly, feeling like a jackass.

But not so much of one that I'd miss out on the opportunity my wife is presenting me.

Ivy

I'm waiting for my husband in our bed, naked. He's taking an extraordinarily long time putting Jackson in his crib, and I'm starting to think he's stalling.

Silly man. He's worried I'm not recovered enough for any physical contact. The doctor informed me I could engage in sexual activity approximately four to six weeks after childbirth. I'm focused on four.

Extremely focused, considering Jackson is exactly a month old as of yesterday.

Besides, I feel like my body has bounced back from childbirth pretty quickly.

Parenting, however, was a difficult adjustment at first—always having to get up every few hours to feed the baby. After a while, I felt like a baby-feeding machine and that was it. I was tired, I was cranky, and I felt decidedly unsexy. As in, I felt like a mama. That's it.

The last week and half though, something has changed. I've got a routine going on, and Jackson is doing well. I've slowly started exercising, and it's reenergized me. My body's not in perfect shape, but I think Archer will ignore any imperfections. It's been too long since we've had sex. His horniness will most likely outweigh any notice of my lingering flab or stretch marks.

"There you are," I say when Archer magically appears in the doorway of our bedroom. But suddenly it's like he can't even cross the threshold. "What took you so long?"

His expression is uneasy. "I . . . Babe, are you really okay to do this?"

"Do what?" I blink up at him innocently as he moves into the room, stopping at the foot of the bed.

He shoots me a skeptical glance. "I can tell you're naked under that sheet, Ivy. You brought me in here to seduce me."

"You're so perceptive. Don't tell me you're protesting?" Because if he is, I'm calling bullshit. The guy usually can't keep his hands off me. Now he's all Mr. Shy. He needs to get over it.

"I'm not." He steps closer, reaching out to grab at my foot

beneath the sheet. "But I don't want to hurt you if you're not up to this."

"Oh my God." I reach out and snag his hand, pulling him until he's practically collapsing on top of me. With a strength I didn't even know I had, I push him onto his back and straddle him, completely naked. "Stop being such a weenie and just do me."

He stares up at me with a frown, looking startled. "You just had a baby. You're exhausted. You might have postpartum or whatever."

I rest my hands on my hips. "Do I act like a woman who has postpartum?"

"No." His gaze falls to my chest and heats to a sexy smolder. "Your boobs are huge."

Rolling my eyes, I shove at his shoulder. "So romantic. Glad to see you haven't lost your touch."

"Damn woman, you're full of it," he mutters, his hands settling on my waist, his fingers light as they skim my skin. A shiver moves through me, and I'm *seriously* glad my husband hasn't lost his touch.

"It's called sexual frustration," I murmur as I bend over him, my lips right in front of his. "As in, I want my husband. And I'm going to be really sad if he rejects me."

"Sad?" One of his hands goes to the back of my head and brings me closer, our mouths brushing against each other as we speak. "I can't have you sad, Ivy."

"I know. So why don't you have me screaming your name in, say, ten minutes?"

Chuckling, he kisses me, his tongue darting out for a lick. "You sure?"

"Definitely," I assure him. "Let me control it though. I don't want you to make a wrong move and then it's over."

He kisses me, his tongue thrusting deep, one hand holding my hip to him, his other hand in my hair, fingers pulling tight. I whimper against his hungry mouth, moan when his hand slides over my backside, his fingers dipping gently between my legs from behind.

"You're wet," he murmurs, sounding shocked as he slowly strokes me.

I release a shuddering breath. My entire body feels strung tight as a wire. "I want you, Archer. I've wanted you for days. Weeks."

"Hmm." He hums against my lips, inserting just the tip of his finger inside me. "Does that hurt?"

I move against him, flexing my hips. "No. It feels good," I whisper.

He flips me over, and I'm sprawled on the bed, Archer's mouth pressed hard against mine. Then I'm left shocked when he leaps away from me, and quickly strips off his clothes. He's erect and just seeing him like that sends sparks of heat scattering through me. My nipples tighten and an incessant ache begins to throb between my legs.

"Come here," I whisper, holding my arms out. "Hurry."

Grinning, he rejoins me in bed, positioning himself above me, his mouth on my neck, nipping and tasting my skin. "If I'm on top then I can control how deep I go," he whispers just before he licks my ear.

I shiver. "But I like being on top."

"Next time," he promises. "I just want to feel you beneath me, wrapped around me."

His words touch my heart. I curl my legs around his hips, anchoring myself to him as he moves downward, blazing a hot, damp, path along my skin with his lips and tongue. He lashes at my nipples before sucking first one, then the other inside his mouth, and I cling to him, crying out when he sucks one particularly hard. "Careful," I murmur. "I'm sensitive there."

"Ah, right." He smiles and adjusts himself above me, his erection nudging my belly. "You sensitive here?" He grabs hold of his cock and gently pushes just the tip inside.

I suck in a sharp breath, holding it as he slowly enters me. "Yes," I whisper in encouragement, but which only makes him stop.

"I'm hurting you?" He sounds pained, his expression tight, his gaze dark. He's waited a long time for this too, and I immediately feel bad for him.

"No. I'm fine." I kiss him hungrily, wanting him to realize that I'm all for this. "Just . . . go slow. No abrupt thrusts okay?"

"Okay." He nods almost frantically. "I'll go slow, I promise."

We move cautiously in unison, me because I'm trying to get used to his size again and he because he's afraid to hurt me. There's something so sweet about it though, how gently he's making love to me. His touch is featherlight, his kisses deep and delicious and so incredibly soft.

I feel like I'm in a dream. Everything is hazy and blurred, my skin tingles when he touches me, my body trembling as he moves inside of me, and I feel so protected, so loved.

Within minutes Archer increases his pace, his breathing heavier, and I can tell he's already close. I'm close too, and I whisper it in his ear, wanting him to push me right over that delicious edge so I can fall into oblivion along with him. "Touch me," I encourage and he does, his hand going straight between us, his fingers playing nimbly with my clit.

I bite my lip and arch into his touch, sending him deeper which makes him groan. The pace becomes frantic, and he's not being as careful any longer, but it doesn't matter. I'm caught up completely, seeking my orgasm just as ferociously as he is. Until we're both tumbling over the brink and falling headfirst into climax, our bodies shuddering and shaking together.

He falls atop me, his heavy weight a comfort. I breathe into his neck, rubbing my hands up and down the wide expanse of his back, as he tries to gather himself after such an amazing orgasm, no doubt.

Oops. Realization dawns, and I shove at him so he has no choice but to roll over on his side next to me.

"What's wrong?" he asks, sounding put out.

"We didn't use a condom." I slap my hand against my forehead, feeling like an idiot. "God, I'm so stupid."

"What's the big deal? You won't get pregnant this quick," he says, sounding pleased with himself. Looking pleased with himself too, like he always does right after he comes. His hair is a mess and his eyes have a satisfied gleam to them, but I sort of want to slug him.

"There are horror stories out there, Archer. I've met women who after having a baby, get knocked up again within months. Sometimes weeks." I shudder in horror. "That sounds awful."

"What, having another Jackson? That kid is the best." He slings his arms behind his head, that smug curl to his lips both attractive and irritating. "He's amazing. Don't tell me all you want is one."

"Oh, I want more," I tell him, walking my fingers across his sweat-dampened chest. "But I don't want babies ten months apart. What a nightmare." I tug on his nipple a little too hard, making him yelp.

"I'd help you," he says, leaning in to kiss me.

I dodge his lips. "I'd need two nannies at least."

"You don't even have a nanny now," he points out. "You refused when I offered you one."

"I can do this on my own." I've taken a temporary leave of absence from work so I can concentrate on taking care of Jackson.

"Right. And you could take care of two babies too if you had to," he says, pulling me close so I can lay my head on his chest. "You can do anything. That's why I admire you so much."

"Aw, you're just sucking up to me because you might've knocked me up." I gaze up at him. "You're so romantic."

"You're the romantic one." He drops a kiss on the tip of my nose. "Don't sweat it, babe. Whatever hand we're dealt, we'll make it."

I snuggle close and close my eyes, my arm slung over his middle. "You're right. With you by my side, we can do no wrong. Even if that means having three babies in two years."

"Three?" His voice sounds strangled and he clears his throat. "Uh, what do you mean, three babies?"

"What if we have twins next time? They run in my family," I say.

"They do? Huh. Wish you would've told me this before. I might've reconsidered our marriage knowing that."

"You pompous jackass." I tweak his nipple again, earning another yelp from him. "You know you couldn't survive without me."

"So true, babe," he murmurs sleepily against my forehead just before he kisses it. "So very freaking true."

About the Author

Monica Murphy is a *New York Times* and *USA Today* bestselling author of over sixty novels and writes mostly contemporary, new adult, and young adult romance. She is both tradition-ally and independently published and has been translated in over ten languages. She lives in central California near Yosemite National Park with her husband, children, one dog, and four cats. When she's not writing, she's thinking about writing. Or reading. Or binge watching something.